WHO KILLED BIG AL?

ALSO BY CARROLL BAKER

Baby Doll

To Africa With Love

A Roman Tale

WHO KILLED
BIG AL ?

CARROLL BAKER

ARCHWAY PUBLISHING

Archway Publishing books may be ordered through booksellers or by contacting:

Archway Publishing
1663 Liberty Drive
Bloomington, IN 47403
www.archwaypublishing.com
1 (888) 242-5904

ISBN: 978-1-4808-7157-1 (sc)
ISBN: 978-1-4808-7158-8 (hc)
ISBN: 978-1-4808-7156-4 (e)

Library of Congress Control Number: 2019932333

Printed in the United States of America.

Archway Publishing rev. date: 03/20/2019

To Sharon Nettles and Foster Hirsch
with thanks for their encouragement and assistance

PART ONE

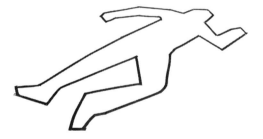

CHAPTER ONE

I t was early summer of 1970 on Escape Island. The morning winds off the Pacific were always chilly. Baron Carlo Alfonso Edmundo Tarrall and Dorothy Saks walked briskly from one end of the rock-strewn beach to the other. Or rather the Baron walked briskly and Dorothy was forced to waddle behind him in an attempt to keep pace. She was plump, with short legs that supported more weight than they were meant to carry, especially on a fifty-year-old frame. Her energy and enthusiasm were boundless, but her shortness of breath made it impossible for her to say all she wanted to say during these hikes. *These damn hikes,* she thought. They took place three times a day, first thing after every meal. It was almost impossible to conduct business on these hikes and yet there was so much to do and so little time in which to do it all.

Baron Tarrall walked fast and well for a man of seventy. His physical condition was exceptionally good. It was his mind that was no longer a match for his body. He was forgetful a great deal of the time and needed to be reminded of things that had happened sometimes only moments before. His long-range memory, however, was very good and so he didn't fret about his short-term memory loss. What he had started of late to fret about was loneliness. He'd never married, and had long ago left family and friends in his native Italy. He claimed it was these recent feelings of loneliness that had given birth to the concept of developing his island into a resort complex with a hotel and bungalows for people like himself who were looking to escape the trials and stresses of the modern world. Only the best people, of course. People of means, who were well bred, and hopefully amusing.

It was Dorothy's job to find such people. The Baron had advertised in the *Vancouver Press* for a Sales Manager/Public Relations person. Actually, his lifelong butler and companion, Foster, had placed the ad. Foster was more informed about current expressions and had specifically chosen the word "person" for the "Situation Available" column. Both Foster and the Baron had visualized a man filling the position, but Dorothy Saks had presented excellent credentials and an amazing enthusiasm for the project. She was also the only person, male or female, to respond to the ad.

Dorothy pulled her muffler up in an attempt to shield her ears from the bitterly cold sea breeze. She regretted not wearing her woolen cap this morning, but she had such a round face and that cap seemed to emphasize her pudgy, red, chapped cheeks. Appearances were important and she wanted with all her being for this job and this enterprise to be a success. It would certainly be unusual for a woman to pull off such a huge project. Especially a Canadian woman from Alberta, where she had had so few opportunities. There was also the large commission to be considered, a commission that could bring her the kind of money she had never known before.

If she were honest, she would have to admit that the island was not very attractive. The land was rocky and uneven, the beaches were of brown coarse sand, strewn with jagged boulders, while the sea, for the most part, was treacherous. In short, it was the antithesis of the calm, smooth, white West Indian islands that she had only read about, but that were her idea of an ideal resort.

However, Vancouver was only half an hour's boat ride away, and Vancouver was a beautiful, modern city. By 1970 the modernity of Los Angeles had exerted the most influence on this part of Canada. Also, the island had its share of mystery. No one quite knew why it was called Escape Island, but rumor had it that the wealthy and noble Baron Tarrall was escaping from some dark secret in his Italian past. For nearly thirty-five years he'd been in seclusion here. Oh, he owned a yacht with a full-time captain and crew, but only Foster went to the mainland; the Baron never left, not even for short visits.

Then there was the glamour and wealth surrounding Escape Island. There were dozens of small islands like it dotting these waters off the coast of Western Canada, but most were barren and would probably remain that way because of the problems and expense of providing water, electricity, telephone, et cetera. Baron Tarrall had reportedly spent a fortune to acquire these amenities.

The Baron seldom had houseguests, but when he did, there were wild speculations about the wealthy and famous who visited him. It was thought that they included everyone from princes to movie stars. None of the local people had stepped foot on Escape Island for the past thirty years or so, not since the house and dock were completed, the furnishings and art delivered. And many of the workmen who had built the island dwelling were now deceased or had moved away. Therefore there was much talk of the grandeur and elegance of the house itself.

In truth, the house was a rather ugly and immense Victorian relic that had just about survived the ravages of time and salt air. But within its walls were well-preserved antiques, tapestries, and paintings. Of these, few were truly beautiful, and had only become valuable by the passage of so much time.

"We should talk about the guest list, Baron," Dorothy said, loud enough to be heard over the howl of wind and waves.

"Remind me, Dorothy, which guest list?" he replied with some confusion. He had begun to doubt his memory to such a degree that he questioned even those things that he knew full well he remembered.

The strain in Dorothy's voice as she answered was mainly because of the effort to be heard. She both liked and respected Baron Tarrall, and had infinite patience with his lapses of memory. She said, "As you will recall, we are inviting prospective investors over most of the summer weekends. The invitations for the first weekend should go out by tomorrow, latest."

"Yes, of course, of course," the Baron answered. "But surely we have already made those decisions."

"You're quite right, Baron. I just wanted to double-check before proceeding. Of our list of potential investors, you ask that Mr. Alan Silver, the wealthiest recommended name we have, be invited on the first weekend. Are you quite sure you want Mr. Alan Silver?" She hesitated. "…Also known as 'Big Al'…to be included?"

"I'm not going to be put off by a nickname. It is no doubt a harmless one, referring to his size, and perhaps the size of his pocketbook," the Baron chuckled.

"Well, if you are absolutely certain, Baron."

"We are just beginning to work together, Dorothy. Understand that while my mind has lapses, I do not readily change it. You can rely on what I say the first time round, to be what I mean."

"Oh, Baron, of course, I didn't mean… I just like to…"

"…to double-check every instruction," he said, finishing the sentence for her. "You are conscientious about the work, and I appreciate that, but you have no need to be so painstakingly careful around me, you know."

Then, halting to take her gloved hand in his own, he said, "Try to relax about the job. I approve of what you are doing and you will be here for the duration of the project."

"Oh, thank you, thank you, Baron. I do so want to please," she said with great relief.

As he let go her hand and strode out in front again, she added, "So then Big Al…ah…Mr. Alan Silver and guest will receive an invitation. And if I'm correct, you wish for me to choose, from the list, the others to be invited?"

"That is what I said, and that is what I meant. End of subject."

"Certainly, Baron, end of subject."

Their walk proceeded in silence, although Dorothy was not only naturally talkative but fairly bursting to get back to the things on her mind. However, she waited for the Baron to speak first.

"I think the maid you hired is going to work out satisfactorily," he said. "The breakfast she made was most agreeable. Remind me again of her name?"

"Trish… That's short for Patricia and what she prefers to be called. I'm so pleased that you find her satisfactory."

Dorothy scurried around a rock that the Baron, with his long legs, had merely stepped over. She came up close behind him to be heard. "I hope Foster approves of Trish."

"He doesn't as yet, but give him time. Foster has been working alone, doing everything in the house on his own for so many years. But you were quite right to recommend a full-time maid/cook. With guests coming over the summer weekends, we certainly will need more help."

The Baron turned to see Dorothy had lost ground and was well behind him. He retraced his steps. "Why not go back to the house, Dorothy, and work on the invitations? I shall join you shortly."

"Well, Baron, if you wouldn't mind?" she said, with a question in her voice.

She was most anxious to finish the invitations and give them to the yacht's captain when he returned to the island, bringing Foster back from shopping on the mainland, at about eleven-thirty this morning. Most anxious. But she was also fearful of not keeping the Baron company on his walks. The first time she suggested accompanying him, he seemed so pleased to have her along. However, now that the work was becoming demanding, perhaps she could skip a walk once in a while without the Baron minding. If only she weren't so unsure.

The Baron, sensing her uncertainty, turned over his shoulder, calling, "Do return to the house, Dorothy. I shall join you shortly."

Back at the house, Dorothy settled at the desk in the study and checked for the final time the invitation to be sent. She had composed most of it, but the Baron had added some personal touches toward the end, and it was, after all, to be from him. It read:

> We wish to invite you as our guest to Escape Island, simply a paradise.
>
> We are planning to build dream villas for the privileged few.
>
> The project is also to include a hotel and the finest recreational facilities.
>
> We have borrowed the idea from the late Noel Coward's plan for the famous Round Hill Hotel in Montego Bay, Jamaica. Each shareholder/owner will have their own habitat plus a portion of the entire enterprise.
>
> Over the summer weekends, we have invited influential guests, such as yourselves, to test our idea of a vacation co-op here on the island. We believe that some of you, perhaps all of you, will want to

own a villa on Escape Island, which will also include shares in the proposed hotel and resort.

Please rest assured that we have no intention of asking you to invest on the spot. Nor will there be any high-pressure sales pitch. And the elegant, relaxing weekend is completely gratis; we will permit no money to pass hands.

Should you so request, we will also be most happy to arrange and provide for your first-class round-trip transportation, and, of course, our yacht will be standing by on the mainland dock to transport you to our incredibly beautiful island for your weekend of adventure, fun, or just rest, as you prefer.

We believe that you will fall in love with our unique island paradise and wish, personally, to live or vacation here, but if not, we are confident that the investment proposal, alone, will appeal to your business acumen, and you will wish to invest with us. *And we have selected YOU to be present at our very first weekend.*

You are one of a handful of potential investors that we would prefer to have as joint owners. Our first invited guests…on our first invited weekend.

You will be in the excellent and exclusive company of just eight individuals (six of whom make up couples), especially chosen for this event. And what an opportunity! What an investment! Remember, when you are not using your accommodation, the hotel will rent the space for you…for US…as we will all be sharing in the profits of the enterprise as a whole. Do come for a glorious weekend with an exceptional and fascinating group of people. We want your ideas and input, as well as the pleasure of your company.

Together we can build a dream haven of comfort and genteel living. The same sort of comfort and genteel living that distinguished my family, which I add with all immodesty, was one of the most noble and respected families of Europe. Together we will realize in the New World that same gracious lifestyle, using modern state-of-the-art concepts and technology, yet retaining Old World charm and values. I'm longing to have you be one of the select group of guests at my island mansion for this first invited weekend. I'm confident you understand how urgent it is that you let me hear from you at your earliest convenience. I will be anxiously awaiting your reply and standing by to personally have the pleasure of greeting you.

Your servant in anticipation,
Baron Carlo Alfonso Edmundo Tarrall

CHAPTER TWO

Trish, the new maid and cook, was roaming from room to room, trying to recall the instructions Foster had given her. The old house was enormous and seemed like far too much work for one maid. Before really deciding to stick it out for the full summer season, she had to remember in detail what her duties would be: the cooking, of course. That meant three meals a day. Foster took care of the drinks at cocktail hour and the tea at teatime. She wouldn't be allowed to do the shopping, which was really a bummer. She would have loved a boat trip twice a week to get the provisions. She could have taken a long walk through the streets of the mainland, looked in shop windows, seen some young people…her own age, or younger was good, too. Trish was thirty-three but loved to feel like a girl, and to be in crowds. It was so isolated here on the island and the people she'd be around most of the time were ancient. But that old poop, Foster, was keeping the outings for himself. He'd gone over on the Baron's yacht this morning and wouldn't be back until eleven or so. She would use that time to look around good and determine if her duties would kill her with work.

Now, let's see, she thought, *Foster does his own and the Baron's bedroom, and Dorothy also does her own room.*

Trish would have to make her own bed and keep her bedroom and bathroom tidy. On weekends she would have about six guest bedrooms and baths to do. The actual number depended on how many guests came as couples. That was a tremendous amount of drudgery, on top of the cooking and dishwashing for all those people.

On the positive side, she would have from noon on Monday till noon on Wednesday off to do as she pleased. That also included rides to the mainland and back on the Baron's yacht, which she would consider a swell treat. She wondered if either of the two young crew members were married. The captain was too old and didn't interest her.

Trish entered the kitchen and took the huge room into account. The floor alone was a backbreaker. But what had Foster said? "The crew, after swabbing the deck, will devote themselves several times a week to the heavy housework: scrubbing the kitchen floor, cleaning the appliances, washing the windows, and polishing the door handles."

What about running the vacuum cleaner? Had he said they would do the vacuuming? She thought that he had said they would, but she'd better find out.

She looked up at the giant chandelier. She remembered Foster saying that the chandeliers were cleaned twice a year. The one in the kitchen was a heavy brass contraption with many arms. *Ugly,* she thought. *In fact, every one of the downstairs rooms has a huge chandelier and they are all ugly, even the crystal ones.*

She proceeded down the gloomy hallway to the enormous sitting room. There was a winding staircase, leading to the next level. The crew would polish the mahogany banisters when they did the other polishing. The old poop, fusspot Foster, did the sitting room dusting himself, because he didn't trust the antiques to anyone else.

What about the stained glass wall between the sitting room and the conservatory? Well, surely the crew washed that if they did the other glass in the windows.

The fireplace? That could be a very messy job. But didn't butlers always do the fireplaces? In movies they seemed to have that duty. Then again she seemed to remember that in some old films she'd seen, a housekeeper took out the ashes. Well, she wasn't a housekeeper. She was a cook, and yes, although she hated the term, she was a maid.

She wouldn't mind doing some gardening in the conservatory. It was a spooky old place, except during the lightest times of day, with its huge bamboo, fruitless grapevine, and weird branchy things that looked like man-eaters. Still, she loved to dig in the earth, always had, and was looking forward to planting some herbs.

Trish tiptoed past the study where Dorothy was concentrating on addressing invitations. She tiptoed because Dorothy might consider the looking-around she was doing as goofing off. Although she didn't really anticipate any griping from Dorothy. In fact, she was looking forward to some advice from her. Dorothy had promised to make up the menus and show her anything she couldn't understand in the cookbooks. If she stayed on Dorothy's good side, which shouldn't be hard to do, Dorothy would be very helpful, maybe even do some of the cooking preparations.

Foster was the one Trish had to be on her guard against. She could tell he didn't want her there, didn't like her. She certainly would never sass him, although the effort would take all her willpower. He was just the kind of man she detested—always thinking they could tell women what to do.

She started down the second gloomy hallway, leading to the dining room, but stopped in front of the large antique mirror. She'd been shaking her head as she thought about Foster and had caught a glimpse of those shiny auburn curls in that mirror. *I do have beautiful hair,* she thought, *and a pretty face and a terrific figure. So what am I doing working as a domestic?*

Well, money was what she lacked. This job paid very well and she'd gotten stuck on her trip to see Canada and Alaska. She'd started out from Brooklyn, New York, with a sleeping bag, a couple hundred bucks, and high hopes of a great adventure. But a little over halfway through the trip, when she'd gotten as far as Vancouver, she'd run out of money.

She had no experience and no references but Dorothy had hired her anyway. Why? She had this strong feeling that they'd accepted her because she was from so far away. If she'd been a local from Vancouver, she felt sure they would never have even considered her. Because they were a strange group with things to hide. She got the job, she felt, because she was a foreigner, and of course because she made such a good appearance. Appearance was important on account of the special guests they had arriving.

She only hoped she could keep herself looking good, if she had a killer load of work to do. Still, here she was, and she didn't have much choice. If her husband hadn't died, if she'd had family—but why dwell on that? Those were the cards she had been dealt, and who knew, she was about to meet a lot of rich people, maybe some rich guy would fall for her and take her away from all this. She giggled and then stopped dead at the dining room door. It was humongous! Who had to clean this room? Surely not auburn locks, pretty face, with the terrific figure?

Still, she was getting oodles of Canadian dollars each week and two days of freedom out of every seven. She'd treat herself to the best beauty salons for hair and nails and facials. She'd take an aerobics class on one of those days, relax and get a stunning tan.

Another aspect of the work occurred to her: would she have to do the laundry? Maybe not. Maybe they'd send it out to a launderette. With all those guests, they'd surely have it done professionally, at least the bed and table linen. But maybe she'd have to do all the small stuff…that could add up to a couple of baskets full.

Her thoughts were interrupted by Dorothy, standing in the dining room doorway. "Trish, I was looking for you. What are you doing?"

"I'm not wasting time, if that's what you mean," Trish said defensively.

"Of course, you're not. I'm sure you're trying to get the lay of the land," Dorothy said kindly. "I was looking for you because I'd like to show you the guest list for our first invited weekend."

"I'm sorry," Trish said. "I know I owe this job to you. I was looking around because I'm worried."

"Of course, you are, but there is no need. Foster will teach you how to serve and I'll help all I can with the preparation of the food. In fact, I've had a few ideas already. Should we sit down at the kitchen table with a paper and pencil and a midmorning coffee?"

When they were in the kitchen and seated at the table with their coffee, Dorothy outlined some menu ideas. "I've included on today's shopping list some great solutions for new cooks."

"Swell," said Trish, trying to appear more interested than she really felt. "Like what?"

"Well," said Dorothy, smacking her lips, "secrets for wonderful, already prepared dishes like this canned Vichyssoise I know about. Also some other wonderful canned soups like Turtle with Sherry. They taste homemade. No one will know the difference and there are at least half a dozen kinds of the brand I have in mind. Then, of course, these waters are full of incredibly delicious salmon. It is great fixed so many ways…and so easy."

"You boiled the Baron's egg this morning," Trish pouted, "but how will I time it just right when you're not in the kitchen?"

"There is a timer, silly girl. Put the egg in once the water boils and set the timer for three and a half minutes. It comes out perfect every time."

"Oh," Trish said, surprised. "And are there really enough already prepared foods to get me by? I mean, I can make some things…like hamburgers."

"When Foster arrives with the groceries I've ordered, I'll show you everything I have thought of…which is a long list, not only of canned and smoked goods, but also frozen entrées and whole meals."

Dorothy pushed her coffee cup to one side. She then placed the guest list she'd been working on, so that Trish could see the names.

"This is what I'm bursting to share," Dorothy gushed. "I've made up the most incredible guest list for the first weekend. The most incredible guests. It's going to be dynamite. I have no doubts about my choices. See, I've already addressed the envelopes." She showed Trish the beautifully hand-addressed envelopes that were safely sealed in a clear plastic bag.

The kitchen double doors swung open and Foster entered. He scowled at Dorothy and Trish, saying, "Having a ladies' coffee klatch, are we?"

"What are you doing here?" Dorothy said, jumping up in alarm.

"I'm about to prepare a cup of hot consommé for the Baron. He often takes one after his morning walk when the sea breeze has been chilly."

"No, I meant, it is only a quarter to ten by my watch. You weren't due back till eleven or so. Where is the Baron's yacht? I hope it hasn't returned to the mainland already?"

"No," Foster said, "the captain does not depart for the return to the mainland until eleven-thirty a.m., no matter how early he arrives on the island."

"Oh, thank goodness," Dorothy sighed. "I must give him these invitations to mail. Where is the captain?"

"He stays with the yacht, unless requested to come up to the house," Foster said.

"Want me to run the letters down to the landing for you, Dorothy?" Trish asked.

"That's a good girl," Dorothy said, handing Trish the envelopes. "Thank you. I'm sure your young legs are better up to it than mine."

Foster watched Trish with distaste as she skipped from the kitchen. "Any excuse," he said flatly. But his voice was always cold and stern. He was completely steel gray, tall and gaunt, and draped himself at peculiar angles while talking or serving. Still, he had a certain elegance.

Foster was older than the Baron, but in even better physical condition. Also, his mind was sharp. And he was an exceptionally strong man. On his day off, he devoted himself to karate on the mainland. He was already a black belt, but enjoyed the practice, as well as a little bit of teaching whenever worthy pupils presented themselves.

His speech was normally polite, but underneath Dorothy seemed to sense something sinister, perhaps because his mouth was cruel.

Ignoring the slur Foster had made on Trish, Dorothy asked, "Where is the Baron?"

"It is his habit, after his walk, to spend some time in the conservatory," Foster replied.

Dorothy asked if she might take the Baron his consommé, as she needed to discuss business with him. Reluctantly, Foster handed her the silver tray. She excused herself and headed for the conservatory.

The conservatory entrance was off the main hallway, a few yards from the front door. Inside the house, one entered by a sliding metal panel in the wall of this hallway. The other three walls and the roof were of glass, and there was an outside door, leading in from the rock garden. The conservatory was visible from the front porch and the South side of the house, where the glass was clear.

From the sitting room, one saw only the shadows of trees and plants through the decorative stained glass wall.

Dorothy entered to find the Baron puttering with his geraniums. He had the tool chest open and several sizes of gardening shears laid out in the watering trough that ran the length of the flowerbeds.

It was always hot and moist inside the conservatory. The glass roof captured the heat of the sun, even though part of the glare was cut off by a gnarled and ancient grapevine that bore no fruit. And eerie, menacing plants shaded the glass-enclosed outside walls.

"We've got a very exciting guest list for the first weekend, Baron, and Trish is taking the invitations down to the captain so that they can be mailed today."

"Good, good," he said. "Is that my consommé on the tray?"

"Yes, would you like to sit over here on the bench and drink it?"

The Baron removed his gardening gloves, moved over to the bench, and sat beside Dorothy to drink his broth.

The bench was of ornate cast iron, painted white, and with individual throw cushions on the seat and at the back. Once she had arranged her cushions, Dorothy found the bench comfortable, but was oddly disturbed by the imposing plant that surrounded the bench on three sides, dominating all but the seating area itself. She imagined the plant was holding her in place: its large overhead fronds curved over her head and its arms enfolded her side, so that she had to be careful not to let her arm stray an inch off the armrest or she would have touched it, and the leaf edges appeared to be razor sharp.

Dorothy proceeded to tell the Baron in detail of the guests she had invited. However, she did not go into detail about Big Al Silver. He had been the one guest the Baron himself had chosen and so she presumed the Baron had the necessary information about Big Al. She was still amazed that the Baron had made that choice, but it was not for her to contradict him or question his wishes.

CHAPTER THREE

Within ten days of the invitations having been sent out, all the responses had come back, and all, to Dorothy's delight, were positive. Big Al Silver would be arriving with a lady friend, known simply as Cheri. It was this Cheri who had accepted on Mr. Alan Silver's behalf. Two guest rooms would have to be made up for them because this Cheri had not indicated whether or not she and Mr. Silver would be sharing the same accommodation. Dorothy felt she knew the answer but without a clear indication, she would have to have two rooms available. Fancy anyone calling themselves Cheri. Dorothy imagined that she must be Big Al's blonde bimbo. She probably didn't have a brain in her head.

Dorothy was absolutely thrilled by the fact that Babs Cunningham, the famous daytime soap actress, had accepted. Miss Cunningham was looking for a secluded retreat. All the supermarket papers had said that…and what better place than Escape Island? Babs Cunningham was still very beautiful and under forty years of age, but she had been forced to retire. A fan's bullet had wounded her, damaging her spine. She would never walk again, and would forever be confined to a wheelchair. Her fans (like Dorothy) were hoping she would accept the part, offered to her by a rival soap, of a woman in a wheelchair, like herself. But she had money and didn't wish to go again before the cameras. Every station still played her aspirin commercial, and there were reruns of her twelve years of soap episodes, but once those were over, no one would see her image again. Dorothy thought that, too, was a tragedy. And to think her would-be assassin was never even captured!

Mr. Renato Silvestri, like Mr. Alan Silver and Cheri, was coming from New York City. Actually, it had been Mr. Silvestri's father who had been invited, but he had replied that his son was coming in his place. He had also made it clear that his son had the authority to buy shares if he liked the deal that was being offered. Dorothy thought a bright young man would be a cheerful addition to the weekend. He was also bringing with him a companion, Jacqueline Le Roir, and it had been clearly stated that they would be sharing the same room. Dorothy had some difficulty getting used to this concept of unmarried people sleeping together, but she realized she was old fashioned and would simply have to learn to accept this type of modern behavior. What worried her was that Jacqueline Le Roir was obviously French…and she knew how immoral the French were…. Québec was the only place one found topless swimming and an abundance of "love children." She only hoped this French girl showed some modicum of modesty and decorum.

A wealthy British couple had accepted, Major and Mrs. James Hurley. Dorothy was so happy that she had someone from overseas, for the Baron's sake. The Hurleys were a mature couple. And they were sure to be refined and amusing, and would provide good company for Baron Tarrall. Perhaps they'd even buy, providing him some permanent company from people of his own class.

Then there was the wealthy and highly thought of American surgeon from Boston, Doctor Harlan Armstrong. He, too, was mature, in his fifties. And he, also, would be erudite, interesting, and good company for the Baron. Doctor Armstrong was very seriously looking for a quiet place in which to retire. Perhaps Escape Island was the place!

Four men and four women, plus the Baron and Dorothy as host and hostess. It was the perfect number for an intimate weekend. There would be the opportunity to get to know everyone quite well, even in a short period. The guests were due to arrive on Friday afternoon, and leave on Monday morning. Two-and-a-half days only. But there would be two lunches, three cocktail hours, three dinners, three tea-times and three breakfasts…perfect. The nice thing about an island was that it discouraged prospective buyers from taking excursions away from the site of the proposed development. However, just to make certain, Dorothy was going to see to it that the Baron gave the crew of his yacht the weekend off.

On Friday evening after dinner, the Constable from the mainland would be joining them to give a speech about community relations. When he first telephoned proposing the after-dinner speech, Dorothy had not been in favor of his presenting himself. The Constable was most insistent, and the Baron did not seem to care one way or the other. But Dorothy was afraid of boring the guests on their very first night, and she wanted to send the crew away on Friday. However, the Constable kept calling and calling, and even agreed to spend the night and have a police boat fetch him the following day. She still wasn't too happy about this intrusion, but one thing did make sense: the Constable pointed out that even the minimum share would be a large investment and that those putting money in would be anxious to know about the security provided locally, and to meet a law enforcement officer. Dorothy thought those were valid points and finally agreed to allow the Constable to come after dinner and stay the one night only.

CHAPTER FOUR

I n the sitting room at tea-time, on Friday afternoon of the first invited weekend, Trish was pouring and Foster was serving. The Baron was comfortably ensconced in his easy chair, smoking his pipe.

Dorothy was addressing two guests, Babs Cunningham and Doctor Armstrong, as if they were a crowd: "The Baron is so delighted that you have accepted his invitation. We are all looking forward to a simply marvelous weekend. You who have arrived so far, and gotten settled into your suite of rooms, may have noticed that a brochure and prospectus has been placed on your scrivener. Look it over at your leisure."

The Baron seemed quite happy to simply nod pleasantly while watching Dorothy take charge of the proceedings. His only contribution was a grunt of approval now and then to the things she was saying: "At any time the Baron and I would be fascinated to hear your ideas and of course to answer any questions you may have. We will also be most happy to take you on a guided tour, either in a group or individually. Of course, we would also encourage you to explore on your own. While awaiting the arrival of the other guests, the Baron thought you should not be deprived of your afternoon tea."

Here she paused and laughed rather stiffly before continuing: "It is, after all, tea-time. That is Trish, pouring the tea, and the Baron's devoted, lifelong butler, Foster, is serving."

Then Dorothy made the mistake of addressing Foster directly, to give an order: "Foster, perhaps you would be kind enough to step into the conservatory and see if the Major and Mrs. Hurley would care to take their tea out there, or would prefer to join us in here."

It was an uncomfortable moment for everyone as Foster glared at her, rather than responding. Finally he turned to his master, the Baron, for instructions.

Only when the Baron waved his pipe in the direction of the conservatory did Foster assume his normal polite appearance. "Very good, if it is your wish, sir," he said, and exited.

Dorothy watched him go and again laughed nervously.

"The conservatory is lovely," she said. "You must all take advantage of its beauty. Of course some people prefer the brightness of the outside. The brightness of the outdoors."

"I don't see why," Doctor Armstrong spoke up. He was emptying a packet of powder into his tea, stirring it slowly and looking piercingly at everyone present.

"There is comfort in gloom," he continued, "certainly in the reassuring gloom of this mansion. A sense of tranquility pervades this habitat...with its connections to a more stable and secure... distant past."

Babs Cunningham, who had been very much to herself since arriving, moved her wheelchair in order to face the Doctor. She suddenly seemed fascinated with him.

"I couldn't agree with you more, Doctor Armstrong," she said, turning her best profile into the light and striking a lovely pose.

"Due to the violent circumstances that have confined me to this wheelchair…" and here she paused for dramatic effect.

Dorothy, in her eagerness to promote the conversation that had begun between the two guests, inappropriately jumped in by saying: "I'm sure everyone present is aware of that terrifying episode when a psychotic fan shot and wounded Miss Cunningham, tragically bringing to an end a brilliant career. The Baron and I feel strongly that Miss Cunningham will find a seclusion and peace of mind…here…by, hopefully, becoming one of the *first* residents of the new Escape Island project."

"It is certainly a possibility," she said to Dorothy. Turning again to the Doctor, she continued, "As I was saying, I feel easier…more at home…in the gloom."

Then she became startlingly dramatic in delivery: "Whereas I once desperately wanted the glare of spotlights, in the days of my fame as the leading daytime soap opera star of my generation."

The Doctor immediately rose to his feet and crossed briskly to her, taking her hand, studying it, and then studying her eyes. After a moment full of expectation, he kissed her hand. He kissed it for a long time and with a slow, lingering delight.

"Indeed you were the undisputed queen of daytime, and with good reason," he said in a low voice full of passion.

"Permit me," he said, and gently touched her face with his fingertips.

She did not mind.

"How great the temptation must be for a cosmetician—for any cosmetician—to make all dull faces resemble the divine features and matchless expressions of Babs Cunningham," he sighed.

The Doctor then settled into the chair nearest her.

Trish watched this scene between Babs and the Doctor with sneering disapproval. Then she quite deliberately put her fingers in her open mouth and pretended to regurgitate, growling, "*Barf!*"

Dorothy was outraged by Trish's behavior. She noted with

much relief that the Doctor and Babs were too engrossed in each other to have registered Trish's rudeness, but she was affronted by the behavior. Her back raised, she headed for Trish.

"What? What?" she exclaimed in a harsh whisper. "What was that sound? Did someone go '*Barf!*'?"

Trish also raised her back, and like a threatening cat, hissed at Dorothy. "Hissssssssssssss!"

Foster could hardly believe how the relationship between Dorothy and Trish had deteriorated in just a few short weeks. His relations with Trish, while still not ideal, had at least improved. But she and Dorothy, who had started out so chummy, had begun to get on one another's nerves. They were not even behaving with tolerance. Instead, they were acting like a mother and daughter who irritated each other.

Dorothy, forgetting her place, hissed back at Trish. "Hissssssss!"

Trish went further—not only hissing again, but showing her red fingernail claws and making a quick catlike clawing motion in Dorothy's direction. "Hisssssss!"

Seeing the raised claw, Dorothy made a small, frightened hiss, and backed off. Almost as if for protection, she moved toward the Baron. He had been snoozing, and was not paying attention. She sat on the arm of his chair and gave Trish a defiant look.

Foster had arrived through the door to the conservatory, that ominous looking jungle of plants, herbs, tall shrubs, and vines, where one corner was hidden by a virtual wall of bamboo. He walked over to the Major and Mrs. Hurley, who were seated on a bench beneath a tall, spreading plant that looked as if it might devour them at any second.

"Beg pardon, sir," he said. "But the Baron wishes me to ask if you will be joining the others for tea, or would you prefer to be served out here?"

The Major replied, "Thank you, Foster, Mrs. Hurley and I will be joining the others shortly. Oh, and Foster, out of curiosity— I mean, I'm sure Lorraine and I are still much too full from lunch… but what I was wondering was…is any sort of staple being served?"

"Sandwiches and cake are being served, sir. At any time you may also request a more substantial meal. Just inform me of your wishes."

"Oh, that's splendid. Isn't it, Lorraine?" the Major said. "Not that we are hungry at the present time, mind you, but it is good to know. And you say that any such request…request for nourishment…we make directly to you?"

As Foster was heading for the door, he turned, replying, "Yes, sir, you may inform me directly."

"Splendid. Splendid, thank you, Foster."

After Foster had gone, the Major turned to his wife and said, "Lorraine, I'm starving, the breakfast served on the airline was hours ago. Let's go in and have some of the tea sandwiches, and perhaps I can find a suitable moment to suggest to Foster that we might, after all, be able to manage a spot of something more substantial."

"James, I know I agreed to this weekend, but I just don't think I can face these people," Lorraine said, close to tears, and her right eye began to twitch uncontrollably.

"Don't be ridiculous, my dear," the Major said. "They are delighted to have us. As indeed they should be. They are a grim lot, so far at any rate, and we shall treat them to our charming best."

"Yes, delighted to have us because they have mistaken us for some wealthy couple with a similar name. Once they discover that we are destitute, merely looking for yet another free room and free meals, they'll soon throw us off this island. I just can't bear these constant humiliations. My nerves can't take much more." Her right eye twitched even more violently.

"Nonsense, my dear, we are thousands of miles from any of the people who know about our temporary unfortunate financial circumstances."

"Temporary? James, we have been destitute ever since the army retired you eight years ago. We have nothing of our own, and have long ago worn out our welcome with friends and family alike." She paused before adding, "I know that you've never even looked for a job."

"You know perfectly well that I am waiting for the right career opportunity to present itself. With my background, I can't be just your ordinary laborer. Now, please do smile, and let us go inside."

"What will I do in the evenings?" she asked. "How can I possibly go down to dinner with nothing to wear but this traveling suit?"

"I have a plan that might provide us with the proper evening clothes. Leave it to me. Let us begin to enjoy this lovely weekend. Just leave it to me, dear."

"Oh, James. James." And she gave a sigh of resignation.

In the sitting room, Foster was leaning over the Baron, whispering something. He then rose and headed toward the serving table.

Trish, who was still at the serving table, began to make a jerking motion, because, shoes off, she was massaging one foot then the other on the table legs. As she saw Foster coming, she turned her head away from him in order to make a nasty face, referring to his body odor.

The Baron gestured to Dorothy, who had been chatting with Doctor Armstrong and Babs Cunningham. She saw the Baron summoning, and excused herself.

As Dorothy neared the Baron, he said in a confidential tone, "Foster tells me that the Major and his wife will be joining us shortly. Now, remind me, who else are we waiting for?"

"We are waiting most of all for Mr. Alan Silver and his companion," she replied in an equally confidential tone.

"Remind me. Why are we waiting most of all for this Mr. Silver?"

"Because he is a billionaire. The wealthiest guest we are likely to have this summer."

The Baron nodded, still looking puzzled.

"And Mr. Silver has shown a decided interest in your development," she said, pausing for a response from him that did not come. So she continued, "Remember, I told you…if he chose to, you would not even need other investors."

"No, no, I made it quite clear. I do not wish to be dictated to by just one partner. I desire many investors. There is safety in many."

"Of course, Baron, I understand your wishes, I was just saying…" Dorothy was at a momentary loss for words. It was the Baron who had chosen to invite this "Big Al" person, although she had questioned the wisdom. Surely, he wanted Big Al Silver as a guest because he was capable of financing most or all of the enterprise?

"Anyway," she continued, "it is only Mr. Alan Silver and his companion who have not yet arrived on the island."

"Everyone else is here, then?" the Baron said in surprise. "It doesn't look like many."

Dorothy said, ever so pleasantly, "If you remember, Baron, we agreed to keep these weekends exclusive…particularly this initial one."

"But surely this can't be everyone? Are we having so few guests?"

With extreme kindness and patience, she answered, "No,

Baron, it is not everyone. Most are on the island but not present here in the sitting room."

"Dorothy, I seem to recall that the local Constable from the mainland promised to come. That chap isn't the Constable, is he? I thought you said he was some kind of a doctor."

"The Constable is due to arrive only after dinner…for coffee. He wishes to give a short speech about good community relations."

"Then who in blazes is that chap?" the Baron asked irritably.

"That is Doctor Armstrong."

"Doctor?" the Baron asked, with concern. "I don't recall feeling ill. Am I?"

"You're fine, Baron," she replied, patting his hand. "Doctor Armstrong is wealthy and retired. He is a prospective investor. And so is the lady he is conferring with, the famous actress, Babs Cunningham. She is most interested in the island development."

"Are they the only two guests?"

She laughed gently. "No, Baron. Mr. Alan Silver and his companion have yet to arrive on the island. The Major and his wife are still enjoying your wonderful conservatory, and that young fellow, the one whose father sent him, the one whose father is an investment banker…he and his lady friend went to their bedroom over an hour ago."

"Oh, yes, that young fellow," the Baron said, suddenly remembering. "Father's an investment banker. Yes. Boy has an unusual name…?"

"Ren…. Ren Silvestri."

"Ren? Never heard that name before. Brought with him a most attractive young woman. Doesn't wear much clothing."

"French," Dorothy said, as if that were all the explanation needed.

"Ah, yes." It obviously explained the Baron's observation. "Where are they?" the Baron again wanted to know.

"They went to their bedroom over an hour ago," Dorothy said, "and have not yet deigned to come down and join the rest of us."

"Been in their bedroom for more than an hour. How odd. This is the middle of the day, is it not? What could they possibly be doing?"

CHAPTER FIVE

As the Baron was asking Dorothy what the two young people could possibly be doing in their bedroom at this time of day, in one of the guest suites upstairs, Ren Silvestri and Jackie Le Roir were tearing the bed apart with their lovemaking…two naked forms thrashing and bouncing. Their violent love-play was veiled behind the curtains of the old-fashioned draped bed, their movements large and athletic. The ancient four-poster squeaked and the springs positively screamed with the unaccustomed activity.

Suddenly, Jackie howled as Ren entered her.

Their movements turned rhythmic.

In a flash he had ejaculated. It was over.

There were loud sounds of satisfaction. His were genuine, hers fake.

They fell to the floor, laughing, and their beautiful young faces and bodies were covered in perspiration. Their breathing, between giggles, was heavy.

Ren was delighted with his performance. Jackie smiled at him, but turned her head and looked to heaven with an "I Don't Believe

This" expression. She turned back to Ren, smiling, kissing him lightly on the lips, then rolled over onto her stomach and rose.

"I'm going to run a bath for us," she said breathlessly, and started into the bathroom.

Ren remained on the floor, admiring her from that position. As she entered the bathroom, the back view of Jackie's naked form made his loins react.

She headed toward the bathtub, a huge old-fashioned iron one on balled legs, and began twisting her hair into a knot on top of her head.

"Ren, wait till you see this funny old-fashioned tub," she said.

He was still looking at her tight buttocks and wondering if he should have her, again, right now, or let her get on with her bath.

"After our bath I'd love to have a swim while it's still light. Or do you think we have to spend some time with our host before we can go outside?"

He was still considering getting up and grabbing her, so he didn't answer immediately.

"I'd love to put on my bikini and go for a swim."

"Then do it, Pussy Cat," he said, "and without the bikini if you want. When you're with me, you do as you please."

"I just thought I'd love to get in a swim while the sun is shining. Or do you think we have to stay and socialize with the others? We haven't even said 'Hello.' Won't Count What's-His-Name think we're rude?"

"Baron. Baron Tarrall," he said. "And stuff him. You want to go swimming, we go swimming. My papa told me he's ga-ga and broke. In fact, so broke…if *I* decide this is a good deal…I go back to Papa, tell him my decision…he buys the whole thing right out from under the old ga-ga Baron."

He had risen, and was lighting a cigarette. He'd decided to make love to her later. The idea of having to please anyone or be polite to anyone had put him right off the prospect of sex. Obeying rules, or being dictated to by anyone but his Papa, always made Ren angry—unreasonably angry.

Looking out the window, and inhaling deeply, he said again, with an edge to his voice, "You want to go swimming, we'll go swimming. Stuff the old Baron." He had exhaled, and dragged deeply again on his cigarette.

Jackie was always alarmed by Ren's mood swings, the way his anger flashed, seemingly over nothing. He had never hurt her, never even threatened her physically, but she felt the potential was there. He was seething with suppressed anger that might one day turn on her.

"Hey, Pussy Cat, don't put any of that sissy bubble bath in the tub, if I'm bathing with you," he said, still looking out the window.

Jackie's face got a "whoops" look. She was already holding a bottle of bubble bath under the faucet and bubbles had started to mount in the tub.

In the sitting room, the shadows of afternoon had begun to deepen. Major Hurley and his wife had joined the others. And, at the moment, the Major was piling whipped cream high on a piece of chocolate cake. Trish looked on in amazement at the mountain of cream. The Major smiled charmingly at Trish, and for once she dropped her perpetually sour look, and replaced it with a hesitant smile.

The Major took the cake over to his wife, Lorraine, seated alone on the far side of the room. As Hurley crossed the room he saw that the Doctor and Babs were in deep conversation, and that Dorothy was sitting on the arm of the Baron's easy chair, explaining something to him in whispers.

As Major Hurley arrived with the chocolate cake, Lorraine was being handed a cup of tea by Foster. The Major did not seem to sense his wife's utter discomfort. Handing her the cake, he said, "Here, my dear, I know how full you are, but this is your favorite."

He then turned around and walked a few steps toward Foster. "I say, Foster, old man," he said *sotto voce*, "I find that I am a bit peckish after all."

"Certainly, sir, what may I get for you?"

"Oh, something light…just some small tidbit…nothing that's any trouble.… Some ham and eggs perhaps."

"Very good, sir," Foster replied, and turned to go.

"Oh, and Foster… Perhaps a small salad to follow…with some cheese, perhaps. Nothing elaborate…some small selection, and with biscuits, of course."

"Very good, sir," he said, and moved toward the serving table.

As Foster walked away, the Major rejoined his wife, picking up his own cup of tea from the side table. He glanced again at Babs and the Doctor, still engrossed in each other. Then he smiled warmly at his wife, who sat stiffly holding the cake. Her eye twitching, Lorraine sighed unhappily, and looked away from him.

Arriving beside Trish, Foster told her, "Leave the tea things. I'll take charge of getting more hot water for the pot. Go into the kitchen and make a portion of ham and eggs, a mixed salad, the cheese board, and biscuits."

Trish gave Foster a look that could kill. "You've got to be joking. I've been on my feet all day. This is far too much work for one person. I've got to start dinner soon. What joker wants a full meal at this hour?"

"The Major. And none of your lip, girl. Get to it, and do as you're told," Foster said sternly. "I'll diplomatically inquire if the Major would mind, considering the lateness of the hour, eating his meal at the kitchen table."

Trish looked over toward the Major, her expression softening, and she purred, "Oh, the Major, huh? Well, maybe such a light meal won't be too much trouble." She reached down and put her shoes back on.

Trish then exited for the kitchen, followed by Foster, who carried the empty teapot.

Dorothy rose from the Baron's armrest and headed toward the Hurleys.

As Dorothy approached, Lorraine felt even more ill at ease. She tried to appear dignified, but was unable to stop her eye from twitching. Also she could not bring herself to rise and cross to the serving table, and the tiny table beside her did not have the space for the huge piece of cake, so she felt obliged to just keep holding it on her lap.

The Major saw Dorothy coming and pulled up a straight-backed chair, placing it next to them, so that Dorothy might sit.

"Thank you," Dorothy said, accepting the chair the Major held for her. "I want to tell you how absolutely delighted the Baron is to have you here. We all are," she gushed. "Please let one of us, Foster or Trish or me, know if there is anything you need. I don't believe you've seen your accommodations as yet. Please let me know if they are satisfactory."

"That is very, very kind of you, Ms. Saks," the Major said. "Isn't it kind, Lorraine?"

"Oh, please call me Dorothy. Everyone does." Dorothy laughed nervously. "I'm just the hired help, you know." She laughed again, taking a sideways look at the Baron, who was still dozing.

"Dorothy," the Major said, "we have not as yet visited our rooms, because, as you may have noticed, our luggage has been lost."

Dorothy suddenly panicked. This sort of thing could lose them an investor, and her...her job. "Oh, dear, was it the airline?"

"Yes, I'm afraid so," the Major replied.

Dorothy was preoccupied, wondering how much of this might be considered her fault. "Oh, dear, I feel responsible. After all, I chose the airline, when you answered positively to our offer to provide all of your transportation needs," she said. "I must telephone them immediately."

"Please don't trouble…eh, Dorothy. We have filled out all the necessary forms, and been assured by the airline that our luggage will be brought here…if it is located. But you see…the awkward thing is that now Lorraine will have nothing suitable to wear to dinner."

Dorothy was visibly relieved. The problem was something she could solve. "That's easily taken care of. Oh, my, yes indeed. We have a superb boutique on the mainland. I will have them send over a selection in your size."

Now it was the Major's turn to be worried. "We were thinking perhaps my wife might borrow a frock from one of the other ladies." He began to stutter. "This boutique…I wonder…I mean, will they take a foreign check?"

"There will be no need for that," Dorothy reassured him. "The Baron will insist upon providing substitutions for the items you have lost."

"Oh, that is kind. Isn't that kind, Lorraine?"

Dorothy turned to Lorraine, asking, "May I take that cake from you? I see there is nowhere handy to put it down."

Gratefully, Lorraine handed the cake to Dorothy.

Dorothy took it, saying, "I'll have Foster bring you a pad and pencil. Take your time. Make a list of the toiletries and so forth that you'll need to make your stay comfortable. The captain of our yacht can have one of his crew members purchase them."

Lorraine never approved of the way James shammed people, but she also never ceased to be amazed at how often he got out of a mess.

James saw that the Doctor had begun wheeling Babs in their direction, and called out to him. "Well, Doctor Armstrong, there you are. We men of the world really must have a lengthy chat."

The Doctor ignored him and stopped Dorothy, who was on her way to put down the plate of cake. She was aware that his movements were jerky, that his eyes darted about. He was definitely agitated. Dorothy was afraid, both of him and of how he might threaten her position.

"Ms. Saks, I should like to know what we are waiting for. Why have you requested that we remain in this particular vicinity?" he asked.

Dorothy stared at him in fright and could not think of an answer.

He continued, "We have been thoroughly saturated with your promotional harangue…as well as with innumerable cups of tea."

Dorothy didn't know how she could possibly respond to the criticism and continued to remain silent.

"Now," he said, "Miss Cunningham and I would like to enjoy the seclusion of the conservatory." He added with emphasis, "And we wish to be there on our own."

"Yes, of course, Doctor. Call me Dorothy, please." Her laugh was even more nervous than usual. "I'm merely one of the hired help, you know," she again said, and again looked to the sleeping Baron.

The Doctor followed her look and said quite flatly, "The Baron is a most boring man. Does he sleep continuously?"

Dorothy was shocked by this slander of the Baron and quickly changed the subject. Indicating the Hurleys, she asked, "I have introduced you to the Major and Mrs. Hurley, haven't I?"

The Major was anxious to ingratiate himself, and said, "Yes, yes, we have had the pleasure. Tell me, Doctor, what do you think of the island? Are you enjoying—"

The Doctor not only ignored him but also rudely cut him off by turning to Dorothy. "My question, Ms. Saks, was 'What are we waiting for?' Do you wish us to remain here in this acute discomfort?"

"Oh, no. Acute discomfort? My goodness, no," Dorothy stammered. "Well, you see, we are waiting for the arrival on the island of our missing guests…Mr. Alan Silver and his lady companion… Cheri…eh, just Cheri." She paused and swallowed hard to gain control. "The Baron did so want everyone to meet this afternoon… get acquainted. Know one another before cocktails and dinner tonight."

Babs asked in the politest of fashions, "So everyone is here except Mr. Silver and his companion, Cheri?"

Dorothy stammered on, "Yes… Of course, Mr. Ren Silvestri and Miss Jacqueline Le Roir, although present, have not come down from their bedroom as yet. And after dinner we are to be treated to a speech from our local—"

The Doctor silenced her by saying, "Please stop babbling, Ms. Saks. My question is answered. If you will excuse us, Miss Cunningham and I are going to the conservatory."

With that he wheeled Babs toward the doorway, but he stopped before exiting. There was a great racket at the front door and inside the entrance hall. The Doctor waited to see what the commotion was about.

CHAPTER SIX

The loud sounds at the front door and then inside the entrance hall actually came from a deep, booming male voice, so that the arrival of "Big Al" Silver was heard long before it was seen.

It was difficult for those in the sitting room to tell if Big Al Silver was complaining, making jokes, or both. He was saying of the conservatory: "What's this? The indoor Amazon? Where are the bare-breasted babes?" He laughed heartily. "Damned creepy place. Why did I come? I hate traveling. All I like is women." And at the mention of women, he made what sounded like a slurping noise. "Like any red-blooded man, I like women, good food, bourbon, and my Havanas. But above all, women." Again there was a slurp. "This place looks like it'll fall apart before the weekend's over. How'd I get talked into this? You told me it was going to be some kind of mansion."

He then burst into the gloomy sitting room, where he stopped abruptly and squinted his eyes as if it were impossible to see. "I can't see," he said. "What is this, a funeral parlor?" And he laughed again, but somehow wickedly this time.

Big Al was followed by a breathtakingly beautiful blonde, who everyone surmised was the much-spoken-of "Cheri." And Cheri was followed by Foster and Trish, who were struggling with what appeared to be dozens of suitcases, hatboxes, makeup cases, and so forth.

Cheri had been sauntering sexily behind Big Al, stopping when he stopped. Now, in the sitting room, she posed, one hip jutting out, so that her already tight white dress stretched to its limits. Her figure, which was voluptuous, was revealed to the fullest.

Big Al flung his arms forward like a partially blind man reaching out in the dark. "You ought to get some light in here," he said. "The first thing I'd do, I'd tear out that wall and those windows with the colored glass…. No, the first thing I'd do, would be fumigate." This he thought so funny that he roared with laughter. "Then I'd shoot the bigger animals and uproot the jungle." His laugh continued but again turned wicked. "Then I'd tear out the colored glass and the walls. Hell, why not demolish the whole place and start again?" Now he was so overcome by his own wit that his laughter made him choke.

Cheri sauntered up beside him, saying, "Those are called stained glass windows, Big Al. People in the know think they're special and beautiful. They cost a fortune."

Dorothy was the first one to approach the Vaudevillesque couple. She arrived to stand beside Big Al, her enthusiasm positively bubbly. "Mr. Silver, we are so pleased that you and your companion have arrived. I do hope your trip was not too tiring…"

Now Dorothy froze because Big Al, never looking at her face, was staring only at her breasts. He studied them, and then reached out to hold one, testing it for firmness.

"Nice and firm," he said. "Good feel. Like that size." He made his slurping sound.

Dorothy was totally shocked. She stood staring at him in disbelief.

"*Ooohh*," she finally uttered. "My. Well, I never."

Everyone remained in an embarrassed silence except for Trish. Trish giggled.

Big Al turned at the sound of Trish's giggle, and like an automaton, put his hand up the front of her skirt. "That's a very, very nice feel. Thank you, Ma'am," he said, roaring with laughter.

Now it was Trish's turn to be stunned. She said quietly, "This is what they must mean by sexual harassment."

Cheri looked at Trish and smiled sweetly. "Big Al is such a bad boy. He can't keep his hands off any female."

But Doctor Armstrong was indignant at the behavior and spoke up. "I'd say he's a blackguard. An uncouth barbarian."

Big Al was flabbergasted by the remark. "Barbarian! You crazy," he said. "This is a hand-tailored suit...Saville Row The Bronx. My tailor, Mannie, keeps me on my feet for hours so that there isn't a crease." He smoothed his jacket front. "You see a crease?"

Dorothy, ever the peacemaker, quickly said, "Certainly not. It is a very fine suit. No one sees a crease."

Cheri said, "Big Al always dresses sharp."

Big Al further defended himself. "A pure silk shirt made to order." Adjusting his tie, he continued, "A two-hundred-dollar tie. And tell me, wise guy, when did you ever see a barbarian in a pair of thousand-dollar two-tone alligator shoes?"

Dorothy interjected, "Never. I'm sure. Never."

Cheri said, "When it comes to Big Al's appearance, money is no object."

He felt his chin. "I have my own barber...comes in every day... shave and a trim." Holding out his hand, he said, "Look at that manicure." And he shined his huge diamond ring on his jacket front.

"He even has his handkerchiefs handmade," Cheri added.

"That's right. And if you wanta talk *couth*—one for *show*..." Big Al fluffed up the red hankie that was on display in his breast pocket. Then, taking a crumpled hankie out of his pants pocket and showing it all around, he laughed, "...And one for *blow*."

Dorothy laughed with him, although her laughter was forced. "How droll," she said.

But Big Al misunderstood the word. "What?" he growled.

"*Amusing...* Droll... Amusing. Very amusing," Dorothy explained.

Big Al shrugged, then walked over and stood in front of the Baron, obliging him to rise. "Well, Tarrall, we're finally here. Lousy trip. If I buy this island, the first thing I'll do is put in a landing strip for my jet. I hate boats. Lousy way to travel, even a short distance. This place looks pretty bad to me. This business deal worth coming for? Worth coming across in that rocking tub of a boat for?"

Cheri came up beside Big Al. "I'm Cheri, Baron. Pleased to make your acquaintance." She held out her hand. The Baron kissed it in the best European manner.

"Big Al," Cheri said, "the word for the Baron's boat is *yacht*, not boat."

Big Al's voice had a hint of menace as he said to the Baron: "You start spending money on these chicks...make them look like a million, with a wardrobe that costs you that much, or more... and these chicks...all of them, of course, with sexy, drive-you–nuts bodies, but with pea brains...they start tellin' ya how to speak... how to behave." He slid his hand onto Cheri's bum in a show of possession. He continued, "So you gotta keep putting them in their place. Otherwise their pea brains begin thinking, 'Let's take the guy over.'"

Foster and Trish, still loaded down with cases and waiting for instructions, were becoming impatient. Trish was shuffling her feet but keeping her distance from Big Al. Foster, however, was disdainful of Big Al and boldly stepped closer. "Excuse me, Baron, but may we have permission to take Mr. Silver and Miss Cheri's luggage to their suite?"

"Yes, yes, Foster, you may proceed," the Baron said. But suddenly he was unsure, and not wishing to presume too much, said to Big Al, "That is… I trust that you will be staying with us, Mr. Silver. I do hope everything is not too unsatisfactory…that you will be spending the weekend with us, as planned."

Dorothy became frantic at the suggestion that Mr. Silver might leave without investing. She hurriedly interjected, "Oh, I'm sure Mr. Silver and Miss Cheri will wish to get settled in, freshen up before cocktails." Addressing Cheri, she said, "Perhaps you'd care to have tea in your rooms while you're unpacking. Of course, Trish will be happy to unpack for you if you so desire."

Trish shot Dorothy a dirty look. "I think Miss *Cherry* better do her own unpacking, I'm going to be busy in the kitchen."

Foster nudged Trish with the corner of a suitcase, forcing her toward the staircase. "We'll just settle these things in your suite. If you'd care to follow me, sir."

Trish led the way to the staircase, followed by Foster, and once in motion again, both had new struggles with the luggage.

Big Al walked behind Foster, taking a cigar out of his pocket, licking it and putting it in his mouth, unlit, to suck on. He was looking the place over, and remained unimpressed. Cheri followed him, her hips moving with exaggerated motion. She seemed curious about the tapestries and portraits on the walls, and paused occasionally to study them. The group was trailed by Dorothy, who seemed hesitant, not knowing what she should do, and afraid to get too close.

Giggles came from the floor above and Jackie appeared on the stairs in the tiniest of string bikinis. "*Bon jour.*"

Everyone froze to observe her, but Big Al, jolted by the sight of her, froze in place, the cigar hanging out of his open mouth.

Jackie attempted, on that narrow staircase, to squeeze by Trish,

Foster, and all the luggage. Big Al continued to watch Jackie's every move, his eyes undressing her all the way, his breathing heavy.

Cheri paid no attention, but Dorothy was rigid in anticipation of what Big Al might do.

As Jackie approached the bottom of the steps and started to move past Big Al, he reached out for the ties of her string top and pulled. The bra ties gave way, leaving her chest bare.

Trish stopped midway up the staircase and blurted out, "Look! She's bare-chested!"

Foster said dryly, "French."

Trish understood. She answered, "Ah, yes."

Retrieving the bra and holding it in her hand, Jackie continued across the room, exiting through the far right door.

Dorothy felt faint, but was also obliged to be a good hostess. She searched for something to say to ease the tension. Big Al was staring into space, watching the door Jackie had left from. Dorothy stepped a little closer to him. "Is there anything I can do for you, Mr. Silver? Please let me know if I can be of service in any way."

In one swift motion, Big Al extended an arm, swooping Dorothy into his side and holding her there with her feet inches off the floor. "Yeah. Yeah, ya can do it yourself, or you can get that sexy piece to service me," he said, and then slurped repeatedly.

Dorothy, her feet dangling, was completely helpless until Big Al set her down. Now flustered beyond all control, she backed away, stammering, "Oh...oh, well, I don't think...I could...if...well... enjoy your afternoon. The Baron looks forward to seeing you in the sitting room at six-thirty this evening for cocktails."

Just then Ren appeared at the top of the stairs, dressed in a designer beach robe. His hair was slicked back and he was tapping a cigarette on a gold cigarette case. Not seeing Jackie, he called out, "Pussy Cat?"

"She your Pussy Cat?" Big Al asked, making at the same time

his slurping noise. "Don't look to me like you could handle a Dark Pussy Cat like that one."

Ren's face turned a vivid red. He looked for a long moment at Big Al, but then decided not to challenge him. So he raced past Big Al, past the people in the sitting room, and, ignoring them all, rushed outside after Jackie.

Big Al had a nasty grin on his face as he watched Ren exit. Turning to Cheri, he said, "Come on, Blonde Pussy Cat, let's go upstairs."

CHAPTER SEVEN

At precisely six-thirty on that same Friday, the cocktail hour had begun in the sitting room. Already present were the Baron and Dorothy, the Doctor and Babs, and the Major and Lorraine.

Only Ren and Jackie, Big Al and Cheri had not yet come downstairs. Trish was in another part of the house, but Foster was standing by to refill the glasses. The ladies each had a glass of sherry and the gentlemen a whiskey and soda.

The ladies were in evening gowns and the gentlemen in black tie, with the exception of the Major, who was still wearing his grey trousers and navy blue blazer, claiming his luggage had been lost. They were gathered around the fireplace, in which Foster had built a good hot fire with steadily burning logs. And as the evening was overcast, damp, and cold, the fire was proving to be most welcome.

Dorothy, as was her habit, was addressing the small gathering as if they were a crowd: "Well, isn't this lovely. Everyone is now present on the island. At least all of our weekend guests. Later this evening we are expecting an interesting local visitor, for an after-dinner speech and discussion."

The Baron looked puzzled and asked, "We are? Who?"

"Yes, Baron," Dorothy said. "I believe you will recall that the local Constable is paying us a visit. If you remember, we wanted him to brief our guests about local rules and regulations, perhaps answer any security or other official questions that they might have."

The Baron nodded but it was apparent he did not remember.

Foster came up to the Major and spoke confidentially. "Excuse me, Major, but I believe your light repast is now ready. Perhaps you wouldn't mind taking it at the kitchen table. Forgive me for suggesting it, but it is only because of the lateness of the hour."

The Major replied in an equally low voice. "Certainly, certainly, Foster. That would be the appropriate place at this hour."

The Major then turned to his wife and held her at arm's length to observe her. "Again, let me tell you how lovely you look." He kissed her on the cheek and whispered into her ear, "Excuse me, my dear. I'm just going to slip into the kitchen. Are you sure you won't join me?"

Lorraine said, "Heavens, no, James, dinner is not far off." She said it with an unaccustomed lightheartedness, because she did, indeed, look lovely in her new flowered chiffon gown. She was feeling good about herself: younger, prettier, and more self-confident than she had felt in years. The famous Babs Cunningham and even the cranky Doctor Armstrong had each complimented her on her appearance. When James left for the kitchen, Lorraine stepped over to the Baron and Dorothy, there to receive more compliments on her appearance.

The Baron said, "How lovely you look this evening, Mrs. Hurley. I was just remarking to Dorothy that I feel fortunate indeed to be surrounded by a bevy of beautiful women this weekend."

Dorothy was smiling with satisfaction because she had saved the day by providing Mrs. Hurley with a gown. "You do look absolutely marvelous," Dorothy added. "I'm so delighted that our local boutique was able to provide some substitutes for your missing garments."

Suddenly there was lightning, followed by thunder. The huge chandelier overhead flashed off and on, as did the other lights in the room. Everyone looked first up at the chandelier and then toward the windows. Again there was a lightning flash, followed by an even louder clap of thunder.

Babs said, "Oh, dear, I'm afraid we're in for quite a storm, and I hadn't heard anything about the approach of bad weather."

The Doctor agreed that it looked nasty and hoped it would pass quickly,

Dorothy tried to put a good face on it by saying, "Well, we are warm and dry in here. Isn't the fire wonderful? And if the lights go out temporarily we have romantic candlelight to eat by."

A roar seemed to mix with the next clap of thunder, as Big Al made his entrance down the stairs. He was dressed in a garish silver and black tuxedo, a garment reminiscent of gangster attire in Chicago during the Thirties. He was followed by Cheri, whose skin-tight silver dress matched his tux and shone brightly even in the dim light.

Big Al was roaring, "A thunderstorm! This island is isolated enough without help from the weather. Butler! I need a large bourbon on the rocks. The first thing I'd do is build a bridge to the mainland."

Cheri spotted Babs. Her eyes grew as big as saucers, and she made straight for the famous actress, where she fell to her knees. "Babs Cunningham, the famous Babs Cunningham! I can't believe I'm in the same room with you, actually face to face with my favorite soap star of all times. You'll never know how sad I was, how I cried when I heard about that crazy fan shooting you."

Big Al got curious about Babs. Like an ape might, he put his hand on her head and tilted it back to get a better look at her pretty face. A startled Babs looked angrily at him. His audacity! But Big

Al smiled, slurped, and moved away to hurry up the pouring of his bourbon. He felt any woman should be flattered by his attention.

Cheri seemed oblivious to what went on between Big Al and Babs, and continued to gush. "How I waited for news of your condition. Then when you recovered, I felt like my own life was good again. You know, and this is the truth, I just don't enjoy the daytime shows anywhere near as much as I used to…anywhere near as much as I did when I used to be able to watch Babs Cunningham."

"Thank you, my dear," Babs said. "Those are such reassuring words. I have always been devoted to my fans. Never has one of my fan letters gone unanswered. I even sign all cards and photographs personally. That's why, perhaps even more than the injury, I have never been able to understand why a fan should want to do me harm." Here she paused to effect a lingering, dramatic look of hurt. Babs' expression was not lost on Doctor Armstrong. He bent over to kiss her hand.

"Oh, my dear. My dearest dear," the Doctor said.

Babs looked at him gratefully. "Thank you for your ever-present kindness," she said.

Big Al returned, drink in hand, to stand directly behind Babs. With his free hand, he slowly turned Babs' face toward him, and observed it. "Beautiful!" he declared. Then he let go of her face. But he wasn't finished with her, and before she could react, he had reached over her shoulder, and out of curiosity had begun to feel her leg. "Any sensation in the vital parts? Can you feel that, Beautiful?"

With one quick movement, the Doctor grabbed Big Al's arm and moved it to the side of Babs' wheelchair. Then he moved his body around to stand with his face straight into Big Al's face, addressing him in a quiet but intense voice: "Never touch her again. Never say a word to her. Never even go near her again. If you do, you are a dead man."

They looked at each other viciously, but then Big Al backed off with a laugh. "Okay, okay, Doc. Hey, I like you, Doc. Hey, I like this guy. The Doc's got guts."

The chandelier grew brighter for a second and then dimmed. There was more lightning and thunder. Foster began to light the large candelabra that rested on the mantelpiece.

Big Al again called out, "Where's the butler? I want bourbon!"

The Doctor took a glass and reached toward the bottles, one of which was clearly marked *BOURBON*.

There was a huge flash of lightning that seemed to be very close by. Then came a tremendous thunderclap. All the lights went out and everyone was grateful for the fireplace and the candelabra.

In the kitchen, Trish was also lighting a candelabra. The Major was seated at the table, his place already set, and Trish began putting a large array of food in front of him: a plate with bacon and eggs, a large serving bowl with salad and a salad plate, a well-stocked cheeseboard, a bowl of fruit, a basket of bread and crackers, and a decanter of red wine.

The Major was saying, "You know, Miss Trish, I have rarely seen a finer meal. You have the gift of the great cooks of the world." He began eating with relish. "During my years in Her Majesty's Service, I was called upon to be in many parts of the Empire…had the opportunity, you know, to partake of some of the finest and most exotic of dishes. But there is nothing like plain country cooking. Nothing compares." He looked up as the lights came back on.

Trish replied, "Well, I'm glad you're enjoying it, Major. That makes me feel good. And there aren't many things around here that make me feel good. I don't like this job. They work me half to death."

Both Trish and the Major turned at the sound of the swinging kitchen doors opening. Ren and Jackie entered, wearing their evening clothes. "God, we're starving," Ren said.

"Oh, did you miss out on tea?" the Major asked, rising at Jackie's approach. "Allow me to present myself, Major James Hurley, at your service. And this young woman is our most excellent cook, Patricia, affectionately known as Trish. You are?"

"*Bon soir,*" Jackie said, as she took a seat. "I'm Jackie Le Roir and this is Ren Silvestri."

The Major bowed and sat down again. "Pleased to meet you. I did see you earlier as you dashed through on your way to sunbathe."

Ren seated himself at the table and began eating directly from the serving dishes. Trish looked at him in disgust and went to get two more place settings.

Jackie waited politely for the place settings to arrive. The Major continued his conversation with her. "Can't say as I blame you… for sunbathing, I mean. It was a most pleasant day, earlier. Lorraine and I were enjoying the warmth of the conservatory. Looks now as though we're in for a bit of a storm."

Trish returned with the napkins and silverware for Jackie and Ren. "That conservatory is the Baron's pride and joy," she said. "But he doesn't do much work in it anymore. Dorothy's been looking after it, and I planted a few herbs of my own."

As Trish turned to get two more plates, the Major said, "It is a marvelous pastime, a conservatory. When I was stationed in India—"

Ren interrupted him by asking, "What's a conservatory?"

"Why, that lovely glassed-in garden just off the main corridor," the Major replied.

"Yeah, well, I didn't see it," Ren said. "When my Pussy Cat is in her bikini, I don't see anything else but that sexy bod."

The Major thought it best to change the subject. "Yes, well, and to what do we owe the honor of your presence in the kitchen?"

Jackie replied, "We were on our way to join the others when

the lights went out. It gave us an excuse to escape to the kitchen and get something to eat."

"Speak for yourself." Ren continued to be rude. "I don't need an excuse for anything."

Picking up the decanter, the Major asked Jackie and Ren, "May I pour you a glass of this most excellent red wine? It seems quite appropriate for a light repast, a subtle but not overly intrusive bouquet for early evening."

"Yes, thank you," Jackie said. "I hope no one else catches us here. So far we've been a bit ill mannered. We haven't even said 'Hello' to our host, the Count."

Ren held his glass out for wine and received it from the Major without saying "Thank you." What he did say was: "The Baron, not the Count. Baron Ga-Ga. And who cares if we're rude. All the old penniless poop is interested in is our investment money. If we shell out the loot, he won't even notice that we forgot to say 'Hello.'"

The Major was taken aback by this piece of gossip. "So, then, it's your opinion that the Baron is, in fact, without money?"

"Papa said he was, and Papa has ways of knowing about anybody he wants to know about. Papa is rich, sure, but more than that, he's very well connected, informed, if you know what I mean. Papa sent me here to look over the deal. For investments, he listens to me."

Trish said, mostly to herself, "I only hope the Baron isn't so broke that I won't get paid. I'm not doing this drudgery for the love of it."

"Your father must think highly, indeed, of your judgment," the Major answered. Then, turning his attention to Jackie, he said, "And, tell me, Miss Le Roir, did you find this afternoon's sunbathing enjoyable?"

"Lovely, absolutely lovely."

A burst of thunder seemed to rock the kitchen.

"Let's hope tomorrow is sunny," Jackie said.

Ren got annoyed. "It better be. We're not staying if there's bad weather. If it rains tomorrow, we're out of here."

Jackie was all at once, and quite surprisingly, concerned at the mention of leaving. "But…what about deciding on the business proposition that your father sent you to consider?"

"I'll just make up my mind fast. Because…no sun…bye-bye Ren, and bye-bye Ren's Pussy Cat."

The Major attempted to comfort Jackie. "Island weather is highly changeable. This storm could pass quickly. They often do. Tomorrow we may not see a trace of it…but instead, glorious sun."

Suddenly all the lights went out again, and they would have been in a total blackout if not for the candelabra.

Trish was proud of her foresight. "Good thing I left these candles burning. I gotta go into the sitting room for a minute. I'll be right back."

With that, she picked up the candelabra and headed out the swinging doors, leaving the Major, Ren, and Jackie in darkness at the kitchen table. Ren started to protest, but it was too late. Trish was gone.

CHAPTER EIGHT

In the dining room, Dorothy was nervously hovering in the doorway, while guests were standing around waiting to be seated. The Major, Ren, and Jackie were still in the kitchen. Both the Doctor and Big Al had positively insisted that since the three were late, dinner should commence without them. Dorothy hoped that the latest blackout would keep everyone in the sitting room for a while longer, but it hadn't. Foster had been pressed into leading the way, holding aloft another candelabra. Now poor Dorothy was frantic. She certainly did not wish to begin serving without all the guests being seated at the table.

Trish entered, holding a candelabra, just as the lights returned. Dorothy took her by the arm and demanded that she find the missing guests and tell them urgently to come to the dining room.

Trish told her that the three were in the kitchen, eating. With that announcement, Dorothy had to grab the dining room door to keep from falling over in a faint.

The Doctor excused himself from Babs and took quick steps over to Dorothy. Ignoring her state of distress, he continued to harangue her. "We agreed cocktail hour was over. Everyone has had more than enough to drink. I wish my dinner now. I'm not in the habit of eating late."

"Neither am I. I'm hungry now," Big Al said as he approached her. Then he reached over and tweaked her nipple. "So let's eat."

Dorothy held tightly to the door as she swooned with nerves and embarrassment, but Big Al took no pity. He continued, "Let's eat or I could gobble you up." And he made gobbling sounds.

Although in shock and visibly sweating, Dorothy managed to speak. "We were hoping to have all our guests together for drinks, together, before even entering the dining room."

Lorraine turned and noticed Dorothy's distress. She hurried to Dorothy and took her arm, giving her much-needed support. "I'm so sorry to see you upset," Lorraine said. "I'm also sorry that James is not present. However, I know James is ready to come at any time. I just need to call him to join us."

Dorothy's voice came out in a thin rasp. "I'm sure the Major will come as soon as called. It is only Mr. Ren Silvestri and Miss Jacqueline Le Roir missing."

The Doctor heard this and spoke loudly. "I suggest you call them at once or they are in danger of missing out on the meal. I have no tolerance for tardiness or inconsideration."

Big Al roared good-naturedly. "I'm not always sure what you're talkin' about, Doc, but I agree. Now let's eat, or I might take a bite out of one of these here dames."

The five guests who were present seated themselves by checking their place cards. It was a rectangular table. The Baron was at the head of the table, with Cheri to his right and Babs to his left. On the right side, Big Al was next to Cheri. On the left side, the Doctor was next to Babs. Lorraine was next to the Doctor, and there was a free chair for the Major. And on the right side, there were vacant chairs for Jackie and Ren. Dorothy's place was to be at the foot of the table next to Ren and the Major:

	Right		_Left_
		Baron	
	Cheri		Babs
	Big Al		Doctor
	Jackie		Lorraine
	Ren		Major
		Dorothy	

Although the others sat, Dorothy was still hovering nervously in the doorway. Foster passed by her, entering the room with a decanter of wine. She asked him, "Where are the three? Did you find everyone? Do they know that the other guests are seated at the table?"

Foster slowed his step in order to answer, "They are on their way, Madam." Then he proceeded to the table and began pouring the wine, first for Lorraine, then Babs, then Cheri.

The Baron began a discourse about the wine, one of his favorite subjects: "I do hope you will enjoy the wines. This white one is light and tangy, one the ladies should find most pleasing to the palate."

Dorothy, still nervous, was unnaturally bubbly. She interjected, "Oh, Baron, I'm sure they will. I know I will. It's marvelous. I've tasted it before…obviously. It will be just right with the delicate white fish appetizer that is planned."

The Baron ignored her and continued with his train of thought: "On the other hand, the red will be a most special vintage. Heavy and satisfying. A wine that has been in the family for a number of years. A very good year. We are in the habit of serving it only for the most special of occasions. The most special of occasions. Fine wine."

Big Al said to Foster, "You can skip the wine for me. Never drink the stuff. Bring me another bourbon…and keep the bottle nearby." He then shouted to Dorothy, "And you at the doorway,

Big Tits. If you're in charge here, how about getting the food? The Doc, there, and me, told ya—it's time to eat. So let's see something on the plates."

Dorothy was insulted by his ordering her about, but as she was also afraid of Big Al, her voice would only come out in a squeaky protest: "I beg your pardon, sir, but I am not a domestic."

All at once the three missing people came down the hallway toward the dining room. Dorothy's spirits rose. "Oh, here they come. Here they come. Isn't it lovely, we are all about to be together for our first meal of the weekend." As they filed past her, she squealed with delight, "Come in. Come in. Please be seated."

Lorraine indicated for the Major to take the chair next to hers. Dorothy pointed out the chair for Jackie, and Ren sat next to her. Foster began pouring wine for them, and Trish entered with a tray on wheels, which held the individual fish appetizer dishes.

Dorothy, who hadn't sat yet, couldn't seem to stop babbling. "Well, isn't this lovely. All together. At last. Simply lovely."

Then a terrible thing happened. The Doctor, after having insisted that everyone sit down to eat, actually got up and excused himself from the table. He kissed Babs' hand and turned to the guests, saying, "If you'll excuse me, I must make a telephone call."

Dorothy could hardly believe that the stressful situation was to continue. "Oh, dear, oh, dear," is all she managed to utter.

The Major took her elbow, held the chair for her, and smiled. "I'm sure the good doctor will be back shortly, and would in the meantime give us permission to begin," he said reassuringly.

Babs said, "Yes, I'm sure he won't be long, and would not want us to wait for him."

Dorothy thanked the Major for assisting her into the chair, and turned to the guests to introduce Jackie and Ren. "Everyone, meet Miss Le Roir and Mr. Ren Silvestri."

There were polite murmurs of acknowledgment to the

introduction, all except for Big Al, who drooled over Jackie. She moved closer to Ren. Ren gave Big Al a dirty, if impotent, look.

Big Al laughed wickedly and pulled out a cigar.

Dorothy decided to convince Big Al to behave by being coquettish. "Oh, please. No smoking until after dinner, when the gentlemen will retire into the study for their brandy and cigars."

Cheri said, "He won't light it now, will you, Big Al? He just likes to have something in his mouth. Don't you, darling?" Her purse was open on the table in front of her, and she had taken out a very large compact and was carefully replacing first powder and then bright red lipstick. She had also taken out bottles and packets of medicine, and they too littered the place before her.

Big Al said, "Hey, what I like most is you on toast. But, what's takin' so long? Maybe I should phone out for a Chinese takeout?"

Cheri pointed to Trish and Foster, who had begun to serve. "There it is, Big Al. Look. They are serving the fish appetizer."

"That better be an appetizer. It's a puny little dish for a sissy." He slapped the table in Ren's direction and said pointedly, "Looks like your speed, Sissy." Then Big Al noted Ren's frightened look and began laughing cruelly.

The Major quickly rose to avert an incident. "I should like to offer a toast to our host, the Baron. And to the charming and helpful Ms. Dorothy Saks. And to us all. May we all have a weekend to remember."

Big Al's fish arrived, and without waiting for his hostess to begin, he took a big mouthful.

Everyone raised their glasses in the toast, except for Big Al. He was eating rapidly, big mouthfuls, and was just about finished with his fish when there was another blackout. Some flashes of lightning lit up the windows for a moment and there was a thunderclap. The thunder was loud, but not loud enough to cover the distinctive sound of a body falling.

The thump of a body was unmistakable and several of the

women screamed. The Baron could be heard to ask, "What happened?"

"It's only a power failure, we must all try to remain calm," the Major said. But everyone instinctively knew a body had fallen.

"But I heard a thump," Babs began to whine and then to cry.

Dorothy pleaded, "Please, everyone, as the Major said, we must remain calm. I'm sure Foster is seeing to some candlelight."

The lights came back on. Everyone was in the exact same position except for Big Al. He was slumped over the chair onto the floor. There was a stunned silence as they observed Big Al's motionless form. Everyone caught their breath and moved toward him to see if he was breathing.

Suddenly Big Al came back to life, violently choking, pulling himself onto his chair.

Cheri stood and lifted Big Al's arms in the air, a useless gesture. Big Al continued to choke.

Ren hit Big Al several times on the back. Big Al seemed to recover, but an instant later he stopped breathing, grew red in the face, and grabbed his throat.

The Major pushed Big Al's upper torso onto the table and gave him artificial respiration, as you would to a swimmer. Big Al was silent and again appeared dead.

Jackie pushed Big Al's torso back into a sitting position, leaned over him, and pounded his heart. Big Al came to life and began choking.

Babs stuck her fingers down his throat, probing for a foreign object. It was difficult to do because of the large cocktail ring on her right hand. Big Al stopped choking but also stopped breathing.

Lorraine courageously began giving Big Al mouth-to-mouth. The other women watched with distaste; apparently they wouldn't have touched his lips even to save his life. Big Al took a breath and again started choking.

Foster gripped Big Al from behind, administering the Heimlich maneuver. Big Al seemed momentarily to recover.

Again there was a blackout, and this produced a chorus of screams and a confusion of voices.

The lights came back on. Doctor Armstrong entered the room. Moving to Big Al, he felt his pulse. He looked steadily around at the faces and declared, "This man is dead!"

There followed screaming and cries of disbelief. Everyone began to gather around the corpse.

A voice shouted from the hallway, "*Stay where you are! No one move!*"

The guests froze in place and turned to look at the entranceway.

The Constable entered the room.

"If this man is dead, it could be murder," the Constable said. "And each and every one of you is a suspect."

There were gasps but no one moved or spoke.

He continued, "I am the local Constable, just arrived from the mainland. From this moment on, I am in charge, in my official capacity."

There then occurred lightning, thunder, another blackout, and an onslaught of screaming.

CHAPTER NINE

They were in the dark, an almost total blackness. There was no fire in the dining room fireplace, and Foster had previously taken the candelabra away. The meal had begun in such a rush that the candles in the candleholders on the dining table had remained unlit. The heavy rainstorm cast a dark grey-black reflection of the sky on the windowpanes, not nearly enough to see by. Only the occasional flashes of lightning illuminated the room where the dead body of Big Al Silver still sat upright in his chair. Moments before, he had been roaring and stuffing himself with the fish appetizer. It was a spooky atmosphere that gave most of the guests a feeling of foreboding and queasiness. One could sense a panic that was in danger of erupting.

Slanting rain pounded the windows and thunder broke loudly. Mixed with these sounds was a chorus of sounds expressing human discomfort. Babs Cunningham and Jackie Le Roir were whimpering in fright, Dorothy Saks was giving tiny moans, and Cheri was crying loudly. Lorraine Hurley's eye was twitching badly but she bit her lips and made no sound. Some of the men gave an occasional sigh, and others seemed to be breathing irregularly. However,

Doctor Armstrong remained unmoved, as did the Constable, both being accustomed to death on account of their professions.

The Constable's thick accent was French. His voice should have been, but was not, soothing. "Stay calm. Please, everyone stay calm."

The Baron was one of those breathing irregularly, but when he spoke, his voice definitely showed annoyance: "Foster, where is that candelabra? What did you do…blow out the candles?… Take it away?" He kept talking, as if the sound of his own voice might help to settle his nerves. "Why blow out the candles or take the flaming candelabra away, when we keep having these blasted blackouts? Now we are in the dark with a corpse among us. Have you lost your common sense, man?"

Foster's voice rang out in the darkness with some indignation at being spoken to in such a manner. "It is in the hallway, sir."

The Baron's voice said, "What is it doing in the hallway? There is no one in the hallway. We need it in here."

Foster's voice said, "Sorry, sir, I was busy serving. I had the candelabra with me in the hallway during the last blackout, in order to see the tray. My hands were too full to bring it back in here at the same time that we were serving the appetizer dishes and the wine."

The Baron's voice had a touch of apology, "Well, get it, man, this is no time to be in the dark."

Babs' voice was a whine. "Please hurry. Please, please give us some light. This is so distressing. My nerves are frayed, and I can't bear to be in the dark with a dead body."

The Constable's thickly accented voice should have been, but was not, reassuring. "Everyone, I say again, please remain calm."

Dorothy's voice was pitched high, with an edge of hysteria. "Constable, thank God, you are here. What are we to do now? Please tell us what to do with this dead man."

The Doctor's voice was matter of fact. "The only sensible thing to do is to remove the corpse so that we may continue with our meal."

Cheri's voice was full of tears. "Poor Big Al, I wouldn't want him to see us eating." Then she again broke into sobs.

Lorraine's voice was motherly. "Now, now, dear, he can hardly see us if he is dead. But it would be appropriate to remove the body and cover him decently. I am so sorry for your loss."

The others joined in with condolences, and Cheri's sobbing abated.

Foster, who was in the process of feeling his way along the wall to the doorway so that he might enter the hall and retrieve the extinguished candelabra, was practical. "May I suggest that we place him on a flat surface like the kitchen table, and cover him with perhaps a large tablecloth. However, the problem will be moving him. He is a very big man. How are we to get him out of the dining room?"

Trish said, "The serving tray is large and on wheels. I'll hold it steady; put him on that, and you can wheel him out."

The Major and the Doctor groped their way to the body and began attempting to lift it under the arms. Both men were grunting under the strain, and failing to lift the corpse of Big Al onto the serving tray. Trish was holding the tray so that the wheels would remain still. But it was no use; Big Al could not be budged.

The lights came back on. There were audible sighs of relief. Foster entered a moment later with the candelabra. He placed it in the center of the table and relighted the candles, just in case.

"I say, this fellow is big indeed. All give a hand," the Major said. And all the men except the Baron and the Constable struggled to lift the corpse onto the large serving tray on wheels.

The Baron said, "Lead the way, Foster, that's a good chap. Let's get this unpleasant sight out of the dining room and into the kitchen where he can be placed on the table and covered."

"Couldn't we put him somewhere else?" Trish said. "I don't want him on the table in my kitchen."

Dorothy reassured her. "It will only be temporary, until we've had time to get our bearings. This has been quite a shock. So unfortunate, unfortunate indeed. Now, please, let's move the body away."

The Constable spoke up as if his opinion had been sought. "I don't mind placing the body in another room. The kitchen for now…until I familiarize myself with these surroundings."

They had not consulted the Constable, who should have been considered the prime authority, nor had they given him the respect called for by a person of his stature or years. Once the lights were back, once they'd finally gotten a good look at him, they seemed to dismiss the Constable. Even Dorothy, who had asked him earlier about moving the body, had begun to ignore him.

Perhaps they failed to give him his proper due because of his appearance. The Constable, who could have been in his late thirties or early forties, was an odd-looking little man with a French accent and a funny pencil-thin mustache. He wore his dark hair parted down the middle, and it was slicked back with Brylcreem. His spats and striped suit reminded one of a dandy from the early 1920s. He also looked very much like some of the illustrations of Agatha Christie's detective, Hercule Poirot.

The Constable continued, "You must try not to disturb the corpse any more than is absolutely necessary."

"Fiddlesticks," Doctor Armstrong said. "There is nothing to disturb. A corpse is a corpse."

Cheri gave one loud howling cry and then grew quiet.

The Major, Foster, the Doctor, and Ren now began holding Big Al's body steady on the tray, and wheeling it carefully out of the room and down the hallway toward the kitchen.

The ladies followed in grim procession: Dorothy, Lorraine,

Trish, Babs in her wheelchair, Jackie, and Cheri, who sniffled now and then but was also combing her hair as she walked.

Jackie observed Ren, red in the face and straining to push the tray with as much force as the other men, although he was much slighter. "Be careful of your back, Ren," she called. "Try not to strain it…you don't want to be laid up in bed for weeks again."

Ren was embarrassed and annoyed. "Shut up, Pussy Cat," he snapped. "Only sissies have bad backs. I'm strong as an ox."

The Major, as always, tried to quell any argument. "Not to worry, Miss Le Roir," he said. "I believe the weight is evenly distributed on this tray. Only a bit of guidance seems necessary. Exceptionally good idea, this tray on wheels. Our Trish is a clever girl."

"Thank you, Major," Trish said. "I'm glad someone appreciates me."

Dorothy turned to look for the Baron. He and the Constable were slowly bringing up the rear. Dorothy went back to take the Baron's arm and escort him the rest of the way. This left the Constable isolated. He walked briskly to the front of the procession and took charge, even though he didn't know where the kitchen was located.

As Dorothy took the Baron's arm and began to walk with him, he asked, "Tell me, where is it we are all heading?"

"We are going to the kitchen, Baron. To place the corpse on the table and cover him for decency."

"Ah, yes, I see. Proper thing to do, cover the corpse. Decent thing to do. Tell me, when is the Constable due to arrive?"

"The Constable has already arrived, Baron," she said with a touch of sadness in her voice. "He is the gentleman you were just walking with…the Frenchman with the slicked-back hair and funny mustache?"

"He has already arrived? Excellent…excellent. And you say we are taking the corpse to the kitchen.... Remind me," the Baron said, "which guest is now a corpse?"

An hour later, after having finished their meal, the group gathered in the sitting room. The storm was still raging outside and the atmosphere in the room was eerie. They were in semi-darkness, the lights having gone out yet again. The sources of illumination were the fireplace and the two candelabra (one in Trish's control and the other in Foster's). Trish was sitting on the floor with her candelabra beside her, and at the back of the room. She had her shoes off, rubbing her feet. Foster was standing at attention by the fireplace, holding his candelabra over the Constable's shoulder in order that the Constable might see to make notes in his pad.

The Constable, notepad in hand, was standing with his back to the fireplace, addressing the room: "Now, then, is everyone accounted for? There should be nine of you, myself, and two servants, makes twelve." Here the Constable paused to look meaningfully at everyone, and make sure that they were all paying attention.

The Baron was in his easy chair, smoking his pipe, and did not seem too concerned about the police investigation that was about to take place under his roof. Dorothy was seated on the armrest of the Baron's chair, and she, too, seemed uncharacteristically calm.

Jackie was seated on the couch, and Ren was stretched out with his head in her lap. Perhaps everyone was just relaxing after a most satisfying meal, which had been accompanied by an abundance of aged red wine.

Certainly Cheri, who sat apart from the others in a small antique chair, had put her grieving behind her by now and was concentrated on repairing her makeup. The entire tiny table beside her was spread with a vast assortment of cosmetics.

The Major sat between Lorraine and Babs, and all three seemed soporific. Only the Doctor was unaffected by the richness of the meal. He had eaten in moderation and allowed himself only two glasses of wine. He was annoyed by the Constable's assumption of murder, and was pacing in preparation for doing battle.

The Constable, once he felt he had everyone's attention, said, "The dead man has been murdered, of that I am, now, certain."

"I beg to differ with you, Constable," the Doctor was quick to say. "In examining the corpse, I saw no signs of foul play."

"A superficial examination means little. You should know that, Doctor…ah…"—he looked at the notebook for the name—"…Armstrong."

"In my professional opinion, Constable, it was simply a heart attack, no doubt brought on by the severe bout of choking."

The Constable uttered, "Ah…huh…choking," and wrote the word down. "And why? Why did he choke?" he asked pointedly.

The Doctor was having difficulty being even a tiny bit patient. "For the same reasons any of us choke," he retorted snidely. "But this man had a history of heart problems. He wore a medical alert bracelet. You will remember, I pointed it out to you."

"Too simple, Doctor," the Constable said, gleefully rising to the challenge. "We must ask ourselves, by what means did the murderer cause the victim to choke, thus inducing his heart to fail?"

Now the Doctor lost control. "That's piffle!" he sneered. "The man drank heavily, then caused himself to choke by gorging himself with food. It was something I'm sure everyone noted."

"Piffle? On the contrary, Doctor," the Constable said. He was calm and felt in total control. "It is my firm belief that there is a murderer among you."

This statement got a reaction of shock from the group.

Now the Doctor was furious at the assumption. "If you persist with this theory, Constable, our only course of action is to request an official determination as to cause of death. However, it would require us to telephone the mainland. And that is not possible at present, as the telephone line is down."

Ren spoke up but did not move from his prone position on the couch. "Now there's no telephone. What a bummer." Jackie stroked his head, which was still resting on her lap. Ren reached up, pulled Jackie's face to him, and kissed her passionately and at length. Then he said, "I don't want to be stuck on this island with nothing to do."

The Constable considered Ren's behavior inappropriate and crude. "The sooner you all agree to cooperate with this investigation," he said sternly, "the sooner we may resume normal activities and, of course, rest easier."

Babs, in a half-hearted attempt to ease the situation between the Doctor and the Constable, said, "I'm sure none of us has anything to hide. I certainly don't."

Cheri sat to attention when she heard her idol speak. "Oh, Miss Cunningham, I remember when you were on trial for your life. You'd been accused by that hateful Klaus of murdering his wife."

"Soooo," the Constable said, looking at his pad and beginning to write. "Miss Cunningham, you were once tried for murder?"

"Ignoramus!" the Doctor shouted. "How dare you not recognize one of the world's great actresses!" He was so overcome by anger that he found it necessary to pause and collect himself. It was impossible to calm down, so he began to pace. Finally he said, in a semi-controlled voice, "I refuse to go along with this poppycock. We need to get a pathologist here to determine the cause of death. We must send the Baron's yacht to the mainland with an urgent message."

Dorothy interjected, "The Baron granted permission for the yacht to return to the mainland."

"I did?" the Baron asked.

"Yes, Baron, earlier today you told the captain that once he brought the Constable ashore, he could have the weekend free.

However, the police boat will collect the Constable tomorrow at noon."

"Oh, I see," the Baron said. "Well, if you say so, I must have." He woke slightly from his wine-induced stupor and took charge as the host and master of the house. "Perhaps in the meantime, while we are waiting— Remind me, Dorothy, what are we waiting for?"

Dorothy reminded him. "We are waiting for either the telephone service to be restored, or the return of the yacht."

"Yes, yes," the Baron replied with dignity. "And while we are waiting, we might cooperate with the Constable."

Dorothy seconded that by adding, "The Baron is right. Why not answer a few simple questions?"

The Baron said, "Yes, do let us proceed in order to finish this unpleasant business."

Foster felt obliged to speak. "Under the circumstances, it would seem the Constable is in charge."

However, Ren felt that he must now express himself and in no uncertain terms. "I say nothing without a lawyer. And I gotta talk to Papa," he declared. "None of us have to listen to the Constable."

The Constable treated this youthful rebellion with a warning. "I advise you not to join in the obstinacy, young man. Remember, I am the only person here who is above suspicion."

That struck another chord with the Doctor. "How is it that you have suddenly appeared out of nowhere, Constable?"

Dorothy felt she had to defend the Constable, it being what the Baron would have wished. "But the Constable *was* expected," she said. "The Baron felt that prospective buyers might appreciate knowing about the security of the island. Even those buyers taking a minimum share will be making an investment of seven figures."

The Major became flustered, as he always did at the mention of money. "Seven figures?" he said, unable to conceal his surprise.

"Yes, Major, the minimum investment will be three-and-a-half million," Dorothy answered him.

"Three-and-a-half million, you say, huh," the Major stammered. "Is that pounds or dollars?"

"Dollars," Dorothy replied.

"Dollars?" the Major again stammered. "Canadian or U.S.?"

"Canadian," she said.

"Dollars? Not pounds? Canadian, not U.S.?" The Major was beside himself at the thought of such a sum. "My, my that is a bargain. Isn't that a bargain, Lorraine? I hope the phone comes back so that I may call my bankers."

Lorraine gave him a dirty look, as if urging him to keep quiet. What she said was, "The banks are closed until Monday, James."

Ren, again without rising, said, "I'm out of here before Monday. I'll go on the police boat if I have to. Monday I'm in New York."

But the Constable was quick to reprimand him for his cocky attitude. "That will be up to me, young man, and I'm afraid none of you will be permitted to leave—not until we determine which of you murdered…"—he referred to his notepad—"…Big Al."

The Doctor was still angry, impatient, and in a mood to taunt. "At the very least, Constable, I should like to know why you are to be considered above suspicion?"

"I am Monsieur Le Constable. This is not about me," he replied.

"And why not?" the Doctor demanded. "When the lights came back, you were already among us. I, myself, opened the front door to you. You had the same opportunity, while the lights were out, as any of us, to commit murder. If there was a murder. An assumption I, as a medical man, refute."

The Constable looked at him a long time before answering, and the look he gave the Doctor was piercing. "Doctor Armstrong, I must insist that you cooperate."

"I shall not, sir," the Doctor said defiantly, "not when you dismiss my professional opinion. An opinion backed by twenty-five years of firsthand medical experience."

The Constable studied him long and hard. Many in the room

began to think that the Constable might buckle under to the older man. But when the Constable spoke, it was with renewed authority. "I'm afraid we have only your word...that you qualify to judge the condition of the corpse," he said, and he smiled condescendingly.

This attitude made the Doctor even more furious and determined to win the argument. "You challenge my qualifications, sir?" He virtually spat out the words. "Well, I challenge yours. I intend to telephone your headquarters on the mainland and inquire into your credentials—as soon as we have a telephone."

The Constable stood his ground and retained his calm. "Your attitude is most unhelpful. You seem to be forgetting that you are a murder suspect."

The Doctor lost all decorum, and raged, "I am a renowned medical practitioner!"

"Doctor Armstrong, in what field are you a renowned practitioner? What type of doctor are you?"

The Doctor waited a very long time before answering, then said, "A plastic surgeon."

CHAPTER TEN

A plastic surgeon," the Constable said with disdain, and then paused to consider. Finally he declared, with a demeanor of supreme authority, "In that case, I disqualify your opinion of the corpse."

Ren, who had been reclining on the couch with his head in Jackie's lap, sat bolt upright at the insult to the Doctor. "Don't take that, Doc. Punch out his face. Smack him one. You're bigger than he is, you could slaughter him if you wanted."

The Doctor, although shaken, was going to find a way to put a good face on things, especially in front of Babs Cunningham, the gorgeous actress that he had become infatuated with in a few short hours. Holding his head high, he said, "I am a civilized man. Not a brawler. And there are ladies present." Then, with an air of authority, he stated, "I hold firm to my opinion, however—the man died of natural causes. It is ludicrous for anyone to speak of murder."

Ren said, "That's good, Doc. If you don't want to whip his butt, you got the words to whip him with your tongue."

Dorothy pleaded, "Please, please, gentlemen, the Constable is in charge, and I thought we had agreed to cooperate."

Babs took the Doctor's hand and patted it gently. Her eyes shone with a pleading for a peaceful solution. The Doctor looked at her adoringly and permitted himself to be more subdued. However, his next response came out petulantly. "I agreed to nothing," he said.

Ren was egging for a conflict, and took his cue from the Doctor. "I didn't, either. Just like the doc said. And as soon as the phone is fixed, I'm calling Papa. He'll tell you where you can get off."

Jackie whispered into Ren's ear so that no one else would hear, "Ren, please, it won't hurt to answer a few questions."

"I, myself, would be willing to answer whatever questions you might have, Constable," Major Hurley said. "What about you, Lorraine, would you be willing to answer the Constable's inquiries?"

Lorraine said, "Wouldn't getting on with the investigation be less painful than this unpleasant bickering? I'm sure, in the end, the Constable will get his way, so arguing is, in any event, useless. After all, he is a law enforcement officer."

The Baron was losing patience. He said in a strong, clear voice, "Let us get this blasted questioning started, and over with."

The Major concurred. "I would consider that a most sensible attitude. Lorraine, wouldn't you consider that a sensible attitude?"

Lorraine nodded her approval, as did the rest of the women and most of the men. It was Dorothy who said, "We consent, Constable."

The Constable studied his notes for a moment and then cleared his throat, preparing at last to begin a questioning of the suspects.

However, Dorothy interrupted him, saying, "Before we proceed with the questioning, Constable, I should like to thank you for your kindness in allowing us to finish our meal. And ask if Foster might not provide us with some after-dinner drinks?"

The Constable took this further delay with good humor. "I

don't see why not," he said. "I myself would appreciate a strong coffee."

"Certainly, Constable," Dorothy said. "But Foster will have to leave the room to prepare our beverages." She turned to the guests, assuming her good-hostess manner, and addressing them as a group. "I suggest for the ladies a crème de menthe frappé. Perhaps for the gentlemen, a liqueur, brandy, or aged scotch." Turning again to the Constable, she said, "And I would also ask your permission, Constable, as we don't want to leave an untidy sink for the morning…for Trish to be able to go to the kitchen where she can begin the washing-up."

Trish howled, "Oh, no, I'm not going in there. Not by myself. Not with that dead body stretched out on the kitchen table."

The Constable had a solution in mind. "Until a coroner arrives, I suggest that we remove the corpse from the table in the kitchen and place it in the deep freeze. I assume you have a deep freeze?"

Foster said, "There is a long one with large capacity located in the basement. If I may say so, it is the perfect size for a body."

Trish said, "That old thing's broken. Well, you know, sort of broken. It doesn't keep stuff frozen, only cold."

"Even so," the Constable said, rubbing his chin in thought, "storing the corpse in the basement is desirable." Then he paused for a moment to construct his plan. Finally he declared, "The servants may carry on. Everyone else, however, must remain here, in full view."

Foster departed for the kitchen but Trish refused to budge.

The Constable was frowning at the gathering with an accusing look. "I have noted," he said, "that not one of you was so distressed by the victim's demise that you were unable to finish your meal. It would indicate a definite callousness."

Again he took them all in with his severe look. "Once the body had been carried away, every person at the table ate and drank most heartily. Most heartily…considering the circumstances."

The Doctor said, "Not I. I always make it a strict practice to ration my intake of food, and I never permit myself more than one scotch and soda before dinner, and two glasses of wine with a meal." The Doctor, who was still stewing over the insult to his profession, could not help but recommence his battle with the Constable. "Plastic surgery is an honorable profession, sir." For the others, the Doctor's statement seemed to come out of the blue and to no longer be pertinent. Nonetheless, the Doctor continued, "While you seem to me, sir, not so much a policeman as a buffoon. A French buffoon."

The Constable said calmly, "French, *oui*, monsieur. From Québec, *oui*, monsieur. And so? Would you care to justify your comment?"

"If you're not a buffoon, how can you present yourself in such a ridiculous light? Why are you coiffed and dressed so very strangely?"

The Constable, with a knowing smile, proudly rolled the ends of his pencil-thin mustache. "Strange, perhaps, monsieur...to those persons unfamiliar with Hercule Poirot, my hero—the master detective who inspired *me* to become a detective."

The Doctor countered with, "How absurd!"

The Constable came close to chuckling; at least, for the first time that evening, he displayed a broad grin as he said, "I would not expect you to appreciate such a great man as the master detective Hercule Poirot, monsieur."

Cheri had no idea what the two of them were talking about, and saw no reason not to interrupt. "What about going to the little girls' room?" she asked. She thought it a sensible question. "Not now; I don't have to go now. But what about later? Is it okay to leave for that?"

The Constable looked at her harshly, resuming his official demeanor. He readied his pencil and pad, and said, "State your name for the official police record."

"Cheri."

"Cheri what?" the Constable asked.

"Just Cheri. I use only one name, you know, like Cher or Twiggy."

"State the full and proper name of your male companion—the victim," the Constable said, and again his voice was harsh.

Cheri was not intimidated, and answered simply. "Well, everybody called him Big Al, but proper, I guess, was Mr. Alan Silver."

The Constable wrote down the name she gave him and continued to study it, staring at the pad in front of him as if it were of some great significance. Then he looked at her accusingly. "Mr. Alan Silver. So if you refer to the deceased by this name, then your proper name would be Mrs. Alan Silver? You were married to, not simply the mistress of, the deceased. Correct?"

Without hesitation or a sense of guilt, Cheri said, "Well, yes."

There were murmurs from the others present.

"I must inform you that as the wife of the deceased, you are the prime suspect," the Constable said.

Now there were gasps all around.

Cheri, however, was seemingly unfazed. "Just because I was sitting next to him when it happened? That doesn't mean much, does it? And why would I murder my own husband, Constable?"

The Constable looked at her with a gaze full of meaning. "Your husband was extremely wealthy, was he not, Mrs. Silver?"

"Sure," Cheri replied.

"As his widow, you stand to inherit a vast fortune. So you have what is known as one of the classic motives." He added with a frown, "Also, you have seen fit to lie not just once…but twice."

Babs felt it her duty to defend the young woman, who was, after all, an ardent fan. "I object to these tactics. How dare you call anyone here a liar? Also it is ridiculous of you to accuse this lovely young woman of murder."

The Constable was unrelenting. "But thus far, she has lied

twice. And," he added meaningfully, "lied for the record. So why should she be telling the truth about her innocence?" He turned again to Cheri. "Have you considered that I might be in possession of your real name?"

It was Cheri's turn to gasp. "Gosh, how would you know that?"

The Constable took from the mantelpiece behind him an official-looking folder, held it out in front of him for all to see, and said gravely, "The Canadian government does a security probe on all arrivals destined for Escape Island. The proposed island development involves millions of dollars, and as a matter of precaution each person's identity and background is verified."

The Major was panic stricken at the news and unable to keep himself from asking, "So you have at your disposal a profile of everyone present? How fascinating. They have a profile of us all, isn't that fascinating, Lorraine? Of course, it's possible in some cases a mistake could have been made. They often make mistakes. Don't they, Lorraine?"

Lorraine was better able to keep the panic from her voice. She sounded almost normal, but her twitching accelerated to an alarming degree and she had to place a hand over her eye to hide it. She said, "I don't know, James. I honestly don't know."

Babs sat up very straight in her wheelchair and became the star. "If you have information in that folder about me, that is a blatant infringement of my rights. I shall contact my lawyer."

Ren joined in and expressed his indignation. "Wait till Papa hears about this," he said, striking an angry pose. "You can't just spout off and accuse people. We have a right to a lawyer."

The Constable was unimpressed by their protests. He was in control and knew he had the authority. "I think you will find that under these unique circumstances…being completely isolated from the outside world…I am the sole custodian of law and order." He walked to the couch and stood over Ren. "Now, would you state your full name, sir."

Ren pointed to himself. "Me? Renato Silvestri." He didn't feel as brave as he sounded and decided a smirk would give him the upper hand. So he gave the Constable his best smirk as he said, "Try and say it's not my real name. Silvestri is an old, respected Sicilian name."

"And what was your association with the deceased?"

Ren again smirked. "I never saw him before in my life."

The Constable turned his back on Ren and returned to the fireplace, where he again faced the room. "On the contrary," he said, addressing his remarks to everyone present. "I suggest that you not only knew the deceased but that you were closely related to him."

Cheri felt that was her cue to confess. She told the Constable, "Silvestri was Al's real name...and mine...our real name." Then a startling thought came to Cheri and she turned to Ren, asking, "Oh, my God, was Big Al your uncle?"

"Ladies and gentlemen," the Constable declared smugly, "there we have the second of this young woman's lies uncovered. She not only concealed her marital status, but also the true name of the victim, as well as her own. We may note that Mr. Ren Silvestri had some reason for covering up his family tie to the deceased."

Ren became flustered. "I didn't lie. I said, 'I never saw him before in my life.' That's the truth. I never saw him before today."

It was not the Constable but Cheri who next asked a question. "Was your father really Big Al's brother? The one that he hated so much from the old country? He didn't seem to recognize you."

"That's what I said. He'd never seen me before. He and Papa despised each other. So we'd never met."

The Constable again took control, peering at Ren. "If that is the case, state your reason for coming here this weekend."

Ren had lost most of his cockiness by this time and answered meekly, "Big Al was interested in this deal of the Baron's. Papa wanted the lowdown. If Big Al was interested, maybe Papa should grab the deal out from under him."

Cheri asked, "But you used your real name. Didn't you think Big Al might wonder?"

"Nah," Ren said, trying to make light of it. "The name *Silvestri* is too common. He didn't wonder, did he?"

Cheri began to attack. "We'll never know, now," she said pointedly. "But you could have had the motive, Ren," she continued. "Your papa hated Big Al, and your papa could have sent you here to kill him."

Ren attempted to laugh. "Now, after all these years? Papa could have had Big Al taken out, any time he'd wanted. Nah, Papa just wanted to know what made this investment interesting to Big Al, and I was sent to find out. That's all. You're the one who really stood to gain from his death, Cheri."

Cheri's face was flushed with anger but she managed to control herself as she answered Ren, "But...he was my husband...my husband!"

It was Jackie who now spoke with uncontrolled emotion. "Don't try to tell us you married that disgusting slob for love!"

Everyone stared at Jackie in utter surprise. Up to this moment, she had appeared to be one of the calmest of the group, with little or no interest in the dead man.

The Constable was prompt to challenge her. "Miss Le Roir, it would seem that you are not just a disinterested spectator to this affair. Such a passionate outcry would indicate more. Perhaps a hithertofore undisclosed intimacy with the deceased?"

Ren was livid over the Constable's insinuation. "What the hell are you trying to say, Constable? That Jackie knew my uncle? How could she? You must be completely nuts!"

Doctor Armstrong took the opportunity to add, "I told you we should not be giving any credence to this man."

Cheri raised her hand for the Doctor to be quiet, because she had sensed some unrevealed relationship between Jackie and her dead husband. It would not have surprised her. Big Al had scores of involvements with women—women who now despised him. She asked, "Did you know my husband before? Is there some dark secret in your past, something about Big Al that made you want to kill him?"

Ren jumped to his feet in a threatening manner. "Don't try to shift the blame onto me or my Pussy Cat. You wanted him dead, so you could collect the money. You haven't shed a tear, lost your appetite, or stopped painting your face since he croaked."

Dorothy was horrified at the turn of events—first a dead body, then a suspected murder, and now the guests were beginning to accuse one another. Dorothy pleaded, "Please, we must not stoop to accusing one another. We must remain civil in these trying times. Tell them, Baron."

But the Baron, stunned by the developments, was no longer concerned with civility. He confronted Dorothy, blaming her for the choice of guests. "Dorothy, oh, dear, what have you done? What sort of people were invited? It would appear that we have, so far, no less than three possible criminals."

Foster had returned with the tray on wheels. It now served as a drinks table for the after-dinner beverages. He returned just as the Baron was expressing his concern over Dorothy's choice of guests. Foster spoke up on behalf of his master. "And it sounds as if the murdered man had a very shady past indeed," he said.

Dorothy wanted to protest, tell them all that Big Al had been the Baron's choice. That the Baron had then insisted that she select the others to be invited. But she dare not defend herself and risk her job.

The Constable now revealed some of his information from the Canadian Immigration Folder: "Big Al, Alberto Silvestri, from Sicily, has been for years the subject of an FBI investigation. He is believed to be the *capo* of a crime organization in New York City, with its roots in the old country."

Again Jackie became excessively emotional, wrung her hands, and bit her lip as she said, "But they never did lock the monster up. All these years he's gotten away with ruining lives."

The Constable raised his voice to gain Jackie's full attention. "As he ruined yours?" Then he took a calmer approach by appealing to her common sense. "You might as well tell us, Miss Le Roir. I assure you that the details will come out during this investigation."

Ren was at his wits' end. "What the hell is going on? I don't believe this!" He turned to Jackie, demanding, "Did you know Big Al?"

Jackie stood to face the others. She tried to speak but tears rolled down her cheeks and she shook with emotion. No one moved and everyone remained quiet, as they watched the young woman with an almost morbid curiosity. Then Jackie's eyes glazed over and she went into a trance-like remembrance. "His organization stole me away from my family in Algeria, kidnapped me. I was a child, a girl of eleven. They smuggled me into the States and forced me to be the sex prisoner of Big Al Silvestri. He was demanding...brutal. At thirteen I was too old for him and he placed me into one of his houses of ill repute."

Cheri was the first to break the spell. "He forced you to be a whore? He kidnapped you? Ruined your life?"

Ren could scarcely believe his ears. His Jackie with Big Al? His Jackie actually saying these things. This was one of the worst blows ever to his ego, to his very manhood. "Why did you hook up with me?" he asked in a whisper. "You must have known who I was all along?"

Jackie confronted him with spirit and bravery. "Of course, I knew," she replied. "I made it my business to get to know you... get you interested in me...get within reach of Big Al." Then she addressed herself to the Constable. "I did have some sort of revenge in mind. But I didn't know exactly what. I thought it would come to me...in time...some opportunity would present itself. But I never wanted to see him dead. Death was far too good for him."

Ren's mouth fell open. He was flabbergasted by the disrespect to him she had just displayed—and in front of all these people. "So you used me?" he said. "You only wanted to get at my uncle?"

"No," Jackie yelled. "We used each other. You had a devoted sex partner, constantly at your side. It took so long for you to come close to your uncle—" She paused to stare at Ren, making no attempt to spare his feelings. "—I almost gave up hope...almost left you. Then this weekend invitation finally brought us together with Big Al."

Cheri said, "Jackie, how can you claim that you didn't kill him? You waited all that time to meet him, to get your revenge."

The Baron rose from his easy chair. "Well, Constable," he said, "there you have it. Obviously one of these young people did the foul deed. Retain the three of them, but allow the rest of us to go to the comfort of our rooms and get some sleep."

The Constable shook his head and indicated for the Baron to return to his seat. "There will be no sleep for any of us tonight," he said. "And I must point out, Baron, although three suspects have surfaced so far, it does not mean that the rest of you are above suspicion."

Babs gasped for air. "Surely, you can't mean every single one of us." She opened a fan and began fanning herself. Her complexion had turned a sickly white. "I'm afraid these alarming proceedings are making me quite faint. Could I have a glass of water?"

As Foster was in the process of serving everyone their after-dinner drink, it was Cheri who ran to the drinks table and poured a glass of water for her idol.

The Doctor rummaged through his pockets and produced a capsule of smelling salts. He gently administered them to Babs and then held to her lips the glass of water that Cheri had handed him. Then he turned vicious toward the Constable. "When we have managed to contact the outside world, you will pay dearly for any emotional distress you have caused Miss Cunningham, or any of the ladies. Beware, sir."

The Baron concurred with the Doctor when it came to the ladies. "Please do choose your words more carefully, Constable," the Baron said. "I, certainly, consider myself free of these accusations."

But the Constable was relentless. "I am sorry, Baron, but until we have established conclusively the relationship of each and every one of you to the victim, we cannot uncover the motive. There is also the question of the murder weapon, the cause of death, which I intend to address shortly."

"I protest," the Doctor spoke up. "This is an exercise in futility. And, Constable, how is it that you claim to have such extensive knowledge of murder?"

The Constable was unshakable. "I have spent innumerable hours reading case histories," he explained. "My interests have always lain in gaining understanding of the criminal mind, and in solving crimes. In particular, the crime of murder."

Dorothy tried to improve the atmosphere. "The rest of us do not doubt your knowledge, Constable. I suggest we take a short break, refresh ourselves. May Foster and Trish have a long leave now, in order to do the cleaning-up?"

Foster protested. "But, Madam, I'm finding all of this quite riveting. And I, too, apparently am considered a suspect."

Trish moaned. "Me, too. I don't want to miss anything. Foster's already been in the kitchen and doesn't seem to mind. But I do. I'm not washing the dishes unless there's someone with me…the whole time. That dead body's still on the table."

"Major, would you help me remove the body to the freezer?" the Constable asked.

The Major replied, "With pleasure." Then he realized that had been improper and added, "I mean, certainly, Constable."

Lorraine rose and walked to Trish. "I shall come with you, Trish, so you are not alone in the kitchen," she offered.

The Constable wanted to make his instructions absolutely clear. "The servants may carry on with the cleaning up. The rest of you may take turns visiting your rooms to freshen up, but only in the company of a partner. No one is to make a move unaccompanied. And I must warn you all that you are not permitted, under any circumstances, to leave this house."

The Doctor snapped at the new instructions from the Constable. "And where do you suppose we could go, Constable? We are, after all, on an island."

Ren joined in with the Doctor's protest. "I guess none of us are Olympic swimmers…and I doubt if even an Olympic athlete could make that long swim to the mainland."

Babs, in a hoarse and dramatic voice, said, "Not to mention the fact that it is still pouring with rain and that there is a fierce wind outside."

"Oh, dear," the Baron sighed, "I can see that we are to have no sleep tonight."

The Constable repeated his instructions: "No one is permitted to leave this house. We will merely have a short break from the proceedings. It is my duty to ascertain the criminal among you and protect the rest of you, the innocent, from also becoming victims."

Lorraine was the first to express alarm over this threat. "Do you really believe that the murderer might strike again, Constable?"

The Constable said, "I spoke earlier of the murder weapon. I believe *poison* to be a definite possibility. But it is an unreliable method of killing. Often, if administered, let's say, in a meal such as tonight's, some people become only slightly nauseous, some feel little or no effect, and someone else may die."

It was again Lorraine who continued with the train of thought. "Are you saying that the wrong person may have been killed?"

"It is possible. I am saying that we must be exceedingly cautious until we have the guilty person restrained." The Constable paused. He looked around the room, hoping to give weight to what he said. "No one must go anywhere alone." And, turning to the Major, he said, "Major, shall we remove the body? And any of the other men who want to help us…it would be appreciated."

The Major and the Constable started to leave for the kitchen, as did Lorraine, Trish, and Foster. Ren shook his head and hoped it wouldn't seem as if he had been intimidated, but he went to help lift the corpse. Even the Doctor followed, having decided to give a hand.

At the doorway, the Constable stopped. Turning to those following, as well as to those remaining in the sitting room, he warned, "I caution…we must all remain alert and vigilant. We dare not let our guard down…not until we know the identity of and have restrained the murderer."

CHAPTER ELEVEN

The Baron, since he was not permitted to go to bed, decided to spend some time in his conservatory. This had been a most troubling night and he needed some form of repose. Digging in the soil, tending to growing things, was good for the soul, he knew, and relaxing.

After the body of the deceased had been stored in the deep freeze in the basement, the Constable had accompanied the Baron to his indoor garden. One of the Constable's orders had been that no one was to be alone, each was to have a partner for the sake of security, and presently he was the Baron's partner. The Constable hoped that everyone was taking the partner concept seriously. He wanted no more murders while he was in charge.

The sound of rain beat on the glass roof and walls, and an occasional flash of lightning, followed by thunder, acted as a reminder that the storm was not over. There was also a damp cold mist that hung inside the conservatory, at times a visible mist. It would have been a good night to be tucked under the covers in a warm bed, but no one dare sleep while a murderer was at large.

While the Baron puttered with his plants, the Constable closely observed everything in the Conservatory and made copious notes. Detail was crucial to any investigation, and especially in murder cases. He had opened the storage bin and was examining its contents, holding up cans and bottles, and reading their labels one by one.

Dorothy burst in on them with her usual cheery demeanor, saying, "Oh, Baron, there you are. All is well with the others. Your guests seem to be adjusting nicely under the circumstances."

She was acting as if it were still a charming house party where a minor inconvenience had taken place. Perhaps she had not permitted herself to dwell on the seriousness of the situation, for that would have endangered the project, and in turn her employment.

She paused for the Baron to reply, but he was lost in his own thoughts and busy with his plants. He did not answer. Not to be put off, she moved deeper into the conservatory until she stood between the two men, and there she hovered, as if waiting to be invited to participate in the latest parlor game. Finally she said, "I'm sure everyone feels better now that the body is stored in the basement…out of view. That was a very good idea on your part, Constable."

She paused for his reply, but the Constable, too, was concentrating and did not feel obliged to respond. "Yes, indeed," she continued, "Trish is happily tidying up the kitchen and Foster has set another pot of coffee to brew. I'm sure you'll have a refill soon."

There was still silence from the men. Dorothy observed the Constable as he lifted cans and bottles out of the storage bin and carefully read each label. "Are you searching for anything in particular, Constable? Arsenic, perhaps?" He did not answer and she laughed nervously, beginning to feel a little foolish.

At hearing the word *arsenic*, the Baron turned from his gardening work to observe the Constable. He said, "You'll find no products containing arsenic, Constable. I use no insecticides or weed killers. And I allow no one else to use them. Indeed not. I believe in natural methods, only…natural methods." As an afterthought, he added, "Nor do we utilize rat poison."

Dorothy said, "If your theory is correct that we might all have been fed poison in the meal, surely one or two others would have some symptoms. But I saw no one who complained of being un-well." For some unknown reason, she giggled, which was most inappropriate. "I find it very dramatic, this concept of an exotic, difficult-to-detect poison."

The Constable closed the storage bin and began to walk, mak-ing an examination of the various plants. "I have not expressed my theory in those words—'an exotic, difficult-to-detect poison'—but that is exactly what I intend to look for."

Now he turned to face her, a meaningful expression on his face. "The Baron tells me that you, Ms. Saks, have taken to tending the plants for him. Shall I assume that you are adept at gardening?"

"Yes, I love gardening and volunteered to assist," she said. "The Baron does not have much free time now that he is concentrating on the development of the island. We are advertising for a gar-dener." A thought struck her and she hastened to add, "I've added nothing, not a single plant. I merely attend to the existing plants."

The Constable commented on a profuse growth of flowers, hid-den in one corner, behind bushes. "I see the daffodils are plentiful."

Although the comment had been directed at her, Dorothy said nothing. However, her expression showed a recognition of what the Constable might be driving at—and he noted that reaction.

"According to Greek mythology, they grew in the meadows of the Underworld," he continued. "Does that mean they can be menacing?"

Dorothy still did not respond, so he made the next ques-tion confrontational. "Ms. Saks, what do you know of poisonous plants?"

Once put on the spot, she began a rudimentary summary of poisonous plants that she hoped would not prove she had extensive knowledge. "Well, there is the most exotic, the deadly night-shade...the most toxic of all nightshades. It is very beautiful and can be recognized by its purple or greenish flowers and its black glossy berries. Some seeds, like the seeds of the castor oil plant, can be a potent vegetable toxin.... And I remember once reading an account of many people having been taken ill by eating a paté made of figs."

The Baron got slightly annoyed with the discussion. "I dabble a bit in herbal medicine. These storybook ideas of eating poison-ous roots and berries...few realize that the vital alkaloid has to be extracted with much care and preparation. The deadly daffodil or herb, the poisonous bulb mistaken for an onion, is mostly fiction."

But the Constable was relentless. "So, Ms. Saks, both you and the Baron tend the garden in the absence of a hired helper," he said, making a note of that in his notebook. "What about the butler or the maid? Do they ever interest themselves in the plants?" he asked.

The Baron was quick to reply. "Foster has been with me and my family since we were both children, but I've never seen him put his hands in the soil."

The Constable asked, "What about the maid...ah, Trish...who also cooks. Has she planted, or does she come to gather, herbs?"

Dorothy considered this before answering. "Well, I suppose she might. She might have planted a few things for the kitchen. Some dill weed, perhaps, or parsley. And yes, she would pick them, I suppose."

Satisfied, the Constable abruptly turned and headed for the door. "I would like you both present for my next set of inquiries. Would you, therefore, kindly accompany me to the kitchen?" At the door, he stopped and asked, "By the way, what about your houseguests? What do you remember? Did any of them show an out-of-the-ordinary interest in the conservatory? Did any spend time alone in here?"

The Baron's short-term memory had, for once, returned, and

he said, "I seem to recall, the Doctor was rather rude. He wished to take leave of our company in the sitting room in order to spend time alone in the conservatory with Miss Cunningham."

Dorothy added, "Also the Hurleys… I remember it was difficult to assemble the guests in order to introduce everyone. It took a very long time, early in the day, to coax the Major and Mrs. Hurley to leave the conservatory and join the others."

The Constable wrote this latest information down in detail. "Interesting," he said. "That is interesting."

The swinging doors opened into the kitchen, and the Constable, the Baron, and Dorothy entered. Trish and Foster were tidying up. Lorraine Hurley was drying the dishes. And Major Hurley was standing beside Lorraine, drinking a glass of wine, and not lifting a finger to help.

Upon seeing the arrivals, the Major said, "Constable. Thirsty work, that body-carrying business. I seem to be a tiny bit out of shape. Miss my own gym at home. Don't I, Lorraine?"

Ever the hostess, Dorothy said, "Hello, all. Mrs. Hurley, how kind of you to help dry. If your society friends could see you now!" and she giggled. She asked Foster, "Is the coffee ready for the Constable?"

Foster was just rolling down his sleeves and removing a bucket of water and a scrub brush from the kitchen table. "Any second," he said. "Cream and sugar are coming right up. The table has been scrubbed thoroughly. I attended to it myself. If you'd care to sit, sir?"

But the Constable was all business. "Fine. I will have another coffee shortly. But right now, I would like to request that everyone please be seated…for some questioning."

They all obeyed and sat down to face him, by taking the chairs at only one side of the table, and at either end.

The Constable had been closely guarding the official Immigration folder. He had carried it with him from place to place, closely tucked under his arm. He now felt the tabletop to be sure it was dry, and then took the folder out from under his arm and placed it in front of him, opening and studying it while everyone remained quietly at attention. It was impossible for them to make out the print.

The long silence was sustained while the Constable continued to study a certain page of the folder. Soon everyone became nervous and began to squirm. Whose profile was he reading with such concentration?

Finally the Constable began. "We have here some rather curious information." Addressing Dorothy, he said, "Ms. Saks, you had a grown son, William, killed three years ago by person or persons unknown."

The Major wiped beads of sweat from his brow. He was most relieved that the Constable's reason for concentrating on a certain page of the folder had not been on account of him and his identity. The Major tried to lighten the mood at the table by saying, "Ms. Saks, who would believe that you are old enough to have had a grown son? I for one—"

Lorraine wanted to stop her husband from making a complete fool of himself. This was not a time for flattery, and no one was interested in his charming banter. "Please, James, that Immigration folder…" Here her eye twitched so badly that she lowered her head in an effort to hide it from the others. "That Immigration folder," she continued, "has information about us all, does it not, Constable?"

The Baron, who was sensitive both to scandal and the right of anyone employed by him to be protected from needless rumors, said, "Constable, if this is a delicate matter, if Ms. Saks is going to be made to feel uncomfortable, why not question her in private?"

The Constable would have none of it. He believed that all present should have the facts as soon as he'd received and verified them. It was not so much a question of believing in freedom of information as it was a belief that this was the way in which other suspects might be goaded into adding to his knowledge of the crime.

"Because, Baron," he said, "as Mrs. Hurley so rightly noted, everyone is listed in this folder." He paused and his silence was poignant. "And," he continued, "everyone—*everyone*—seems to have something they chose not to come forward with."

This occasioned a chorus of denials.

"Also," he said tersely, "this revelation about Ms. Saks and her son involves yet another person—another seated at this table."

In the next second, the Constable's theory of how a witness could be goaded into a confession was confirmed, as Trish volunteered, "So I was married to William. So what?"

The others were startled and some "Oh's" and "Ah's" were heard.

Trish's confession continued to spill out, as if she could not stop herself. "I didn't tell anyone that Dorothy Saks was my mother-in-law. So what? I needed the job and she helped me get it. So what? What was wrong with that? Okay, we thought that the Baron might not approve if he knew I was her daughter-in-law. And I guess she was ashamed that I needed to work as a maid." Then she laughed bitterly and said, "She puts on a few airs around the Baron."

"Really, Trish," Dorothy scolded, "that statement was at best unnecessary." Dorothy was also taken aback by Trish's openness and tried to soften the effect on the Baron. "However, I did think it might be wiser not to seem to be recommending relatives to the Baron."

The Constable was anxious to have the flow of confession

proceed. "Please let us not waste time with these fatuous statements. You both suspected how William was killed, did you not? And by whom."

Lorraine was so surprised by the revelations that she forgot her place and spoke up, when it was really the Constable's place to speak. She asked, "Don't tell me it was this Big Al person? Did you think that he and his organization were responsible?"

The Constable may or may not have been sarcastic as he said, "Yes, thank you, Mrs. Hurley. That is the question. Had you reason to blame your son's death on Alberto Silvestri and his organization?"

Dorothy, tears glistening at the corner of her eyes, said, "Yes. William had gotten innocently involved with them, as a driver."

Trish added, "When he found out they were gangsters, he tried to quit. He wasn't going to inform…he just wanted to walk away."

Dorothy was unable to keep the tears from spilling as she said, "William couldn't have informed on them. He really didn't know anything, but they wouldn't listen to reason. The very day he left their employ…his car overturned and exploded."

There followed a stunned silence.

It was the Major who spoke first, saying, "How horrible for you both. Please accept our heartfelt sympathy."

The others murmured in agreement.

The Major now adapted an outraged tone of voice as he said, "This Big Al and his organization should have been stopped. Can the law be so helpless in the face of organized crime?"

The Constable said, "I think you *know* the answer, Major." He turned a page of his files. "You've had some contact with the money-lending side of this Silvestri crime organization. You borrowed to pay a gambling debt and then fled. You could possibly be on their hit list because of your disappearance, and this unpaid debt."

Lorraine, a sob catching in her throat, said, "Oh, James. I knew we were in serious debt and I blamed you for borrowing from these shady people. But I had no idea that your very life was in danger."

However, the Major was less concerned about his wife's fright than about his carefully planned front being uncovered.

"Constable, I object in the strongest possible terms to an open discussion of my financial situation," he said. "I find myself in a temporary cash-flow bind." Then, turning to the Baron, he went on, "That is all and it is temporary, I assure you, Baron."

The Baron could be a most understanding man. He liked the Major, liked him very much, and did not really care that he was a phony. He said in a kindly tone, "I believe, Major, that the Constable does not wish to discuss your finances as such. He is, rather, in the process of establishing motive. Is that correct, Constable?"

The Constable took turns playing the sympathetic coach and the cool appraiser. His present role of appraiser made everyone squirm, as he announced, "Correct, Baron. We are concentrating on motive. And it appears that all six of you have a motive for murder."

"Not I, sir," the Baron said. He was indignant at the suggestion.

Foster said quickly, "Nor I…I hasten to add."

The Constable ignored both protests and pressed on. "Foster, you have been in the employ of the Baron and his family all of your life? Is that an exaggerated statement?"

"I can't say that it is," Foster replied. "My family for generations worked at the Tarrall estates and for the Baron's family. From the day I was born it was known that I would become a servant to some member of the family."

"These generations that worked at the Tarrall estates, where was that? Do you mean in Europe? Before the Baron moved to this island?"

Now Foster remained silent.

"Are the Tarrall estates not located in Sicily?" the Constable continued, not wishing to give them time to make up some story.

The Baron raised his hand, stopping the proceedings. "Alt! I have some pressing questions of my own. Ms. Saks, you were in charge of preparing a guest list. We had a reference book listing thousands of names of wealthy prospective buyers. You narrowed that list down to a manageable few." He paused and took a deep breath to calm himself. "It cannot possibly be a coincidence, can it, that you chose to invite these particular guests, all of whom had a strong motive for wishing the man dead?"

"But Baron, I did that only after you, yourself, chose to invite this gang boss, Big Al."

Everyone stared, seemingly pressuring her. She said, "It was then that I conceived of the plan to invite some of his victims."

Again the others silently waited for her to continue. Finally she blurted out, "And I admit...I did hope someone would get him."

The Constable, pleased that his tactics were working, wanted to leave no room for anyone to interrupt the flow, so he pounded on. "Was it not at that time...that you recommended your daughter-in-law for the job of housekeeper/cook—an employment for which she had no previous qualifications?" Then he struck a terrible blow. "I suggest there is a strong possibility that you and your daughter-in-law planned and executed the murder."

Trish gasped, then protested. She felt the blame must be shifted. "Why us? You said yourself that everyone here had a motive."

The Constable made short work of her protest by whipping in the suggestion, "What better cover for your deed, than a house full of guests, each with a motive?"

He went on rapidly to his next point. "So, that brings us to the method used." Here he produced a napkin filled with dried leaves. "Before the servants began tidying the kitchen, I took a sample of the herbs used in tonight's fish stuffing. It appears to be sage. But upon closer examination one detects a mixture." He looked at everyone as if to read their expressions, saying, "Not sage alone, but also foxglove." He held forth one of the foxglove leaves for them to see. "Poisoning by digitalis…found in foxglove."

Just then the kitchen doors swung open and Doctor Armstrong wheeled in Babs Cunningham.

The Doctor's mood had not improved. He had a stern look and seemed again ready for combat. "Everyone has washed their hands and returned downstairs," he said as if it were a challenge. "May I ask why we do not proceed with this bogus inquisition, if proceed we must?"

Dorothy found his attitude disagreeable. She wished only for this night to end with everyone still feeling positive about the proposed investment. Her solution was to alter the mood by making witty small talk. "Oh, we have not wasted time, Doctor. The Constable has not taken even a short break from his work."

The Major tried to help Dorothy smooth things out by adding, "Indeed not, he was just saying that he discovered foxglove leaves mixed with the sage that was used in tonight's fish stuffing. He suspects that the victim was poisoned by digitalis."

"Laughable," was the Doctor's reaction to this news. "Right out of some Agatha Christie story. Digitalis is a useful heart stimulant, and not deadly. Tonight's death was by heart failure that might have been brought about by severe choking. The fish stuffing would not have been the culprit, but a fishbone might have been."

The Constable went on as if the Doctor had agreed with him. "In either event," he said, "the cook is likely to be the guilty party."

"I'm beginning to agree with you, Doc," Trish said with a scowl. "The Constable is talking rubbish." And Trish turned her back on him.

The Baron seemed to concur. "Surely you're drawing conclusions prematurely, Constable."

"Not conclusions, I'm merely stating some conjectures," he said. "Now if everyone has returned downstairs, I should like us next to recreate the events in the dining room, before and after the victim began choking," the Constable announced.

Lorraine said, "Constable, you had begun a discourse about all of us having a motive. But you hadn't finished. Please do continue."

The Major was also curious but tried to state it diplomatically. "It would seem only fair now that some of us have been mentioned, to also mention the others who are suspected, and tell us why."

The Constable explained the turn of events so far to the newcomers on the scene. Turning to the Doctor and Babs, he said, "We have previously discovered that the real name of the victim was Alberto Silvestri. His true identity, we now know, was that of a crime boss…his operation being in New York City, with connections to the Sicilian Mafia. Here in the kitchen it has come to light that the Major was in debt to Mr. Silvestri's organization and possibly on their hit list. Ms. Saks had a son, presumed murdered by that organization. The cook was married to Ms. Saks' son. Therefore, Ms. Saks and her daughter-in-law had a motive for killing, as did the Major and his wife."

CHAPTER TWELVE

When the Constable accused the Major and his wife of having a motive for the killing, the Major felt it could be true of himself, broadly speaking, but not of Lorraine. It was his duty to defend his wife, and yet he couldn't help wondering what he really knew of the inner Lorraine. Their bad times had put such a strain on her that she was often aloof. She definitely had an inner world where he did not enter. And he, of course, kept secrets from her. Lorraine had not known the details of the money he had borrowed from the loansharks. He'd not told her that the loanshark operation was owned by Big Al…so she couldn't have known… could she? Until now, she had probably not been aware that his life was in danger. The reason his life was in danger was that he'd run away without making good on the loan. Had Lorraine known they were running away from a particular bad debt and a dangerous one? He didn't think so. But he couldn't be sure. However, of all the people present, she was probably innocent, he felt. So he told the Constable, "You cannot suspect my wife…. Lorraine has nothing to do with this, whatsoever."

The Constable was becoming a touch exasperated with denials.

"I shall repeat what I stated earlier—thus far, no one is free of suspicion. And I add to that…neither is any couple."

Now that Doctor Armstrong and Babs Cunningham had joined those in the kitchen, only Ren Silvestri, Jackie Le Roir, and Cheri, Big Al's widow, were in another room. The recently arrived Doctor was quick to take umbrage when the Constable claimed that everyone was under suspicion. "What utter nonsense," the Doctor snapped. "Miss Cunningham is completely above reproach."

The Constable said, "You were not here and are unaware that Ms. Saks has previously admitted inviting guests who had a motive to kill the victim, in the hopes, she said, that one of you might—and I quote—'get him.'" With this, he looked piercingly at Dorothy. "Ms. Saks, kindly explain why you invited Miss Cunningham."

Dorothy began without hesitation. "In the three years since the murder of my son, I've made it my business to look into hideous crimes that happened in Big Al's New York territory. Babs Cunningham, I think, was not shot by a fan—" Dorothy offered.

"No. It was not a fan," Babs said. "I was shot and left for dead by Big Al's hoods."

Dorothy felt terrible, sorry that she had been obliged to reveal the story as false. "I'm so sorry, my dear," she said. There was still one aspect of the story that she had never understood, and she asked, "But why did you not put the blame where it belonged? Why throw off the scent by claiming it was a crazed fan?"

Babs moaned, "Because I was afraid.… Having survived the attack, I thought he might try again, in order to prevent me from talking."

The Doctor said, "So that is why this so-called 'crazed fan' was never caught? How dreadful for you, dearest. But weren't you afraid this gangster would come after you again, despite the fact that you hadn't revealed he was to blame?"

"No," Babs said emphatically. "I knew he wouldn't. You see, Big Al had made advances which I'd spurned. He'd wanted me at the height of my fame and beauty. I knew he would have no more interest in me once I'd become a retired cripple."

The Doctor was furious. "The despicable pig, the blackguard!" he said. "He deserved to die. Had I known what he'd done to you, I would have strangled him with my bare hands."

The Constable interjected smartly, "Instead of emptying a packet of lethal powder into his drink, Doctor?"

The Doctor cried out loudly, "Bosh!" He retrieved a packet from his pocket, holding it out for all to see. "I use this for chronic indigestion. I'm often seen with these in my hand. The drink I put it in was my own," he said curtly.

However, the Constable was not put off. "Deny it if you will, Doctor, but there are several eyewitnesses. And I have no doubt that they will all come forward when requested to do so."

Dorothy blushed, saying, "Forgive me, Doctor, but you, too, had a motive. I happen to know that a mistress of Big Al was a patient of yours. When you gave her a less than successful breast implant, he punished you by bankrupting your practice."

"He was instrumental in terminating my practice, I admit," the Doctor said candidly, "but my own funds were never in danger. I can assure you all that I retired quite comfortably." This was said mostly for the benefit of Babs, and he wondered if he had stressed his bountiful means strongly enough. The Doctor would never want to give Babs the impression that he was less wealthy than she herself. Perhaps one day they might have a future together and he would never live off a woman or even become seriously involved with one richer than himself. Never would he be thought of as a kept man—a gigolo.

The Major's curiosity was aroused. "A breast implant? Fascinating. In what way was it unsuccessful?" he asked.

Lorraine whispered, "James, I don't think that is relevant."

The Constable agreed. "Yes, do let us keep to the subject. So, Doctor, while you admit that the dead man put you out of business, you deny that that constitutes a motive?"

The Doctor disliked this line of questioning and growled, "I was about to retire shortly, at any rate. So it was but a minor inconvenience. My own wealth was separate from that of my practice."

The Constable was willing to desist. The point was a minor one. "For the moment, I shall refrain from arguing the point."

Babs said, "You must admit, Constable, the Doctor stumps you all the way in this investigation. He is such a brilliant man." She smiled beguilingly at Doctor Armstrong. She, too, was thinking about their recently formed friendship possibly becoming something more serious, more permanent. The Doctor did not seem to mind her handicap. That was so refreshing that as she thought of it, tears came to her eyes. Perhaps, after all, she could have a life with someone. Perhaps she would not forever be condemned to loneliness.

The Major had been puzzling about something that the Constable had mentioned earlier and felt he would like to have it set straight. "Do forgive me, Foster," he said, "as we have all been labeled suspects...are all in the same boat, so to speak. The Constable was about to reveal your motive when the Doctor and Miss Cunningham entered."

The Constable took up where he'd left off. "Foster's motive is closely connected to that of the Baron."

Now it was Dorothy's turn to protect the Baron, as he had tried to protect her. "As his public relations director, I shall not permit you to say one word about the Baron, unless it is said in private. This is his home, his island," she said. Then she went further, even at the risk of offending the Constable. "And you could be considered as a trespasser, Constable."

The Baron felt she had gone too far with this last statement, and attempted to make amends. Also, her attack made no sense to him.

"I applaud your loyalty, my dear," he said, "but is it not true that the Constable was invited by you so that he might talk to our guests?"

"I'm sorry, Baron," Dorothy said, "but that is not entirely true. It was the Constable who all but insisted on this visit. It was his idea to lecture about security and add to good community relations. At first I was most upset at the thought of the law being present, when there was a possibility of one of Big Al's victims doing away with him. Then it occurred to me that a death under the very nose of the law would be…well, never would be thought of as a murder. However, the Constable immediately cried foul."

Lorraine asked, "Did you come here expecting murder, Constable?"

"Big Al's movements have always been closely monitored by law enforcement," the Constable said. "It is ironic that this Big Al should be the victim. Because, of course, my concern was not for him, but for the safety of the other guests on the island."

"Speaking of the others," Dorothy said, "they will be wondering where we are. May we not proceed to the dining room as the Constable suggested earlier?" Dorothy was becoming anxious about the other investors left to their own devices in the sitting room. They could be getting bored on their own, and nothing was worse than boredom for making a business proposition seem unappealing. Murder or no, her job remained the same—to make the guests happy and sell shares.

Trish objected to moving into another room without finishing the discussion of everyone's association with the dead man. She said, "But he still hasn't told us about Foster's motive. It's always the butler who does the murder, and I could tell Foster hated Big Al."

Foster said snootily, "I merely disapproved of his boorishness. I've never witnessed such a lack of manners and civility."

Dorothy bristled at this attempt on Trish's part to involve Foster, whose motive, it had been established, was the same as the Baron's. No matter what, she must defend the Baron. "It was agreed not to speak openly of the Baron's motive, apparently related to the motive of his butler. So may we change the subject?"

But the Baron would have none of it, telling her, "It is no use trying to protect my reputation, Dorothy, or this front I have been trying to maintain. You see, I was hoping to obtain some investment money so that I might live out my days without worry," he said, going on to make an even more revealing statement: "True, I own this godforsaken island and this wreck of a house…but I will admit it.… I have no means of support."

Foster was the only one who was not astonished by the Baron's admission. He apparently knew the Baron's circumstances in detail and went on to explain to the others, "The Silvestri family wiped out the monetary reserves of the Tarralls. They kept kidnapping members of the Tarrall family and demanding ransom, until the family was close to bankruptcy. Finally each grown male of the Tarrall family was forced to salvage what they could and move away from Sicily…away from Italy, itself."

Dorothy was dumbfounded by these confessions. "Yet you wanted Big Al to be invited," she said. "I did not initiate the idea."

Trish was unclear what they were talking about, and wouldn't let them go any further without explaining things. After all, she was a part of the proceedings. She felt that she had a right to interrupt. She, too, was a suspect. "I don't understand Foster's motive or how his motive is connected to the Baron's," she insisted.

The Baron thought the explanation crystal clear and that Trish must be quite a stupid young woman not to have understood. However, he tried to clarify what had already been said. "When our family was all but bankrupted, it meant no more work for Foster and his family, who'd known no other employment for generations, but that of serving the Tarralls. So both of us were losing our livelihood."

It was Bab's turn to be amazed. "You escaped from them. So why did you want that gangster here, in this, your place of refuge?"

Foster cleared his throat, then almost belligerently explained. "The Baron and I had a plan to swindle money from Silvestri."

Dorothy turned crimson with emotion and thought she was going to faint. The word *swindle* was abhorrent to her. She was an honest woman. She'd placed all her hopes on the success of the island development. Surely Foster jested. Surely the Baron had no intentions of swindling anyone, including Big Al. Of killing him perhaps, but surely not of swindling him. That would be dishonest and make a mockery of the entire development scheme. She stuttered, "Heavens, if there was a plan to swindle…I had no knowledge of it."

The Doctor was outraged and said so. "Outrageous, Baron…. Did you mean to cheat all of us?"

The Baron's face took on a blank look. "I don't think so," he said. "Remind me, Foster, were we going to cheat everyone?"

"Not really," Foster replied. "Our elaborate scheme was for Alberto Silvestri alone. Although I personally question the soundness of this development plan."

Dorothy was again staggered by what Foster had said. Why couldn't he just be a good servant and keep his mouth shut? He was doing more to destroy the success of the weekend than the advent of a murder had. "Heavens! I had no idea! I thought it was a good investment," Dorothy sputtered. "But then I've got no head for business," she said as an afterthought, and to declare herself harmless of their intentions.

For once Trish came to Dorothy's defense, or so Dorothy thought. It wasn't much of a recommendation and was said nastily, but nevertheless Dorothy felt it helped her case when Trish declared, "I'll vouch for that. Dorothy is an overzealous bubble-brain."

Surprisingly, the Major suddenly showed some wisdom, saying, "Foster, I don't think you or the Baron should discuss your scheme, or the merits of the development project. No reason to incriminate yourselves on matters that the Constable isn't investigating. The question here is one of motive. And you *wanted* Big Al *alive*."

"That's true," the Baron said joyfully. "I just wanted to extort money from him…as he and his family had from the Tarralls. That was Foster's wish, also."

However, the Constable said, "Sorry, but I cannot accept that. I consider that you both had motive to kill…. So that leaves out no one. All eight of you could have wanted the victim dead, as well as the three suspects who earlier incriminated themselves."

"Oh, yes, the three young people," the Baron said, happy he had recalled the three other suspects. But then he was forced to ask, "What are their names again?"

Dorothy answered him. "Cheri Silvestri, the widow. Ren Silvestri, the nephew, and Jackie Le Roir, who was kidnapped in Algeria as a child and taken into slavery."

The Baron gasped at the news. "She was? How extraordinary," he said. "I seem to have forgotten that."

The Constable was ready to move on to other aspects of the crime. "Everyone had motive," he said. "Now to discover the method. Of course everyone despised the victim. Perhaps this is another *Murder on the Orient Express*, where all present had a hand in the killing."

The Doctor, who had lifted the phone to find it still dead, was exasperated by the lack of phone service, as well as by the Constable's theories. "Balderdash!" he yelled. "And this line is still down. When will we get an expert to dispel this spurious hare-brained assumption of murder?" To emphasize this statement, he slammed down the phone. "Again we are witness to the idiotic mentality of this man who is trying to emulate Agatha Christie's fictional detective."

The Constable puffed out his chest, at the same time sucking in an angry breath. "Sir, say what you will about me. But never, in my presence, attack Hercule Poirot. If you do, I cannot be held responsible for my actions."

"Doctor, the Constable has done a remarkable job of bringing to light who we all are in relation to Big Al, and our motives for perhaps wanting him dead," the Major said as a peace offering. "Has he not proven his suspicions to be valid?"

The Doctor, still bristling, retorted, "Definitely so…if there had been a crime. But I still say the deceased died of natural causes. A coroner will dispel all of this hokum."

Ignoring the Doctor's most recent jibe, the Constable headed for the swinging doors, saying, "I should like you all to follow me into the dining room for a demonstration. I am encouraged that we seem to be getting closer to the truth. Closer to the murderer!"

CHAPTER THIRTEEN

They followed the Constable through the drafty halls toward the dining room. The Constable remained in the lead and Foster was behind him, carrying the candelabra. The hallway had a few wall lights but they were dim, giving off an eerie glow. Also, Foster had learned his lesson. He did not wish to upset the Baron should the electricity fail and he not be prepared with the candelabra at hand. The others kept pace closely behind Foster. The hallway was not only dim but also damp and uninviting, if not downright spooky. Only the Baron walked slowly, but Dorothy took his arm, moving him along at a faster pace.

The Doctor, who was wheeling Babs, was shaking his head and still repeating, "Again I say, hokum. *Hokum!*"

Lorraine, who along with the Major was just ahead of them, turned to him and asked, "Surely, we can not take a chance, Doctor. Suppose it is murder and the murderer didn't kill the intended victim, or decides to strike again?"

Babs was quick to defend the Doctor's point of view. "Or suppose the Doctor is correct, and we are all suffering from a hysteria created by the Constable…who perhaps has an overactive imagination," she said scornfully. "I, for one, would prefer to be in my bed."

Trish said, "Hah, we'll all sleep better now that Big Al is dead. He's the only one I was afraid of. I'm not scared of a murderer. If there is a murderer...I'm sure he was only after Big Al."

The Major said, "May I point out that through the Constable's efforts we have learned that this development deal may be suspect. Happily, I was unable to contact my banker, so my money is safe."

Lorraine said impatiently, "Please, James, no more pretense. We, too, have been found out."

Realizing he had again made one of his pretentious blunders, the Major attempted to bring the conversation around again to the problem at hand. "Yes, well... What is your next course of action, Constable?"

They had arrived at the doorway to the dining room. The Constable stopped, turned, and addressed the gathering. "To recreate how everyone made physical contact with the victim while he was choking," he said with authority and sternness. "As stated, it could have been poison." Here he made a pointed comment. "Or he could have been killed as he choked and while the rest of you were distracted."

Once in the dining room, every person in the house was assembled: The Baron and Dorothy, the Doctor and Babs, the Major and Lorraine, Foster and Trish, as well as Cheri, Ren, and Jackie; and, of course, the Constable, who seemed to be taking the proceedings well in hand.

First the Constable counted the people present. "Every one of you is present, splendid," he said. "Now I would like you all to take the exact same position you were in, before Big Al began choking."

Now there was confusion as they tried to recall their places before Big Al began to choke. Foster began miming the pouring of the wine. Trish followed suit by miming the bringing in of the fish. The others stood and sat, stood and sat, trying to remember where exactly the action was supposed to begin.

The Constable was walking about observing. He felt everyone would eventually grasp the beginning of the re-enactment in the dining room. But he felt the Doctor was being deliberately disruptive to the proceedings and said, "Doctor, if you were seated, then, kindly sit."

"But I was out of the room," he snarled. "Why should I sit when I stood up almost immediately and excused myself to make a telephone call?" Then he added, with venom, "I opened the door for you, you nit."

The Constable knew he must get the upper hand if his demonstration was to be effective. He took a long and thoughtful pause, then said, "Everyone please place yourselves as you were before the Doctor excused himself to make a telephone call."

The others sat, remembering that they had just found their places at the table and were in the process of sitting when the Doctor had excused himself. The Doctor looked around to see that only he was standing. He grunted, but finally also sat down.

"Thank you," the Constable said with satisfaction. "Now I would like us to relive, one by one, the events before the lights went out…and again when they came back on. In particular, try to re-enact exactly what you did to assist the victim as he choked."

"Where do you wish us to begin?" the Doctor asked peevishly. "I suppose just as I got up to leave the room…now that I have just sat down?"

The Constable held back a contented smile. "If you would."

Still behaving peevishly, the Doctor said, "Do you actually wish for me to go into the other room and pick up the telephone? For everyone to follow, and you make your entrance?"

The Constable's mouth curled into a slight smile, despite

himself. "That won't be necessary. You may tell us what you did upon leaving."

With a bored sigh, the Doctor began. "I rose, leaning to kiss Miss Cunningham's hand, and asking her to forgive me for leaving. I asked everyone to excuse me, as I had a telephone call that I must make." The Doctor now demonstrated by walking to the doorway. "I entered the sitting room and lifted the receiver to discover that the phone was dead. I was annoyed beyond measure."

The Constable said politely, "Thank you, Doctor. Please continue. Then what happened?"

The Doctor continued his account of what had taken place. "My back was to the door that separates the entrance hall from the sitting room. I heard a tapping on the sitting room door."

The lights began to flicker. The Doctor looked up and made a queer sound. "The lights flickered then, as they have done now. And at about the same time that I had ascertained where the tapping was originating." He gestured over his shoulder to an imaginary door. "It was directly behind me. I looked over my shoulder at the sound, then toward the dining room. Apparently no one else heard, because no one came to answer. I slammed down the phone, turned, and stepped over to open the sitting room door." The doctor then pointed almost accusingly at the Constable, saying, "You, Constable, were standing there, shaking a wet raincoat you had just taken off."

The Constable confirmed the Doctor's account. "Yes, I had seen the lights flicker as I came up the corridor. When you responded to my tapping, I was still wet. You are quite right about that, Doctor."

The Constable mimed how wet he had been and how he had removed his coat. "I put the raincoat down before stepping through from the corridor, not wishing to soil the sitting room carpet."

Dorothy said, "Thank you, Constable, that was most considerate."

"It was the civilized thing to do," the Constable said, before continuing his account. "I said to you, Doctor, 'I believe the bell is broken. I'm the Constable. No one responded when I rang the front door bell. May I come in? I'm expected.'"

"And I quipped," the Doctor replied, "'You're already in, aren't you...so why bother to ask?'"

The Constable did not rise to the bait. Instead he said, "At that moment we were thrown into total darkness. From the dining room came a thump, screams, and a confusion of voices."

"Oh, it was a terrible moment," Babs said, shivering. "We were in total blackness when we heard a body fall. I can't remember if I was one of those who screamed. I probably was. One doesn't always recall what one does at moments of fright."

"That is quite understandable," Lorraine said. "I, too, may have screamed, but I couldn't swear to it. Could any of the ladies?"

The Constable, anxious to get back to the exact sequence of events, interrupted, "I believe it is sufficient to say that screams were heard by the Doctor and myself. As well as male voices."

"Yes," the Doctor said, agreeing for once with the Constable. "And when the lights came back, we walked together to the dining room."

"Splendid, Doctor," the Constable said, and he did indeed seem quite pleased. "Now each of you, please, go through your actions."

Suddenly there was a blackout, just like the one that had been described in the re-enactment. No body was heard to fall, but several of the ladies screamed, and even the men gave startled cries. Under the circumstances, these constant blackouts were getting on everyone's nerves, and were especially frightening to the ladies.

Now the lights returned, but only dimly, and they continued to flicker. In this strobe-like atmosphere the re-enactment began.

Cheri stood and lifted the imaginary arms of Big Al above his head. This time, her expression was cold. And in the half-light, some sensed she was wasting time, even allowing him to choke to death.

Ren then began hitting the imaginary Big Al on the back. However, in the flickering half-light, the enactment seemed vicious.

James gave the imaginary Big Al artificial respiration. His movements this time appeared to be far too slow, and he also seemed to be wasting precious time.

Jackie stepped up to the chair where Big Al once sat and pounded the spot where his chest would have been. However, this time, observing the angle, her pounding seemed to be nowhere near his heart or where it might have been beneficial.

Babs wheeled herself over and began pretending to put her fingers down Big Al's throat, probing for a foreign object. Perhaps it was an illusion, but her ring seemed to open and spill contents as it entered his imaginary throat.

Lorraine was next. She arrived at Big Al's chair to demonstrate how she gave him mouth-to-mouth resuscitation. But she now appeared to be emptying his lungs without giving him new air.

Foster replaced Lorraine and mimed the administering of the Heimlich maneuver. Somehow it took on the appearance of an excuse—an excuse to give Big Al a karate chop to the heart.

The Doctor now re-enacted entering the room and going to the place where Big Al was slumped. While feeling Big Al's pulse, he made another movement that looked in the half-light as if he were injecting Big Al with a previously hidden needle.

The lights suddenly came up full without a flicker. The Constable walked to the center of the room and asked everyone to sit. He looked piercingly at each of them in turn.

"Of course, I saw this just now for the first time. I did not see this action originally, as I entered only as the Doctor did, and at a time when you had all finished *assisting* the victim."

The Constable paused to clear his throat but it was a meaningful sound, full of accusation. He said, "Perhaps you all sensed what I sensed...that the assistance was not helpful and might have killed."

Everyone was offended and murmured protests, but the Constable was determined to make his point. "I believe you realize that he may not have choked to death. Any—or all—of you who came into physical contact with the victim, could have killed him."

Again there were murmured protests from everyone, and Lorraine said, "But his choking was very serious, Constable. He could not get air. I think we all were concerned that he would choke to death and that we all did our very best to try and save him."

"Perhaps," the Constable grunted, stroking his chin. "Or perhaps while everyone was distracted by the choking..."— he paused for effect—"...the murderer took the opportunity to strike the fatal blow." He looked closely at each of them. "For example," he said knowingly, "the concealed compartment in Miss Cunningham's ring could have dispensed a deadly powder that was actually the cause of his death."

"Twaddle," the Doctor objected, springing to his feet. "Hidden compartments, indeed," he muttered. Then he walked to stand over Babs, saying, "Babs, dearest, let us examine your ring and put this absurd theory to a halt."

But Babs said, "I'm afraid the Constable is correct about the type of ring. It does have a compartment for ladies who once hid their snuff. But I have never used it for storage and I certainly had no concealed poison."

The Baron disliked this unchivalrous habit the Constable had of accusing the fairer sex, and he protested, "Surely, Constable, you are clutching at straws? Miss Cunningham is far too delicate a creature to inflict bodily harm. Foster, on the other hand, is a black belt, and could kill in one blow if he chose to."

Foster was quick to say, "Thank you, Baron, for pointing that out. I hasten to add that I did not so choose. I deploy my martial art skills solely as a sport."

The Baron said sheepishly, "Sorry, Foster, I merely brought it up to defend Miss Cunningham against these wild speculations. Why, Foster, you administered the most effective first aid. What is that maneuver? I can never remember the name."

It was the Constable who responded. "The Heimlich maneuver. And while preparing the patient for the maneuver," he said pointedly, "Foster could have administered a quick, lethal karate chop to the victim's heart."

Cheri spoke up boldly and rather too loudly, "Well, I know I couldn't have hurt him by raising his arms in the air."

But the Constable did not accept her plea of innocence. "You could have tried to kill him by wasting time on useless maneuvers, thereby depriving him for too long of vital oxygen. I'm thinking not only of you, Mrs. Silvestri, but also of Miss Le Roir's rather anemic chest pounding, Mrs. Hurley's so-called mouth-to-mouth, and certainly of Major Hurley's ineffectual artificial respiration."

The Major said, "I strongly object to the use of the word *ineffectual*."

Dorothy interjected, "That leaves in the clear the Baron, myself, and Trish. None of us touched the man."

The Constable answered her, saying, "True. However, you three were in charge of the conservatory garden, where in one corner foxglove grows beside the sage. One or all of you could have been responsible for adding digitalis to the stuffing."

"But, sir," the Baron said, "you have established nothing by going round in these circles."

"I established previously that every one of you had motive. Now I'm showing that you also had both opportunity and means."

"Not all of us, Constable," the Doctor said. "I had an alibi—opening the door to you. I entered the dining room when the man was already dead."

"Or did you?" the Constable asked.

"You could have had a syringe up your sleeve or in your pocket and administered an injection as you leaned over the body."

Ren took up this argument with harshness. "Yeah, you're a doctor. You could have done that. And you're the one bellyaching the loudest about being questioned."

Cheri said, "You are also the one that threatened to kill him."

The Constable looked startled. "Indeed." And he began to make a note in his notebook. "This has not come to light before," he said. "Mrs. Silvestri, can you remember the exact wording of the threat?"

Babs said, "I can, and it was understandable. Big Al, after putting his hands on me, harassing me in the vilest manner, made an obscene remark."

"I swung that big ape's hand away from Miss Cunningham," the Doctor said, "telling him not to dare say another word to her. In no uncertain terms, I told him that if he insulted her once more, he was a dead man."

The Constable continued to write, saying, "I see."

There was a silence while everyone thought about the Doctor's threat. It seemed an ominous revelation.

At that moment the chandelier flashed off and on...off and on. And in its off mode, only the candelabra gave light, casting grotesque shadows on the walls.

CHAPTER FOURTEEN

The chandelier stopped flashing and returned to its full brightness just as a streak of lightning crossed outside the windows,
and thunder roared close behind.

The Doctor said, "This weather is as intolerable as this drivel
I'm hearing from the Constable." He now moved to the dining
room doorway and started to walk down the hallway, saying, "I'm
again going to try the telephone."

As soon as the Doctor was gone, Ren said, "He did it! So why
don't you arrest him and let the rest of us go?"

The Constable was thoughtful. He put up his hand for silence.
"We may have missed out on something significant," he said. "We
have not yet re-created the earlier events that took place in the
dining room…before the Doctor excused himself."

The others were about to grumble at yet another re-enactment,
but Dorothy volunteered, to be helpful. "Well, where do you wish
to begin, Constable? Not everyone showed up promptly for the
meal. I remember feeling rather frantic because the Doctor and
Big Al were demanding that the food be served." She turned to

Foster, indicating for him to proceed from there. "Eh…Foster? If you would."

Foster took up the story from where Dorothy had left off. "I entered the dining room and reported that they were on their way. Then I proceeded to pour the wine. First for Mrs. Hurley, then for Miss Cunningham, then for Miss Cheri. The Baron was extolling the virtues of both the white and the red to be poured later."

"Yes, indeed," the Baron said. "The white was a light and tangy one, to please the ladies. On the other hand, the red—"

The Constable could not allow the Baron to continue with what was sure to be a lengthy description of both wines. Cutting him off, the Constable said, "Yes, Baron, thank you. I believe we can proceed without a critique of the vino."

Foster then continued. "This Big Al person told me I could skip the wine for him, bring more bourbon…and keep the bottle handy. I noticed that Miss Cheri had used both her own and her husband's water glass for his medicine."

Dorothy interjected, "Yes, I saw Cheri hand a glass of medicine to him. I noticed because I was looking in Big Al's direction. He'd been very rude, ordering me to go to the kitchen and bring the food. 'I beg your pardon, sir,' I'd said, 'I am not a *domestic*.'"

Trish turned furiously at the word domestic and hissed at Dorothy, "Hisss! You didn't want to be called a 'domestic'—a slave like me."

The Constable moved between them as if to break them up. He said loudly, to gain everyone's undivided attention, "We were talking about a very important new element that has just come to light. There was a glass of medicine which was handed by Mrs. Silvestri to her husband. In fact, reference has been made to two glasses, previously with only water in them, being used for medicine. Could someone please take up the story from there, and in particular as it involves medication."

Lorraine began to speak slowly, as she recalled what happened next. "The others entered then. I was certainly relieved to see James. Some had been insisting on eating before everyone was at table, you see. I indicated for James to take the chair next to mine as soon as possible," she said, and stopped without mentioning the medication.

Dorothy, too, said nothing about medication, but rather followed Lorraine's example and spoke of the seating arrangement. "I pointed out the chairs for Miss Le Roir and Mr. Ren Silvestri."

Foster, however, had a keen grip on what information would be most helpful to the investigation. He said, "At that point I poured wine for the late arrivals…and witnessed Miss Cheri mixing another packet of medicine and handing it to him…to her husband."

"I, too, remember that," Dorothy added. "At that point Big Al seemed a bit groggy, a bit heavy of tongue. I seem to recall him asking, 'Didn't I already take this medicine?'"

The Constable had been writing furiously, getting down every word of testimony. Finally he looked up. "Well, well, Mrs. Silvestri, do you admit giving your husband two consecutive doses of medication?"

"I forget. Maybe I did. Is that important?" Cheri asked.

The Constable was surprised at Cheri's casual attitude. "Surely you would consider it important, even grave, to give more medication than prescribed, Mrs. Silvestri?" he said. "What do you next recall?"

"He wanted more bourbon," Cheri said with a shrug, still not seeming to understand the implications of giving Big Al medication, or giving him medication along with all the alcohol he was consuming. "Oh, yeah," she said, "and the fish appetizer had arrived."

Foster cleared his throat for attention. "When Patricia entered with the individual fish appetizers, and began to serve, I set the decanter of wine on the sideboard and picked up the bottle of bourbon. I then walked over to this Big Al creature, filled his glass yet again, and left the bottle," he said with distaste. "It was then I noticed Big Al had emptied the second glass with medicine. One had little sympathy for the man, but one could hardly help thinking the effect of two doses of something, and on top of all that alcohol consumption, must be hard on the constitution."

"I remember that, too," Jackie added. "Big Al had in front of him two empty water glasses. Both were stained with a white residue."

"Mrs. Silvestri, there are witnesses to the fact that you emptied packets of medicine, twice, into water glasses and fed them to your husband," the Constable said. "Apparently he was drunk and unsure, so he swallowed both. What have you to say in your defense?"

"Well, Al made it my responsibility to give him his medicine," she said, and again shrugged helplessly.

"But," the Constable pressed her for more of a response, "you gave him the medication twice, and within a matter of minutes."

Audible gasps of disbelief were heard from the others when Cheri replied, "Maybe I did. I'm not sure. Is it really so important?"

At that moment the Doctor re-entered the room, looking frustrated. He had heard Cheri, and answered her question. "To overmedicate patients can have severe consequences. What was it he was taking?"

"I don't know," she said quite simply. When she saw that the others were still amazed at her responses, she tried to explain. "He took lots of stuff. For different things." In a bid for understanding, she whined, "It was really hard to remember when he took what." When the others still looked disbelieving, she added, "I have it all written down in a small notebook." Still seeing looks of incredulity, she began searching through her handbag for the notebook.

"By the way, the phone is still down," the Doctor said. "We seem hopelessly cut off." He watched Cheri unsuccessfully going through the items in her purse, and commented. "I note that while I was absent the suspicion seems to have shifted."

However, Ren was unwilling to let the Doctor off the hook. He said, "The way I see it, either you or Cheri is *Numero Uno Suspecto.*"

Cheri, still searching through her bag, had decided she disliked Ren. He annoyed her, and she said, "I don't know what that means, but in my opinion, you were the one that killed him, Ren."

Dorothy, at the risk of angering him, said, "Mr. Silvestri, there *was* hate in your eyes when Big Al called you a sissy."

The Constable was most intrigued by this remark. He said, "Please elaborate, Miss Saks. You mentioned hate and the word *sissy.*"

"Well, it was when I invited everyone to meet Miss Le Roir and Mr. Ren Silvestri," Dorothy said.

Lorraine did not let her finish. She jumped in with, "I recall how Big Al drooled over Jackie, and she moved closer to Ren. Closer to him for protection. That's how aggressive Big Al had become."

"What did Ren do?" the Constable asked.

"Nothing," Trish said with a dare in her voice. "Ren gave him a dirty look, that's all. He was too scared for anything else."

The Major unintentionally added insult to injury by saying, "Indeed. And Big Al knew he was frightened. Big Al laughed. And I'd say, he laughed somewhat viciously."

Cheri said, apropos of nothing, "Big Al wanted his food so badly that he offered to phone out for Chinese." She smiled at the memory. "I said, 'Look, darling, there it is…the fish appetizer.'"

The Major interjected, recalling with a chuckle, "And Big Al said, rather drolly, I thought, 'That better be an appetizer. It's a puny little dish for a sissy.'"

Jackie finished the explanation of the episode without regard for Ren's feelings. "And Big Al slapped the table in Ren's direction, saying, 'Looks like your speed, Sissy.'"

"Shut up, Pussy Cat," Ren said miserably.

Trish was not finished with her scorn of Ren. "Big Al knew Ren was scared of him, so he laughed and laughed," she said, laughing herself.

A look of recognition came into Cheri's eyes. "Yeah," she said, "he did pick on you for no reason...unless he guessed who you were. And why wouldn't he, when you were introduced as *Silvestri*."

"I quite agree," the Constable said. "No matter how distantly, all the Silvestri from Sicily could be related. Your uncle had no doubt guessed who you were. So out of fear you wanted him dead."

Ren was now like a petulant schoolboy, his macho reputation having been damaged beyond repair. "Yeah, well, if you're so smart, how did I do that?" he challenged. "And when?"

But the Constable had a theory for that, too. "While he was choking, you pounded him in the exact spot to shatter a rib and have it pierce his heart."

Ren was actually pleased at the Constable's assumption; it went a long way in restoring his self-image—the tough guy who could so easily shatter a rib—and someone with the guts to carry it out. Therefore his protest lacked conviction as he said, "You're dreaming. You're dreaming, if you think I could do that. I'm good. Macho as they come, but... I don't see how that's even possible." And he couldn't help but laugh.

Dorothy was again concerned about the comfort of her guests. They had been in the dining room for quite some time without refreshment. "This is a very thirsty business, and our after-dinner drinks are waiting for us," Dorothy suggested diplomatically and with all her charm. "May I suggest that we move into the sitting room?"

The Constable hesitated only a moment before agreeing. "I have no objection," he said. Then he noticed that Cheri was still digging in her handbag and finding nothing that resembled a notebook. The Constable said to her, "Mrs. Silvestri, please continue to look for the notebook where the medications are listed. It is vital."

"Well, maybe while sitting in the living room with a cold drink, I can empty everything out onto a table. I know it's in here somewhere. I always carry it on me."

CHAPTER FIFTEEN

A few minutes later in the sitting room, Cheri placed herself in a chair, facing a small side table, and began emptying the contents of her handbag, spreading them out for clear viewing.

The Constable again took his standing position in front of the fireplace, in order to face and dominate the gathering. The Baron lowered himself into his easy chair beside the fire. Major Hurley stood behind Babs and Lorraine, after helping Babs to place her wheelchair in the direction she desired, and holding a chair in order for Lorraine to sit. The Doctor, who'd first gone to the telephone to see if the service had been restored and found that it hadn't, seated himself on one arm of the couch, close to Babs' wheelchair. Jackie settled on the couch, and Ren sat on the other arm of the couch, near Jackie. Dorothy decided to sit on the couch next to Jackie.

Foster was quick to enter with a pot of coffee and the cups, which he placed on the drinks table. The ladies were all having a crème de menthe frappé, as Dorothy had recommended. Foster waited while Trish placed the shaved ice into the glasses, then he poured the liqueur over it and served the ladies their drinks. The gentlemen, most of whom were having coffee or brandy or both, were served after the ladies. When everyone had a drink in hand, the servants stood to attention beside the drinks table.

The Constable cleared his throat to call the meeting to order. But before he had commenced, Cheri let out a shrill cry. She had turned the purse lining inside out and found the tiny notebook where she kept a list of Big Al's medications schedule.

"Here it is," she said, holding up the notebook. "At last. I just knew it was somewhere in my purse. Must have gotten stuck in the lining."

The Baron asked, "Why was she looking for the notebook? Can someone remind me? I can't seem to remember its importance."

The Constable was anxious to gain control of the meeting and said, "Because Mrs. Silvestri has a list of her husband's medications." Turning his attention to Cheri, he said in a commanding voice, "Now, Mrs. Silvestri, kindly read for us the particulars."

"Oh, please stop calling me Mrs. Silvestri. I can't stand the name. I like to be called Cheri. Just Cheri. Will you do that, Constable?... And what are particulars?"

The Constable was flustered. "Very well, if you wish…Cheri." Then he sought again to take charge. "Now tell us which medication you were supposed to give Big Al at dinner time. What was the name of it? We may then determine if it was harmful to give it twice, as you did."

Cheri read with hesitation, and broke up the spelling of the word: "*Met-o-clop-ra-mide.*"

Doctor Armstrong was quick to comment. "Metoclopramide. Perfectly harmless. For the colon. Should be taken before meals. One packet, or two, would not constitute an overdose."

The Constable was about to ask Cheri to read the other entries, but then realized that she would probably read all of them with hesitation and not much accuracy. So, walking over to Cheri, he sat in the chair beside her and examined the pill bottles and packets of medicine that were out on the table. There were dozens of them, all seemingly different.

The Constable, in spite of himself, asked, "Did you never get confused with all these different packets and bottles?"

Cheri said, "Maybe I got confused sometimes. Sometimes I ran short and sometimes I had things left over. It was difficult. You can see that for yourself."

The Constable's attitude again became businesslike. "But you did have everything written down, so with a little concentration and some practice you should have been accurate." He reached for the notebook, saying, "I should like to look at the list of medications you were to administer to your husband."

Everyone sipped their drinks and quietly waited while the Constable studied the entries and compared them with the labels on the bottles and packets. He was calm and pensive. People began to yawn.

Suddenly the Constable rose to his feet and marched swiftly to the fireplace. He turned to the group, holding out a pill bottle, a packet, and the notebook with the list of medications for all to observe. His manner was now grave. "Ladies and gentlemen," he said, "I think I can finally name the murderer."

There were gasps all around. Then a hush fell over the gathering.

The Constable hesitated a long time, holding the gathering in his power, as everyone waited with bated breath for his pronouncement. Finally he declared, "Mrs. Silvestri...Cheri...did not give her husband the harmless colon medicine that he was supposed to have before meals. On both occasions she stirred a packet into a glass of water. The Metoclopramide is in pill form." Here he held up the bottle and showed it around for all to observe. Then he continued, "The packets contain something quite different—*digitalis*. The very poison I have suspected."

Cheri was unperturbed. "But he took digitalis all the time," she said with an edge of disgust in her voice at the Constable's silly conclusion. "So what if it was digitalis?"

Doctor Armstrong sprang to Cheri's defense, practically jeering at the Constable. "Precisely. The young woman is quite correct. As I've said previously, it is a commonly used heart stimulant. It is not thought of as lethal…when taken 'as directed.'"

But the Constable was in full swing and threw back at the Doctor, "Exactly, Doctor, 'as directed.'" Then, reading from Cheri's notebook, he added, "According to the medication chart, Big Al would have taken his quota of digitalis by the afternoon, some hours before dinner. But his wife then administered it to him twice again in quick succession."

Trish, who had been standing quietly beside Foster and at the drinks table, all at once said, "Oh, boy, and those doses on top of what was in the stuffing."

"Hey, wait, I missed something," Ren interjected. "What was in the stuffing?"

Lorraine explained, "Apparently foxglove leaves were mistakenly mixed with the sage. And foxglove leaves apparently contain the poison, digitalis. So it was in the herb mixture that was used to stuff the white fish appetizer."

Jackie asked what they had all been thinking. "If it was in the fish, and it's poison, why did no one else feel sick?"

"That does remain a mystery," the Major said.

"I suppose not," Dorothy said with confidence. She was not concerned about being poisoned. "Only Big Al had a huge dose of the digitalis. I suppose that solves the mystery about the rest of us."

The Doctor concurred. "The rest of us might, from a few foxglove leaves, experience some slight heart palpitations. I doubt if it would make anyone really ill."

But the Constable said, "Except a man with a bad heart, who had been drinking heavily, who had already taken his dosage for the day, and then was subjected to a stuffing with digitalis and two more packets of the drug."

Suddenly Cheri, white as a ghost, rose to her feet and cried out, "They'll kill me!"

The group was taken aback by Cheri's violent outcry.

Finally it was Babs who asked, "Who, dear? Who will kill you?"

"Big Al's hoods," Cheri said slowly and with conviction. "They'll kill me. If this gets out. If they hear."

Babs tried to ease her mind. "But your guilt can not be established here on this island. There will be a trial. You are innocent until proven guilty."

Lorraine, too, tried to make Cheri feel better. "You probably just made a mistake by giving him the wrong medication."

The Major said, "Lorraine is correct. It is not murder, but accidental death."

"We have a crime," the Constable said with great authority. "Accidental or intentional is yet to be determined. But we must also learn the names of her accomplices." His gaze swept the room. "How many were party to digitalis being present in the stuffing?"

Cheri was fatalistic. "It doesn't matter," she said, in a flat, resigned tone. "They'll kill me. If Big Al's hoods hear that I'm even suspected of doing away with him, they'll kill me. They won't wait for a court verdict. I was his wife. I inherit his fortune. They will blame me no matter what. I'm a dead woman."

Ren agreed. "She's right. If so much as a whisper gets out, they'll kill her."

Dorothy's nerves gave way. She blurted out, "What about the rest of us who might have been involved? Will the gangsters…will they kill us, too? I mean…even if we are proven innocent?"

"If one of us prepared the stuffing and put it in the fish, let's say?" Trish asked.

It seemed they were all more afraid of the gangsters than they were of the law, which the Constable represented. Even the Baron asked, "What about the person who grew the foxglove and perhaps gathered it?"

"I don't know," said Cheri in a small voice. "All I do know is that the minute they hear Big Al was murdered, they will suspect me. Then if I'm accused by the Constable, they will kill me long before I have a chance to go to trial."

"She's right," Ren said again, confirming Cheri's worst fears. "They won't waste a minute in getting her."

Jackie said, "We better listen to Ren. Be warned. Ren knows how they operate."

The Major was very concerned and asked, "Couldn't you talk to them, Ren? Explain what happened?"

But Ren said, "Are you kidding? Papa is their enemy. They know he hated Big Al."

"Maybe you'll be in danger, too, Ren," Jackie offered, "when they learn you were here."

But Ren pooh-poohed the idea. "Not if Cheri is booked for the murder. Besides, a hit on me would start a gang war. Nobody wants that. But I think Cheri's dead for sure."

Cheri's voice was still small, and seemed to come from a distance. "I know without Ren saying it. The minute they find out, I'm dead."

Babs was most distressed at this discussion. She said, "How dreadful, you poor child. Something must be done. But what?"

Doctor Armstrong attempted to come to the rescue by again being adamant about his opinion. "I'm the doctor and I say the man died of natural causes. He had a bad heart." He looked sternly at the Constable. "This questioning never took place. There was never any suspicion of murder. The Constable must agree to say nothing."

Next the Baron joined in by stating, "I am certainly in favor of forgetting the entire episode and going to my bed. I think, Constable, we must consider the young peoples' lives."

"I think so, too," Trish said. "Forget the whole thing. The Doctor said he died of a heart attack. I say we leave it at that."

Foster unexpectedly put forth a strong opinion. "No one outside this house has any knowledge of how we have spent the night. The doctor said he died of natural causes, the Constable agreed. That is the way we present the death to the authorities."

Trish agreed. "He was a criminal of the worst kind," she said. She added with passion, "So who cares that he's dead?"

Jackie's pent-up bitterness surfaced. "It is good riddance. Think of the money saved by not going to trial."

Babs added, "And the money the taxpayers save by no longer having to support law enforcement to find and punish this criminal."

Lorraine said, "To say nothing of the human misery that has now been spared."

The Major's mind wandered onto another aspect. "What of the money she would have inherited? Imagine all that money and no chance to spend it."

Lorraine pulled him up short, simply saying, "James, really."

"Oh, sorry," said the Major. "I just meant that's a pity, too. It's all such a pity."

"Well, Constable, we all have very good arguments why this should not be investigated as a murder," the Baron said in a strong, clear voice. "Perhaps you will reconsider?"

The Constable was flabbergasted by all he'd heard. "I can't believe what is being suggested," he said. "What about justice?"

Trish let out a hiss of indignation. "Justice. Justice. The fact that he's dead, Constable, that's justice."

"Death was too good for him," Dorothy also hissed. "Justice gave him a big break. More than he deserved. Much more."

Now everyone responded in agreement, leaving the Constable with his mouth hanging open and without a ready argument.

"Cheri, you would have to begin again, dear. Perhaps go away somewhere," Babs said, as if the matter had been decided.

The Constable said in a subdued voice, "I have not changed my mind or my principles."

But Babs, ignoring him, continued with her line of thought. "Have you thought of what you might like to do, Cheri?"

Cheri got a dreamy look on her face, and said, "When I saw the pictures of this island, I fell in love with it. I was the one who coaxed Big Al to come and consider the offering."

Lorraine thought perhaps Cheri did not really know her own mind, and asked, "Wouldn't you find it a lonely place, at your age?"

"Oh, no," Cheri said. "I have always wanted to paint. I could be very happy here."

Dorothy knew about an art institute and was enthusiastic over the possibilities of Cheri's training in Vancouver. She became quite excited at the thought of this lovely child staying full time, actually enjoying the island and the mainland of Canada…and becoming like a daughter to her…a daughter she'd never had. "There is an excellent art institute on the mainland," she gushed. "You could enroll there, study during the day, and be here in the evenings, and on weekends, live here with the Baron until your own house is ready."

The Constable could not believe the conversation he was hearing. How could they all assume he would agree to a cover-up? In a shaky voice, he asked, "Why are we even discussing this?"

The Baron, too, liked the idea that a lovely young woman such as Cheri might grace the island with her presence. He responded to Dorothy's offer, totally ignoring the Constable. "Indeed, I'd be most pleased to have you as my guest, Miss Cheri, and to offer you the service of my yacht to go back and forth to your studies."

The Constable thought he must press for reason. "Do you mean if she is acquitted at trial?" he asked.

Again ignoring the Constable, the Baron went on with his

thoughts for the future…a very agreeable future. "In fact, any of you who sign on are welcome to stay here until your own property is ready."

"I find this seclusion so appealing," Babs said.

"But, my dear, the Baron and his butler have admitted to a scam," Doctor Armstrong cautioned. However, he did not say it with conviction.

"Nonsense," Babs answered. "I have a good head for business. I had already decided to buy, and my mind has not been changed."

"I, too, like the business side of the development," the Doctor said, "and had not actually changed my mind. Perhaps you could explain yourself better, Foster. What exactly did you mean by the scam?"

Foster said, "I was wrong to imply that the entire scheme was suspicious. We had in mind a special revenge for Big Al. A scam for him alone." Here he paused and collected his thoughts, then said, "Under certain conditions, the development could be very profitable."

Dorothy again felt it necessary to stress her innocence. "I have always thought it could be profitable. Very profitable," she said, "but on one condition…that we get everyone's money immediately. We can't borrow, and so are in no position to start without every cent of the capital up front. Then it would work. I know it would."

Lorraine had a faraway look as she thought about the development. "How I wish we had the means," she whispered. "It would be a dream come true for James and me. Wouldn't it, James?"

Her husband nodded and also assumed a faraway look of longing.

Cheri suddenly startled everyone, took their breath away, by declaring, "With the money I inherit, I would like to finance the whole project and share it equally with each and every one of you."

"That is far too generous, my dear," Babs said. "And I, for one, can afford to purchase my own shares."

"What is the meaning of *too* generous?" the Major protested.

Answering Babs, Cheri said, "But I want to do it for every one of you, whether you can afford it or not. We all shared this terrible night together. We all suffered from Big Al's cruelty. That is the way I think his money should be spent."

"Poetic justice," the Doctor exclaimed. "What a startling concept. I am not opposed, in theory."

Once Dorothy realized that Cheri's offer was genuine, she was quick to say, "Oh, I accept, and most gratefully. I never even dreamed of myself as being an owner here. And I would still carry on the work to get it built, and with the greatest of dedication."

"Well, I wouldn't carry on the work," Trish said, "not as a maid. But I'd pitch in and help in all sorts of ways. Boy, how I'd thrive here. You wouldn't see me getting bored. Gosh, a house of my own."

Foster, for once, was able to dream of a possession. "I would never leave the service of the Baron," he said, "not so long as he lives, but a house of my own to return to at night. Yes, I should like that."

The Major still could not believe what he had heard. "Let me try and understand this. Are you offering to buy the entire development plan with your inheritance money, and give each of us an equal share?"

"We think that is what you said," Lorraine added, "but it is just too good to be true."

But Cheri was sincere and determined. "That's what I meant. The Baron will have his house and his profit," she explained. "Each of us will have a house and a share in the profits of the hotel and resort. And I'll still have plenty of money left over."

Ren was flabbergasted. "What about me?" he asked in disbelief. "You'd include me…knowing who I am?"

"You could consider it a present from your long-lost uncle," Cheri said with a lovely smile and a feeling of benevolence toward Ren.

Ren's eyes grew big as saucers at the thought of possession. "Wow," he drawled. "I could be independent from Papa. I wouldn't have to spend every moment here. I could go back and forth to New York."

Jackie had a worried look. "I'm not sure I could accept your offer, generous as it is," she said hesitantly, "knowing where the money came from…how he got it."

Babs tried to persuade her to see reason. "Think where the money goes if Cheri does not inherit it. She has a marvelous plan to share it with us, his victims. Poetic justice."

The Baron attempted to close the deal. "Well, I think everyone should be in agreement?" he said. "Miss Le Roir?"

"Yes, I would adore to be here," she said with tears in her eyes. "You've all become like a family to me."

"So is that everyone?" the Baron asked.

All nodded their consent, with the exception of the Major. He said, "I should like to consult my attorneys before signing."

CHAPTER SIXTEEN

Lorraine scolded her husband. "James…no more conning. From now on, we will be legitimate, have a home at last… stop roaming and living off other people." She stood and faced the gathering, saying, "And I would like to put James and myself forward to manage the hotel. It's a job he'll be good at—charming the guests."

The Baron raised his voice with a newfound energy. "I, of course, could not be more delighted by the plan," he said. "We have gotten to know one another very well in this short period, and have much in common. I foresee a marvelous cooperation and great success."

Cheri looked around the room and gave each of them a personal nod. Her look stopped at the Constable and she said, "That leaves only you, Constable. Will you accept the offer?"

"You mean you're including him in on the deal?" Ren said, unable to keep distaste for the idea out of his tone. "That's a bribe."

"Not entirely," Dorothy pointed out. "This arrangement, in order to work, must include everyone who has shared in the night's events." Looking to Cheri, she asked, "Isn't that what you had in mind, my dear? This generous scheme was conceived with all those of us present in mind…excluding no one."

"Oh, yes," Cheri assured them, "I really do want everyone present to be an equal partner. Everyone."

Foster didn't like the idea and said so. "If he were just another person who had shared this horrendous experience with us, but he represents the law." Foster then cautioned, "He would be committing a crime in accepting and that would place us all in danger."

But the Baron cleared his throat and disagreed, saying, "I don't see how he can be left out. If he accepts, then he must be included, and we all share the same fate…hope for the best."

Cheri said, "So it is up to you. What do you say, Constable?"

"I'm not the Constable," he said in a sharp, clear voice.

There was a profound silence. Everyone just stared at him.

The Baron asked for help, thinking perhaps his mind had played a trick, that he had not heard correctly. "What did you say? I don't think I heard correctly."

Cheri repeated what the Constable had said. "The Constable said that he's not the Constable."

"Then who are you?" Babs asked.

He said, "I'm an actor. My name is Jerome Harrison."

Dorothy had invited him and felt certain she had spoken to the Constable's office. Why, she had returned his call, had dialed the number herself, and asked for him. "But I don't understand. How did you get here? I was expecting…"

"The real Constable," Jerome said. "I know. It was a bad night. I took his place."

"You impersonated him?" the Major said in disbelief. "But you had the Immigration file?"

Jerome said, "I hang around the police station. They all know me. I'm doing research into their behavior. The real Constable said he was going to cancel tonight because of the bad weather. He said he needed someone to take the message to the captain of the Baron's yacht. I offered to carry the message for him."

Jackie filled in the rest. "But instead of telling the captain…you got on the yacht, pretending to be the Constable?"

"Yes."

Lorraine wanted to know, "What about the Immigration file?"

Jerome almost laughed as he told them, "I slipped it under my raincoat…borrowed it, really." Then, on a serious note, he said, "I was more shocked than any of you when I saw what it contained."

Cheri was not really upset that he had fooled her. In fact, she was relieved that he did not represent the law. She also found him appealing. "You're a good actor," she said with admiration. "You fooled us all. What have you appeared in that I might have seen?"

"He did not fool me," the Doctor said sharply, to remind them. "I said from the beginning he was an imposter."

"I haven't appeared in anything professional," Jerome said. "I'm part of a little theater group. We're going to be doing a series of Agatha Christie plays, and I'm researching the part of Poirot."

Doctor Armstrong had an *I-told-you-so* look. "Didn't I say he was quoting from Agatha Christie? Didn't I say that?"

The Baron suddenly realized that he had spent an uncomfortable evening and decided that he was not amused. "You are a very naughty fellow, whatever you said your name was."

"Jerome Harrison," he said. He looked at Cheri in a flirtatious way. "Do you think that's a good name for an actor?"

Cheri did seem to be taken with him. "Yes, I think it's beautiful and sexy," she crooned.

Babs said, "It's a good name, and you are quite a good actor."

The Doctor felt a jealous pang rising to accompany his already deep-felt annoyance with the would-be actor. "He is a scoundrel. He's put us through this long, ghastly night for nothing. He ought to be horsewhipped."

"I am sorry I deceived you all," Jerome said with great sincerity.

"I'm afraid that I just got carried away. My intention was to make the Constable's community relations speech." He took the speech from his pocket and held it up. "I borrowed the written text. I was going to read the speech, have a cup of coffee, and leave tomorrow on the next available boat."

Doctor Armstrong spread his legs and planted his feet, hands on hips, assuming a threatening pose. "You'll not leave before we deal with you for your deceit."

But Cheri came to Jerome's defense. "His plan wouldn't have done any harm," she said. "We would have heard the Constable's own speech, just said by Jerome Harrison."

Lorraine kept harping back to the thing that she had found most disturbing during the evening's mock investigation. She asked, "But then why did you have the Immigration portfolio?"

Jerome said, "It was with the speech. I thought it would be useful to have everyone's name and a bit of background for good relations."

"A birching would be too good for him," the Doctor said.

But Jackie also defended him. "He's already said that he didn't know beforehand what was in the file…that he was more surprised than we were with the information it contained." She added, "I think he made a dull night exciting."

The Baron could not see it that way. "He kept me from my bed and caused us all a great deal of anxiety. Why did you carry on so, sir?" he asked. "Why did you begin by declaring murder?"

"There was the drama of the storm," Jerome explained, "and almost the first thing I encountered was a dead man on the floor. Just like the Agatha Christie play, the first in our series. Poirot took over."

Doctor Armstrong said, "I say we hang him up by his thumbs."

Babs turned to the Doctor and tried to soothe him with a gentle voice. "Do let us put it behind us, dearest. The night has had the most marvelous conclusion. The Baron's conversion for the island is to be a joint venture in which we all share. We must learn to live together in harmony, and that includes this *amateur actor.*" And "amateur actor" was said with disparity by the great actress.

But the Doctor had not really heard her, and said, "If we find an anthill we could stake him on it."

Jerome again said, "I do apologize most humbly. And I also want to make amends by repairing the telephone line." He walked over and picked up his raincoat from the chair by the sitting room door.

Jackie asked, "Do you work for the phone company, as well as act?"

Jerome said, "That is my real job. I'm employed by the telephone company." He put on his raincoat and extracted a wrench from his pocket. "I am a telephone repairman."

Now it was Ren's turn to be annoyed. "We've been without a telephone all this time, and you're a telephone repairman. Why didn't you say something before?"

The Doctor again thought of a punishment. "At the very least we brand him with a hot poker."

Cheri tried to reason with Ren by saying, "He couldn't tell us he was a telephone repairman, and still pretend to be the Constable."

The Major said, "I hope you'll be successful with the repair. I must be near a telephone to keep in touch with my brokers."

Lorraine said, "James!"

The Major said, "Oh, yes, sorry. It's a habit."

The Baron asked, "What is happening now? Someone remind me?"

Foster tried to explain. "The would-be actor is really a telephone repairman. He believes he might be able to repair our downed telephone line."

"Oh, I know I can fix it," Jerome said with complete confidence. "It was me who disabled it to begin with."

"What?" the Doctor exploded. "You deliberately disabled

the line and left us without any communication with the outside world?" He drew in a sharp breath and said, "Extracting his fingernails one by one would not be too extreme a punishment."

Trish was fed up with the Doctor and his persistence on dealing out a punishment. "Why don't we just let him fix the telephone instead," she suggested with biting sarcasm. "I want to make a call and probably everyone else does, too."

"I should have the service back in about twenty minutes," Jerome said as he exited the sitting room for the main hallway.

"I've got to call Papa," Ren said, almost to himself. "And I want a reservation back to New York."

But the Doctor interrupted his reverie. "I believe that I am first in line for the telephone," he said, and then added, "After the imposter repairs the line, I insist we punish him."

"Well, nobody agrees with you," Trish snapped at him, "so why not forget it, and just drop it, Doc?"

Dorothy said with enthusiasm, "Now that we are all going to be owners, would you like to see the plans again? Why don't we move into the dining room so that I can spread them out on the dining table where we can all have a good view. They may be more interesting this time around."

Everyone uttered their agreement and happily followed her into the dining room.

CHAPTER SEVENTEEN

Jerome, AKA the Constable, felt the effects of a strong wind as he opened the front door against its force. The rain was coming down in a slanted sheet that struck his face, stinging his eyes and preventing him from fully opening them. He fought his way forward a few yards to the telephone pole, where one end of the severed cable was dangling, reached, and grabbed hold. He looked up and saw that he would have to climb the pole to get to the other end of the cable so he could attach them. He didn't relish the climb in this rain, but it had to be done.

Meanwhile, in the dining room, maps, blueprints, and big color posters now covered the dining room table. Everyone was gathered tightly together at the head of the table for the best view.

Lorraine, who was standing next to Cheri, hugged and kissed her, saying, "You can't imagine how happy you've made us."

Babs reached up from her wheelchair and affectionately patted

Cheri's arm, adding, "You truly are an angel." Then, pointing to the map of the island, she said, "I would like a bungalow near the hotel path. It will be easier for me to get about."

Doctor Armstrong was quick to say, "I shall have mine immediately next door to Miss Cunningham."

Jackie, great excitement in her voice, cooed, "Oh, I want to be right on the shore. As close to the water as I can get. I adore sunbathing and swimming."

Dorothy, after surveying the happy faces of those gathered around the table, blurted out, "To think that none of this might have happened if it hadn't been for the murder."

Cheri begged, "Oh, please stop calling it a murder."

Dorothy, by way of apologizing, said, "Forgive me, everyone. I forgot myself. I shall never again say the word *murder*. And all of us should forget anything about murder."

Suddenly a booming voice came from the direction of the hallway. "*Murder!* What are you talking about? What *murder?*"

A terrified silence followed. Everyone was in deep shock as they looked in the direction of the voice. It sounded familiar…but surely not…it wasn't possible!

But it was possible. A large man emerged from the shadows and entered the dining room. It was Big Al. He was frowning and hitting himself on the arms and chest. His color was ever so slightly blue, he was breathing deeply, and his large frame was racked with shivering.

Cheri was the first to pull herself together. Although terribly shaken, she managed to smile and say to Big Al, "Oh, it's nothing, just some story." Walking towards him, she added, "Where have you been?"

Big Al stood in place, allowing Cheri to come to him. He was still slapping his arms, trying to get warm. "I'm cold," he said. "I don't know how I ended up in the cellar," he added, shaking his head in disbelief. He caught sight of Foster and yelled, "A bourbon!"

Foster stood to full attention. "Certainly, sir, coming right up."

Upon reaching Big Al, Cheri had taken off her shawl and put it around him, leading him to his same seat at the table. "Come, darling," she said. "Sit down."

The Major then rushed to Big Al and began rubbing his back. "I'm sure you'll be warm in a minute," he offered with concern.

Then everyone gathered close to Big Al to attend upon him.

Big Al began reviving. "I must of tied one on," he said, still shaking his head in disbelief. "I don't know what I could have been looking for in the cellar. Somehow I managed to lie down in this cold box, a broken freezer, I guess."

"Oh, dear," Cheri lisped, "you might have been suffocated."

"Yeah, if the lid had been closed tight," Big Al agreed. "But it was open a crack." He pushed the Major's hands away, indicating that he wanted no more rubbing. He looked slowly at everyone present and they all seemed to cower under his gaze…with the exception of Cheri, who looked her same smiling, vacant self. Finally he exploded, yelling, "Damn, I'm cold! Where's that bourbon?"

Just then Foster arrived with the bottle of bourbon and a glass. "Here you are, sir," he said, and began to pour.

Big Al grabbed the glass as soon as it was full and downed the bourbon in one gulp. Then he smacked his lips with satisfaction. "That's better. Hit me again," he said, holding up the empty glass. He turned a menacing look on Cheri and growled, "Why didn't you look for me? How long was I gone for?"

Now even Cheri showed her fright. She took the bottle of bourbon from Foster and began pouring, but her hand shook noticeably. In answer to Big Al's question, she said as casually as possible, "Oh, no time at all. I think you were out of the room for only a few minutes."

Everyone chimed in, in an effort to reassure Big Al that it was no time at all since he'd left the dining room.

Cheri said, "We thought you were in the little boys' room."

Again the gathering muttered their agreement.

"Why, we haven't even started our main course yet," Cheri said, in a fit of inspiration. "The table has just this second been cleared of the appetizer."

To everyone's enormous relief, Big Al accepted Cheri's time-frame. "That fish was pretty good," he said. "Did I eat all my fish?"

"Yes, you did," Cheri said. "But we don't mind waiting to start the main course. Maybe you'd like some more fish?"

"Yeah, give me some more of that fish appetizer," Big Al agreed.

Trish immediately headed toward the kitchen. "I can get you another piece right away," she said, and left the room.

All at once there was another blackout. But this time the candelabra was still alight.

Meanwhile, outside, Jerome Harrison, AKA the Constable, had successfully climbed the telephone pole and was making good progress in reconnecting the two ends of the severed cable.

Ten minutes later, inside the dining room, the table had been laid. Dorothy had scurried to put on the dishes, and Lorraine had placed the napkins and silverware all around. And Big Al, who'd never paid any attention to the proper manner of serving a dinner, seemed none the wiser when the place settings had been done for a second time.

Actually it was the Baron who looked totally confused, and everyone took turns distracting him lest he ask, "Remind me, why are we about to eat for a second time?"

Most of the guests found it taxing to sit in their places and pretend they had not eaten. But they all made a superhuman effort, as if their lives depended upon being convincing.

The electricity came back on, but no one seemed to notice.

Foster kept looking nervously toward the doorway, waiting for Trish to return with the fish. In the meantime, he filled Big Al's water glass and his bourbon glass, and poured red wine for some.

Cheri now pulled two packets of medicine out of her purse and emptied them into Big Al's water glass, stirring vigorously. "Here, darling, I'm preparing your medicine," she said sweetly.

The other guests froze with fright as Big Al asked, "Didn't I already take my before-dinner medicine?"

But Cheri was calm again, and vague. "I don't remember," she purred. "I don't think so."

They all watched with bated breath as Big Al lifted the medicine glass and emptied it. He then polished off his bourbon.

Foster stepped in smartly and held the bottle. "Allow me to refill your bourbon, sir," he said, then added, "Ah, Trish is here with your fish."

Trish put the appetizer down in front of Big Al and he began to tuck into the fish, cramming one big mouthful after another down his throat…until he began to choke…which was no surprise.

Everyone must have been expecting him to choke, after the way he was cramming the food down his throat, and, after all, he had already choked in the very same way earlier in the evening. However, there was a long, motionless silence in which the entire group seemed paralyzed. Many moments passed in which no one stepped forward to aid Big Al.

Finally, Cheri stood and lifted Big Al's arms above his head. She mouthed a slow count.

Moments later, Ren rose from his chair and walked around the table. Cheri had let Big Al's arms down to his sides. Her arm-raising had not been beneficial in any way, and Big Al continued to violently choke.

When Ren arrived behind Big Al, he hit him viciously on the back. Big Al was choking so hard he had turned purple in the face.

Babs had wheeled herself over beside Big Al. She nudged Ren to move away, reached up and shoved her fingers down Big Al's throat, spilling the powder contents of her ring into his mouth.

As soon as Babs had wheeled herself clear of Big Al's chair, Foster stepped into the space she had vacated. He assumed a martial arts stance, gave a strange cry, and administered a karate chop to Big Al's heart.

Big Al's torso jumped violently and then fell with a crash onto the tabletop. Plates and glasses flew everywhere, and the people stood back from the flying objects.

There followed a long period of silence.

The Doctor had been calmly observing the others. Now he stepped into the slumped, motionless figure of the gang boss and felt for a pulse. He gave no indication as to the patient's condition, but while still feeling Big Al's pulse, he produced a full hypodermic needle from inside his waistcoat and injected it into Big Al's main artery.

Jerome Harrison, AKA the amateur actor posing as the Constable, had successfully made the connection on the severed phone line. He removed a stethoscope from his raincoat pocket and listened to the repaired cable to make sure there was a dial tone and that the service had, indeed, been restored. He heard dialing coming from the house. Someone was already trying to see if the phone had been reconnected.

Jerome was able to see into the dining room from atop the telephone pole, and he had noticed a great deal of activity. The people inside seemed to be scurrying about. He couldn't tell what exactly they had been doing, because the rain was still heavy and had obscured his vision.

He was about to climb down the telephone pole and return to the warmth and protection of the house when he heard words which riveted him to the spot. It was the voice of Doctor Armstrong, telling the police that a man had, only moments before, died of a heart attack on Escape Island.

PART TWO

CHAPTER ONE

Twenty-three years had passed since the demise of Big Al the New York crime boss, who had met his Maker in the presence of his widow and eleven others on that stormy night in 1970. None present were ever questioned by authorities, the incident never investigated as murder. Doctor Harlan Armstrong had put himself forth as the attending physician and was permitted to sign the death certificate. The cause of death was officially listed as heart failure.

The deceased's wife, Cheri, had inherited a huge fortune which she then invested in the Escape Island Development Project, giving all persons who had been present on that fateful night equal shares. In no time, the mansion had been converted into a hotel, and the grounds dotted by lovely cottages. There followed tennis courts, an Olympic-size swimming pool, verandas, garden paths, and an outdoor pavilion for banquets and dancing, weather permitting.

All those present at the passing of Big Al—and, some nasty rumors had it, responsible for his passing—had lived for a time quite happily with the new development, enjoying life on the island. However, presently only three of them were still inhabitants of

Escape Island: Cheri Silvestri, Dorothy Saks, and Doctor Harlan Armstrong.

Cheri never remarried. She'd gone to art school on the mainland and then devoted herself to her painting. Cheri was prolific, if not notably talented. She'd had dozens of offers of marriage, but none that interested her; and she had made (and was still making) dozens upon dozens of pictures, which crowded the walls of all the cottages and the mansion-turned-hotel.

Dorothy Saks, even as one of the owners, never stopped being publicity manager and sales representative for the complex. She'd been a working girl from Alberta trying to make a success in a man's world, and had finally succeeded, but had never realized that she might hire someone else to perform those duties in subsequent years. But she was rewarded for her continued devotion. When old Baron Tarrall, the original owner, passed away, he'd left his shares to Dorothy. The Baron's devoted butler, Foster, who had died— some said of a broken heart—the very day after the Baron's funeral, had also surprisingly willed his shares to Dorothy.

Trish, Dorothy's daughter-in-law, who'd once been the maid, had been the first to tire of island life and had sold her shares to Dorothy. So had Jackie Le Roir tired of the island, deciding to move to France. She, too, had sold her shares to Dorothy.

Babs Cunningham and Doctor Armstrong never became the romantic duo everyone expected. Their romance grew cold even before the island complex was completed. Babs missed show business and had not found the promised fulfillment in seclusion. When the network offered her the starring role in her own soap opera, in which she could play a cruel but glamorous matriarch who was wheelchair-bound, she'd made up her mind overnight to accept. Babs offered to sell her shares to the Doctor and he readily accepted to buy.

Major Hurley and his wife, Lorraine, had managed the hotel for the first five years and had done so with great success. Then, craving a more adventurous lifestyle, the Hurleys had moved to Kenya, East Africa. Each had been given shares, and each had sold out to the Doctor.

Jerome Harrison—AKA the amateur actor whose idol was Hercule Poirot, AKA telephone repairman impersonating a Constable on the night Big Al croaked—had become not a professional actor as expected, but a Senior Vice President of the Western Canadian Telephone Company. He'd spent little time on the island, preferring to work his way up in the phone company, and was finally persuaded by Doctor Armstrong to sell his shares to the Doctor.

Ren Silvestri was presently, as his uncle and father before him, the top hood in New York. Ren's father had succeeded his brother, Big Al, as head of the mob, and then in his old age had turned the "big boss" job over to Ren. Of all the owners who no longer lived on the island complex, only Ren Silvestri had kept his shares. The shares were, therefore, in the hands of four of the original shareholders—Ren, Cheri, Dorothy, and the Doctor. These four owned the island and its enterprise, but not on an equal basis. Ren had only his single holding, as did Cheri. She had never been greedy or sought other shares because she had no desire to gain control. She was content to paint, paint, paint—filling up more wall space—and to remain the little girl on whom the Doctor and Dorothy doted.

The oddest coupling, romantically speaking, was that of the Doctor and Dorothy. Shortly after all the available shares had been divided either by inheritance or purchase, Doctor Armstrong proposed. Now they were a married couple with the controlling interest.

The Doctor excelled in finance, and handled all fiscal matters. Other than that, he was a gentleman of leisure, still a formidable, opinionated, rather handsome fellow at the age of seventy-three.

Dorothy, as stated, was still the same public relations and sales manager she had always been…although, perhaps, a bit more vague at the age of seventy-six, but still enthusiastic, bubbly, and a hard worker. She never ceased being flattered by the Doctor's offer of marriage and was completely devoted, overlooking his sometimes stern treatment of her. Also to her astonishment, the Doctor had not only consummated their union, but did so on a regular basis.

Dorothy had lost her son William, who had been killed by Big Al's hoods; and she and her daughter-in-law, Trish, had gotten on each other's nerves. Trish had moved to the city of Vancouver and opened a beauty salon, after she sold her shares to Dorothy. And though she remained on the mainland just a short boat trip away, she never came to visit and hardly ever telephoned.

Dorothy's maternal feelings turned toward and were lavished on Cheri, the daughter she'd never had. And Cheri wanted nothing more than to be the Armstrongs' little girl. She suggested that the couple legally adopt her. As it happened, Doctor Armstrong's only vulnerable spot was reserved for Cheri, and the Armstrongs became the married couple who adopted a grown child. Both Dorothy and Harlan thought the sun rose and set upon Cheri Armstrong.

Cheri had been twenty-two on the terrible night of Big Al's death. That had been twenty-three years ago, and Cheri was about to celebrate a milestone: her forty-fifth birthday! Dorothy wanted a very special birthday party for Cheri, and had hit upon the idea of a reunion of the former shareholders. She had sent out the invitations over a month ago, and was over the moon now that every one of them had agreed to come back for the celebration. It would, indeed, be a weekend to remember.

CHAPTER TWO

The invitation for the Senior Vice President, Mr. Jerome Harrison, arrived at the main offices of the Western Canadian Telephone Company. Jerome's secretary had placed a large stack of mail on his desk that morning in March of 1993, but the moment he saw the postmark, Escape Island, Dorothy's invitation was the first piece of mail he opened. The invitation stated that next month, on April 17th, Cheri Armstrong would be celebrating her forty-fifth birthday, and a reunion of all the original shareholders was planned as a special celebration.

Jerome leaned back in his red leather desk chair and looked out the window at the lovely panorama of the Cascade Mountains. It was difficult to believe that beautiful young Cheri was about to turn forty-five. He himself could never believe his own age. He would be sixty-one this summer. When thinking of his own age, he wished that he had made a better marriage, one that had not ended in divorce and one that had produced some offspring. It was too late now. He was a lonely bachelor with only his work to think about, and that, too, would end in four more years, when he reached retirement age.

He swiveled his chair and looked at his office walls, hung with plaques of gratitude for his work in many charities. He had climbed the corporate ladder and his professional life could be counted a success. The very walls announced that success, not only the plaques and certificates, but also the expensive red hemp wallpaper and the mahogany trim stretching up to the ceiling and down to the carpeting of finest wool. The customers paid for more than the telephone service they signed up for, they paid for this and other plush offices.

The intercom buzzed. He pushed a button and asked his secretary to hold all his calls until further notice. He stroked his thinning hair and wondered at the mixed emotions he had about returning to Escape Island. Certainly, he would go back. He felt compelled to go back. It had been a very long time since his last visit, but he would not miss Cheri's milestone birthday or the reunion.

He had been sweet on Cheri, no doubt about that. For a time she seemed to return his affections. Maybe he should have pressed harder, been a more aggressive suitor, but he was still married then, and he felt that Cheri needed some time for mourning. Then all at once she dropped him and began dating one of the sailors on the Baron's yacht. That had been quite a blow to his ego.

No doubt Cheri's jilting him had a great deal to do with this climb up the corporate ladder. He moved back to the mainland and threw himself into the affairs of the telephone company. His promotions came one after another, and he worked ever harder. He even gave up his place in the little theatre group, and with that, his dream of becoming a professional actor. Hercule Poirot faded from his memory. He would never appear in an Agatha Christie, or any other, play.

Once he dropped Hercule Poirot as his idol, his own image of himself changed. He began by abandoning his slicked-down hairstyle, opted for a conventional short cut, and shaved off his mustache. His wardrobe, too, became conservative. Charities received his former clothing—although what a homeless man would do with vests and spats was anybody's guess.

The new image made him better material for promotion. But his wife claimed he'd become too dull to bear. Theirs had never been an ideal relationship, and now she had an excuse to divorce him.

He wondered if Cheri would now also find him hopelessly dull. She had seemed to like his eccentric appearance and manner. But then she'd thrown him over for a common, rough sailor. She'd never married again, however. Perhaps, in the back of his mind, if he admitted it to himself, he still had hopes of rekindling their romance. At any rate, he was longing to see her again.

In fact, he was looking forward to seeing all of them. He hadn't been back since the Baron's funeral twenty years ago. Twenty years was a very long time. He had changed, grown old, bald, and paunchy, but they would all have changed as well. Dorothy and the Doctor were in their seventies. Dorothy, being a few years older than her husband, would be closer to eighty, he supposed.

Jackie Le Roir was probably slightly older than Cheri, and Ren would still be a young chap of about Cheri's age, forty-five. As for Trish, she had been considered one of the younger people on the island, but he had no idea what her age was now, maybe fifty?

Babs Cunningham lied shamelessly about her age. He knew for a fact that she was as old as he, but all her publicity releases claimed that she was still forty-nine.

Major James Hurley and his wife, Lorraine, would be in their seventies by now, and no doubt looking craggy but fit because of their lifestyle in East Africa. He admired the fact that they had sold their shares, given up work, and lived as free spirits. How many people could lay claim to a life devoted to adventure and freedom? Yes, he admired them, and looked forward to chatting with them again, as he looked forward to chatting with them all.

He also had this strange feeling of foreboding. Perhaps because of the manner in which Big Al had died. Had it been murder?

The thought of murder sent a chill through him, and he was happy when the intercom buzzed again, disturbing his reverie. This time his secretary reminded him to take his ten o'clock medication.

Jerome rose from behind his grand Regency-style desk and went to his private bathroom, which was done completely in black and gold. He took a glass from beside the sink and turned on the gold-plated faucet. One of those faucets cost more than a half-hour call, during business hours, from Vancouver to China. Not surprising, as socialist societies always unfairly rewarded bureaucrats of any type.

From the mirrored medicine cabinet he took a packet of powder and put it into the glass of water. It immediately dissolved, unlike the powder Cheri had put in Big Al's glass, which had to be stirred, then turned white and left a sticky residue. Had that been digitalis? Odd how he had always wondered and yet never informed himself of what the digitalis would have looked like in a glass. He could easily have had one of the juniors research digitalis and foxgloves, and he would now know if foxglove leaves mixed with sage as a fish stuffing could be considered a poison. But he didn't know, because he'd put it out of his mind...or thought he'd put it out of his mind. Who had grown the foxgloves, who had gathered the leaves, who had put it in the fish?

Lost in thought, he had taken his own medicine without realizing it, until he observed the empty glass. He rinsed the glass and put it back. Then he dried his hands on a black and gold towel and went back to his desk.

Before sitting, he picked up the rest of the mail, intending to open it, but without knowing why, he put it down again, and again turned to study the snowcapped mountains. His mind wandered to skiing. He enjoyed the sport and tried to work in a skiing holiday about twice a year. It never snowed, or almost never snowed, in

Vancouver proper. Perhaps because the sea sent in warmer breezes that discouraged the rain from turning to snow. Once Dorothy had written to him that it had snowed on Escape Island, a rare occurrence. Dorothy was so good about keeping in touch by mail.

Jerome had little time for personal correspondence, but he always dictated a reply to his secretary. Even though Dorothy must have known that he never replied personally, she still continued to write. She must have kept up a more or less regular correspondence with the other former investors, as well, because she was always full of news about what the others were doing or where they had spent their vacations. And Dorothy flooded his office with every scrap of publicity information about the island, and probably sent it to all the others as well.

In his mind's eye he pictured Cheri, of course as she was then, in her early twenties; but Dorothy had also sent photographs of the Armstrong family throughout the years, and it seemed to him that Cheri never aged. He again thought of her being without a husband, and of himself filling that position. Odd how many of the former owners had not changed their marital status. Maybe it was the times they were living in; marriage wasn't a necessity in the Nineties.

The big surprise, of course, was Dorothy and Doctor Armstrong tying the knot...to say nothing of adopting a big girl like Cheri. The Hurleys had been married for as long as he'd known them. Somehow one expected people like James and Lorraine Hurley to be faithful forever. But like himself, Cheri Armstrong, Babs Cunningham, and Jackie Le Roir had chosen to live alone. Trish was in the process of getting her second divorce, Dorothy had written, and he'd detected the pain Dorothy felt in passing on that sad news about her former daughter-in-law.

Ren Silvestri was the exception. Ren had married shortly after that fateful night when Big Al was...murdered...or died of natural causes? He had wed a young Catholic girl from a good New York

Italian family. They had a huge house somewhere in Connecticut, and six children. Apparently it was no secret that Ren had inherited more than just the desire for a large family, he had also inherited his uncle's and his father's shady businesses, and even the title "big gang boss."

What had Jerome seen that night in 1970? When he was at the top of the telephone pole, he'd been able to see in the dining room windows, but heavy rain had blurred his vision. He'd seen a great deal of movement in the room. That had surprised him; they were supposed to be looking at maps and drawings of the proposed development plan. Had he seen Big Al and dismissed that image as impossible? Doctors claim we often see more than we are willing to admit, and sometimes it takes hypnosis to arrive at the truth. The body of Big Al was in the dining room when he'd again entered the house. Had they simply moved him as they claimed, or had he regained consciousness and been murdered again?

CHAPTER THREE

When the invitation arrived at the Tresses By Trish salon, it was tossed in a pile of unopened mail and left there for several days. Tresses was a unisex beauty salon, a messy, run-down place in a poorer section of Vancouver. The establishment catered to the young arty crowd, mostly migrants to Western Canada. Punk styles were Trish Saks' specialty, and they were no longer in vogue with any but the unwashed few. None but unstylish, pubescent rebels still went in for spikes, peaks, and streaks of pink and purple. However, Trish's overhead was low, she made enough to make ends meet, and she didn't seem to crave more. Besides, she wouldn't lose her shirt in her present divorce proceedings, because there was nothing of substance to lose.

Trish had kept the name Saks through both unsuccessful marriages that followed after the death of William Saks, the only man she'd ever truly loved, who had been murdered by Big Al's gang. One of those marriages occurred right after she'd left Escape Island. She'd taken the capital from the sale of her shares in the island complex and invested it in a salon in the best part of town. Then she'd married the flamboyant hairdresser, Josh, who was her partner.

When the marriage broke up after nine years, she discovered that their business partnership was unfairly weighted on his side, and he'd kept almost everything.

Her third husband, George Loom, was an alcoholic who'd always sponged off Trish. He was too lazy or too continuously drunk to protest the divorce or the measly allowance she had agreed to pay him. Her lawyer assured her that she would be free in a matter of weeks, and that the settlement would remain uncontested.

She'd married George Loom on the rebound from Josh, and had stayed with him almost eleven years. He had been a good-natured drunk who had been more or less indifferent both to her wishes and to her scalding tongue. She'd stayed with him because he mainly kept out of her way, and because she couldn't be bothered to go through the legal hassle of another divorce. However, recently his drinking had gotten worse and he'd been fired from his postal job. Idle all day, he'd begun to show up drunk at the salon, put demands on her. Her desire to be free of him had grown irresistible and she'd filed for separation.

Trish did not admit it to herself, but she always waited eagerly for mail from her mother-in-law, Dorothy Saks. Maybe she wasn't that crazy about Dorothy, certainly they'd gotten on each other's nerves, but it was a link with the love of her life, William. And Dorothy was loyal no matter what; she kept up a steady, one-sided correspondence.

There were two reasons why Trish didn't open the mail immediately. Firstly, there were always bills that she had to scrape to pay; and secondly, a letter from Dorothy was a missive to be savored. She wanted to read the latest from Escape Island at a leisurely time when she could savor the words and reminisce.

Monday there was almost never any business and she closed the salon early in the afternoon. So it was on Monday afternoons when she did her own hair, the laundry, the bills, and read the mail. She saved Dorothy's letter for last. The blinds were down, all the menial tasks were done, and she could take time out for her own enjoyment. She went to the tiny refrigerator, which she kept a lock on, took out a bottle of white wine, poured a glass, and sat down in the easy chair to read.

Trish choked on her wine upon reading the first line of Dorothy's letter:

> *You are cordially invited to a special celebration*
> *in honor of Cheri Armstrong's forty-fifth birthday.*

She put down her wine, wiped her mouth on a small shampoo towel, and stormed up and down the closed salon. What was so special about Cheri's forty-fifth birthday? Trish had turned forty-five ten years before, and all she'd gotten from Dorothy was a birthday card. There was no special reunion planned to celebrate any of her own landmark birthdays.

And what was so special about Cheri, period? She was a stupid, baby-like "retardo." Trish always cut Cheri out of the photographs Dorothy sent of the Armstrong family. They were ludicrous images of a cartoon family, a cartoon daughter. Imagine anyone Cheri's age still wearing gingham pinafores, saddle shoes with bobbysocks, and pigtails. It was grotesque. She was grotesque. A child-woman who had begged to be adopted at the age of twenty-six by two elderly people she'd met late in life. Trish was happy she had left the island before the ridiculous adoption had taken place.

Cheri was a major reason why Trish had sold her shares to Dorothy and left the island for good. It was obvious that Cheri would be there forever. She never had any intention of going out on her own after graduating from the art institute. Her only wish was to remain the perpetual little girl, be doted upon by the elderly ga-gas, and paint her uninspired landscapes and flowers.

Trish stopped pacing and admired her recently coiffed hair in the mirror. Her gorgeous, thick red hair had always been a source of pride. Maybe she wasn't as beautiful as Cheri, but she had better hair. Maybe she hadn't made good marriages or a lot of money, but Cheri hadn't remarried at all after Big Al died, and Cheri had never sold any of her stupid pictures.

When they were still all living on the island, Cheri had taken Jerome Harrison away from her, just for the fun of it, because she hadn't really wanted him, and had then dropped him for a sailor. Maybe Trish could have been happy with Jerome, if Cheri hadn't stolen him? Jerome was a successful man now, head of the telephone company. She would not have had the financial struggle if she'd married Jerome. He was the type of man who had the ability and willingness to take care of a woman…just as William would have…had he lived.

Trish and Jerome had a swell sex life while it lasted. And she was sure Cheri was nothing but a passive, you-do-everything-for-me type. But she had bewitched Jerome, and Trish wondered if he ever regretted dumping her for that infantile blonde wimp.

She would like to see Jerome again. After his divorce he had never remarried, and by the time of the reunion she would be a free woman. By now Cheri would no longer have a hold on him, and he would be mature enough to see through the little girl act. He would probably be ready to take on a red-blooded woman. Given an opportunity, she would show him how love was made. Maybe she'd have a chance of becoming Mrs. Harrison. It would be to both their advantages: he would have a partner to look after his needs, and for her part, she could retire and live like a lady. She deserved some comfort and peace of mind. Then Dorothy, too, would appreciate her as a worldly woman who'd made a good marriage.

She hadn't seen any of them since the Baron's funeral twenty years ago. Maybe it was time to go back…for many reasons.

CHAPTER FOUR

Babs Cunningham lived in Beverly Hills below Sunset Boulevard where the land was flat. She felt a need to get fresh air in the mornings and was in the habit of having Miss Jane Tiddles wheel her around the neighborhood at an early hour, five-thirty or six, when no one else was about. She didn't want people staring at the famous wheelchair-bound soap star taking her constitutional. Both she and Miss Tiddles got dressed first thing each morning and took their walk before breakfast.

Miss Jane Tiddles was a pinch-faced spinster in her forties, extremely thin, with mousy brown hair, a nurse/secretary/companion who was completely reliable and devoted to her employer. She never complained about the long hours. She enjoyed being in show business and working for a great television star. She rested or slept only when Miss Cunningham was thus engaged, and often she rested much less than her employer so that she could keep pace with Babs' publicity stories, gossip about others, and the phone calls and mail.

The invitation to Escape Island intrigued Jane Tiddles. Before and since being employed by Miss Cunningham, she had read many gossip items about that mysterious island and a mysterious death that had taken place there over twenty years ago—the death of a notorious gang boss that many speculated was actually a murder. "Cover-up" was the word most often used to describe the police report of death by natural causes. Scuttlebutt had it that Big Al Silver (or Silvestri) was such a vicious criminal that the police did not care if he'd been murdered, and therefore had not bothered to investigate.

Jane knew that his widow, Cheri Silvestri, had purchased the island development with her inheritance money and had divided the shares equally among the people who had been present the night her husband died. That seemed very fishy. If the widow hadn't done in her husband, how else could she have been blackmailed into giving away all but one measly share? People just didn't make gestures like that unless it was to keep others quiet. The papers also played up the fact that the widow had only known the other guests for one night—one night—before she agreed to make them all joint partners.

Also, Cheri Silvestri was a beautiful woman, but she had never remarried and lived in relative seclusion with her elderly parents. Another odd thing was that they had adopted her when she was already well past girlhood. And even in her forties this Cheri dressed, spoke, and acted like a child. Oh, it would be fascinating to meet these curious people. And all were bound to be at the reunion.

Jane knew Babs Cunningham had been one of those present on the night the gang boss met his fate. They often wrote of how Babs had been one of the owners and had lived there for a time, until she could no longer bear the horror…the horror of what the island represented so she fled…fled back to a humiliating job in a wheelchair. Well, that wasn't true. Miss Cunningham adored her role in the soap, adored the attention and fame. Jane never got the feeling that Miss Cunningham in any way found her work humiliating, but that didn't mean the rest of the gossip didn't have some truth to it.

Imagine her, Jane Tiddles, having firsthand knowledge of the scandal? Miss Cunningham had never spoken to her of the event. And Jane wasn't one to pry, but surely in going there, the true story would come out...even if inadvertently. She would know what the scandalmongers were longing to find out. Not that she would ever sell the story to the press, but what a conversation piece it would be for friends and strangers alike. How she hoped Miss Cunningham would accept, and, of course, take her along.

Today was Thursday and not the day to trouble Miss Cunningham with anything unless it was urgent, and the invitation to Escape Island was for one month from now. Thursday was the day that the producers had to finish taping all of Miss Cunningham's scenes for the present week's episode. The other actors would work Friday and perhaps a half-day on Saturday, but not Miss Cunningham. She only worked four days a week. It was in her contract. They did her close-ups before they filmed the scenes proper. And if they got behind, they used her double in an over-the-shoulder shot once she'd been dismissed. Because on Thursday at five p.m. sharp, she expected to leave.

Miss Cunningham was in a position to demand this type of star treatment. Hers was no longer a daytime soap: it had been transferred to the evening network schedule, where its success surprised even the people who'd been responsible for moving it to an eight p.m. slot. It was a nighttime soap, and the number two show in the ratings.

During the four days when she worked, Miss Cunningham would let them schedule her first thing every morning. In fact, she liked going before the cameras early in the day, but her evenings and weekends were sacred. The two of them—Jane went everywhere Miss Cunningham went, even to premieres and star-studded dinners—had a glamorous but always-relaxing three-day weekend to look forward to. Next month that weekend would be in Canada, and Jane saw no reason why Miss Cunningham wouldn't take her… unless the secret was so dark that Miss Cunningham felt even her closest companion could not be trusted with the knowledge. She tingled at the thought of that dark unknown.

Babs was slightly annoyed that Jane had kept back the invitation to Escape Island until Friday. There was no reason she shouldn't have had it Thursday. Sometimes Jane was too overprotective. She should not make these decisions on her own. If she had asked, Babs would have told her that the day's filming was light and that she wished to see all the mail. It was always nice to wake up Friday with the decisions about the mail already made and placed in Jane's hands. Babs liked to spend Friday mornings in her garden, catching up on her reading, and she could only do that once she had dictated her responses to the post, including which invitations to reject or accept.

Today she had given Jane instructions about everything except Escape Island. She had planned to think it over and respond in a few days' time. But it was no good. Something was troubling her. She could not decide whether or not she should go back to the island. It also seemed impossible to think about anything else.

Was it Harlan Armstrong? Was he the reason she hesitated? It was, after all, a special reunion, the first in twenty years, and she would spoil it if she did not return. She was longing to see all the partners again, they had so much to catch up on. Also, she'd still seemed a helpless victim at the time she'd left, but now she was an enormous star, again.

They probably all watched her show and cheered her beauty and acting ability. Well, maybe not the Hurleys. There were probably no American television programs in Kenya.

Was it Harlan Armstrong whom she was afraid to see? But why? She had been the one to leave him. Their romance had lost its spark long before she'd decided to return to Hollywood. Perhaps she could not bear to see him with that fat, ugly Dorothy. How could he have married such a woman? She was in no way his type. Then he'd further made a fool of himself by adopting Cheri, a grown woman. Maybe she didn't want to spend the weekend with that bizarre family. It was embarrassing to think that she had once been romantically involved with the Doctor, when his present tastes were so far removed from what she would consider normal. How could he have romanced her, a star, and then turned around and married an unattractive drudge?

On the other hand, she was curious, and she did want to see the other owners…and allow them the privilege of seeing her. It would be mean-spirited to spoil the reunion by not appearing. Some of them might only be coming in order to be in her presence. Many people were that way about stars. Also there was much to talk about. She needed to discuss the night of Big Al's death, and they were the only people to whom she could be open about her feelings. Yes, she would go…she really had to be present. The only decision now was whether or not to take Jane Tiddles with her. There were things about the island that could not be said in front of an outsider. On the other hand, she always needed Jane's help, she relied on her for so many things she no longer did for herself. Yes, she would go, and she would take Jane.

CHAPTER FIVE

Major James Hurley and his wife, Lorraine, received the invitation in the bush—or what James called the bush. Actually they lived in a quite civilized old English inn just outside Nairobi, where they had a lovely cottage of their own as part of the complex, and all essential comforts. But James told everyone that they lived in the African bush. That was more romantic, and James could not help himself, he did enjoy making up stories and putting on airs. They lived comfortably but that was because living in Nairobi was inexpensive. They were certainly not wealthy people. They were a retired couple living on a fixed income, the income from their investment of the money they had received from selling their shares of the Escape Island complex.

Lorraine had a small cottage garden that she tended, and she did volunteer work for the local hospital. Twice a year she canned fruits and made jellies. These were considered a great treat by her co-workers when received as presents, and they sold well at the annual fundraising bazaar. By contrast, James spent his days in Nairobi at the Hunter's Club. He had a group of cronies who never tired of recounting tall tales of their days as white hunters, and James told the tallest tales of all.

The Hunters Club was a leftover from Colonial days. It had nothing to do with modern East Africa. An actual hunting safari was a rare occurrence. They had been replaced by photographic safaris, which were much less colorful to talk about. Even when the Major and Lorraine arrived in Nairobi in 1978, the old way of life had vanished. So James never participated in the adventures he recounted daily.

The Nairobi Game Reserve was the closest James ever came to big game, and while in the reserve he had never once stepped foot outside the Land Rover. But every day James left his cottage at the English inn and drove the forty-five minutes into town and the Hunter's Club. His uniform was consistent: he always wore grey trousers, an immaculate white shirt, a striped tie, and his blue blazer with the Hunter's Club emblem on the pocket.

He arrived each morning at ten precisely and sat in his favorite leather chair. The waiter brought him a pot of coffee and he read his newspaper for the next hour. A walk around the gardens was the next order of business, and at noon he joined his cronies for a sherry before lunch. Lunch was always a splendid buffet of cold cuts, or one of the typical British pies like steak and kidney; and four days a week, it was curries. Then the afternoons were spent in storytelling.

Many of the club members told the same stories over and over again, but James was the star speaker because he made up his tales and therefore they were endless.

Friday nights were open to wives, and it was traditional to bring your spouse for the one sit-down dinner of the week. The men wore a tuxedo and the women wore gowns. Cocktails were from six-thirty, and dinner was served at eight. Before dinner people stood and mingled, and spoke of a variety of subjects that interested them. Lorraine enjoyed the cocktail hour and dinner in the company of the men. After dinner, she and the other women escaped into a corner of the lounge to speak of family and friends, and receipts and gardens…escaped to where they did not have to listen to more hunting stories.

Both James and Lorraine were thrilled at the idea of a reunion on Escape Island. The money to get there was the bother; every penny they had was budgeted. A trip from Nairobi to Vancouver was a costly one, even when reservations could be made in advance, to take advantage of special fares. They dare not spend their capital, so they would have to borrow the money, and that was awkward. How would they meet the interest payments?

It had been fifteen years since they had retired and left the island. This might be the last time they went back, and the trip seemed essential. Lorraine thought of asking Dorothy if they might stay and work again at the hotel to pay off their fare. However, this might prompt the Armstrongs to offer the trip gratis, and Lorraine could not bear the idea of charity. She had lived for years off charity before Cheri had made them the magnificent offer of becoming shareholders.

The only luxury they could forgo was James's membership in the Hunter's club—the yearly dues were about the same price as that of the trip. But Lorraine could not even contemplate depriving James of his daily activity, what had become his way of life, so she vowed not to even mention the club as a sacrifice for the journey. As badly as they wanted to return, perhaps they simply could not raise the money.

A week later, James arrived home with the solution. They would travel for four months and rent out their cottage while they were gone. The rental money would be enough to pay for the round trip airfares from Nairobi to Rome, and from New York to Vancouver. For the round trip ocean voyage from Rome to New York, they would travel on a luxury liner, all expenses paid—James had gotten himself booked as a guest entertainer to recount to the cruise passengers the tales of a famous white hunter.

CHAPTER SIX

J ackie Le Roir could never again think of living anywhere but
Paris; for her, it was the hub of the chic universe. A weekend trip back to Escape Island would be wonderful, so long
as it was just a weekend. She had her profession to think about.
Jackie was in charge of a prestigious art gallery on the fashionable
Rue Saint-Honoré. The wealthiest, smartest people in the world
sooner or later visited the gallery, and she was considered a leading
art expert. She did not own the gallery, but as the directress, her
commissions were formidable.

Her position meant that she met fascinating people from all
walks of life. She had never married, preferring to have an array of
lovers, both men and women. Although sex itself did not especially
interest her. She simply liked being close to the rich, famous, and
artistic.

Her first sexual experiences had been a nightmare. She'd been
kidnapped from her home in Algeria at the age of eleven and taken
to New York, where she was forced to be the slave of the gang
boss, Big Al Silvestri. When he tired of her, she had been sold to a
house of prostitution, where she remained until her escape at the

age of twenty. Then at twenty-five she had met Big Al's nephew, Ren Silvestri, and become his mistress, in the hopes of one day getting close enough to his uncle to wreak revenge on him. This had led her to Escape Island.

Going back to the island would bring back horrendous memories of the past, but she did not hesitate to accept the invitation. She felt compelled to return to the scene of Big Al's death. That event had been cathartic, but there were still emotions to be resolved, and unanswered questions to be broached.

The biggest question was the way in which Big Al had died. Afterwards she'd remained for four years on the island, and in all that time neither she nor any of the others had ever spoken of the events of that night. Once the police had accepted his death as natural, the subject was never again raised. But this was a reunion and twenty-three years had passed since his death. What happened should no longer be ignored. Jackie thought the others might feel as she did: it was time to sort out the events and finally put that night to rest.

She questioned her feelings about her ex-lover, Ren Silvestri. She knew she would always have a certain contempt for Ren, but she did not hate him and did not have qualms about seeing him again. Their affair had been unmemorable, except for his selfishness and immaturity. He had thought he was using her by making her his mistress, but she had also been using him in order to get close to his uncle. Now he had become the successor to his uncle's crime empire, but it no longer affected her personally, and she was prepared to look the other way. After all, what could she do to stop crime in New York? No, she could not hate Ren even for the serious flaws in his character. And they had shared one momentous occasion together—the death of Big Al.

Ren aside, Jackie had become very fond of the others, and had lived a happy life for the four years that she'd remained on the island. Cheri had been a generous angel...the way she had shared her inherited wealth with all of them. Owning a piece of the island complex and her own little cottage had given Jackie the security and confidence she'd needed to finally face the world. Then selling her shares had enabled her to move to Paris.

Tears welled in her eyes when she thought about seeing Dorothy again. She could never forget the love that Dorothy had lavished on her, making her feel special and wanted. Trish was her daughter-in-law and Cheri was her favorite, but Dorothy still had enough love left over to make Jackie one of her own.

Dorothy wrote all the time. Her letters were a treat, like getting mail from your mom. Jackie had never been able to find her own family since that terrible night when she'd been stolen away from her childhood home. Dorothy had become a surrogate mother and Jackie had the greatest affection for her. She would have made the trip even if it was just to see Dorothy alone. They had been separated much too long, and Dorothy was now seventy-six. Jackie wouldn't have her forever, and while she telephoned at least once a week and Dorothy wrote that often, it couldn't take the place of actually seeing her, putting her arms around her, and enjoying that motherly warmth.

She didn't mind sharing Dorothy. She was perfectly aware that the Doctor and Dorothy had adopted Cheri. Cheri had remained a child and would probably always remain so. She and Cheri had gone to art school together for two years. Jackie hadn't stayed longer at the institute because she was only interested in studying art history and had no ambition to paint.

The one sticky point might be Cheri's so-called "art." It was atrocious. Dorothy had sometimes hinted in her letters that Jackie might like to consider Cheri's paintings for her gallery. She had replied that the gallery was not hers, and that she had no say over what works were accepted for sale. The latter was not true, of course, but it was the easiest way of getting out of an impossible request. She hoped that none of the Escape Island owners or former owners, whom she was so fond of, would press her on the point of accepting Cheri's hideous paintings.

Lorraine Hurley was one of Jackie's favorites. She and Lorraine also kept up a steady correspondence, and Jackie was greatly looking forward to seeing Lorraine and James. But East Africa was such a long way from Vancouver. She hoped the Hurleys would have the money to come to the reunion. Perhaps she might find a way of offering them the air tickets. That would have to be handled very delicately. Lorraine had such a fierce pride. For years James had made a beggar of her, and she had determined never again to find herself in that position.

Jackie felt she could get along with almost everyone. She'd known true brutality as a child at the hands of criminals, and as an adult she was now able to overlook harmless, petty foibles in human nature. She and Trish were only tolerant of each other because of Trish's bitchy disposition, and she and the Doctor kept their distance out of mutual respect for their differences. However, they all had a bond, a strong bond that rested mainly in the events of that fateful night.

Jerome Harrison was the one person she had not gotten to know very well, perhaps because he had been so busy romancing first Trish and then Cheri. But Jerome might now be a fascinating man. Anyone who had worked his way up the corporate ladder must be interesting. She would take the time to get to know him better. Success has a strong pull.

She was greatly looking forward to her reunion with Babs. Dorothy and Lorraine were motherly, but Babs was more of a girlfriend, a pal. Despite the difference in their ages—Jackie was forty-eight and Babs well into her sixties—Babs always seemed more of a contemporary. Babs had style and wit. She had more than regained her earlier fame; she was now a television superstar. Her show played even in France, where they picked up very few American shows. Jackie hoped to have long conversations with her.

She would be fascinating to talk to and the time they spent together would be terrific fun. Yes, she was greatly looking forward to being with the extravagant, dramatic Babs Cunningham.

There was, of course, some sadness to be confronted. How she would miss having the Baron around! Baron Tarrall had been like a kindly grandfather to her. He'd been forgetful and even a bit ga-ga, but nevertheless an unforgettable character and a positive influence. It had been the Baron who had first sparked her interest in art. He had many wonderful art books in his study, as well as a fine personal collection of everything from art objects to paintings to tapestry and antique furniture. It had also been the Baron, more than Dorothy, who had encouraged her to study art history. He had taken the trouble to make her dig into herself and think of what profession might make her happy, and had been responsible for her attending the art institute on the mainland.

In a funny way, she would also miss seeing Foster. He had been reserved and hard to get to know, but in the end they had become friends. Foster had been the epitome of a true gentleman, and she would miss him. Jackie had been present for both of their funerals, but somehow had not put to rest the idea of their having passed away. She wanted to visit the graves, place flowers, and say a prayer.

CHAPTER SEVEN

Ren Silvestri was the number one crime boss in New York. New York was the hub of the universe, or so Ren thought, and he considered himself King of the Universe. He had more money than he, his children, or his grandchildren could spend in a lifetime, and he had power…power with a capital P, power that he didn't even have to work for, because the organization ran without him. His uncle Big Al and then his father had set up the structure so well that he only had to sit back and enjoy. His lieutenants did the planning and the muscle-ing, and they came to him out of courtesy for his approval. Also there had been no gang wars, and none of the other bosses had ever challenged his authority.

Ren had a great office where the door was always locked and his secretary let no one in without an appointment. Inside his office, he had a sliding panel wall behind which were the latest arcade machines. He played those machines all day long. Nobody knew how he occupied his time but his secretary, Mary. She was an older broad with no one but an aging mother to distract her. Ren had placed Mary's mother in the finest nursing home money could buy. He paid Mary a bomb of a salary, but she was worth every penny. She knew just how to answer his mail and take care of his phone calls without having to disturb him with a lot of questions. Except for his signature on letters at the end of the day, Mary left him entirely alone to enjoy his hobby. Neither his underlings nor his wife had any idea how Ren spent his time.

He had a beautiful and well-run home, a devout and devoted wife, and six offspring. What man could ask for anything more? So why should he care about Escape Island? Why should he go back?

But he had a strong tie to the island, which he couldn't exactly explain. For example, he had kept his shares, had not sold them even though he hadn't been back in twenty-some years. And he had an urge to attend the reunion, which he didn't understand… except that he and the others had shared a weird experience the night his uncle Big Al had kicked the bucket. He was strangely tied to them and to that place.

His secretary, Mary, kept up a running correspondence with Dorothy…in his name, of course. He enjoyed getting those letters from the island. They were always full of news. At all times he knew of the whereabouts and activities of the others. Mary always wrote (in his name) that his own activities were hush-hush and confidential, but she went into great detail about his family. In fact, when he read the letters he'd supposedly written to Dorothy, he learned what his wife and kids were up to, something he wouldn't otherwise have known. And Mary made him out to be a perfect gentleman and a good friend to all.

So why would he hesitate to meet up again with Jackie Le Roir? He had never understood why Jackie had dropped him. Well, she'd never found anyone else. She had never married. That said something. Maybe every guy after him had been a disappointment. So he had a tiny problem with premature ejaculation. Jackie had never mentioned it, and his wife didn't seem to mind. Of course, his wife had been a virgin. What did she know? She certainly knew nothing about sex even after all these years. Teresa was passive; she laid back and took him as a duty. If he admitted it, his wife, Teresa, was without personality, and a bore.

His children were boring, too. He had never gotten to know them very well. The first five had been girls and that had been a bummer. And by the time a boy finally came along, he had lost interest. All his kids were goody-good wimps, raised by Teresa and influenced by her and the nuns. Often he couldn't remember their names or who was older than whom. But he'd done his duty to bring them into the world. They were Teresa's responsibility, and he didn't care to know beyond that.

Why shouldn't he go back for the reunion if he felt like going? If he desired it, why question the desire? Then it came to him…his wife. He did not want the former owners, and certainly not Jackie, to see his wife. He couldn't explain to Teresa about Jackie and he didn't want Jackie to meet Teresa. His wife wasn't a woman one showed off with pride. Oh, yes, to other Sicilians, because she was the perfect mate for a high-powered Italian gang boss, but not to the people who were the former owners of Escape Island.

Then an idea came to him: he was a big man, the boss, the king of New York, and wasn't he expected to have mistresses? Of course he was…so he would get himself the greatest woman around and take her, presenting her as his mistress. Madam Betty always found girls for him, not whores but high-class hookers. He would hand the problem over to the madam. He needed a woman who could play the part to perfection, the part of his devoted mistress. She had to be well trained to keep her mouth shut and convince everyone that she was dotty over him. She had to drop hints that he was a great cocksman as well as a terrifying gangster. Madam Betty would also have to make sure that the dame was gorgeous, stacked, well educated, and classy. He needed a woman that even Jackie Le Roir couldn't help but admire.

CHAPTER EIGHT

The reunion was planned to begin on April 16th, when the Escape Island complex would still be out of season. The season picked up in May, but really began in June and lasted through October. Oddly enough, April was one of the worst months weather-wise, as it rained almost every day, and in some years even snowed. Of course there were a few diehards who came at all times and in all kinds of weather. At the moment there was only one guest occupying a cottage, and no one in the hotel.

That one guest was a retired inspector from New Scotland Yard, a Percival Forsythe, who after London did not find the island weather a drawback. Dorothy would rather have had the entire complex reserved for the reunion guests, but Inspector Forsythe had booked the cottage through April and exhibited no signs of leaving early. She had hinted that if he found the deserted island lonely this time of year, they would be willing to return his deposit, but the Inspector had said he was writing a book and found the quiet perfect for his work.

The Inspector was a short, burly man with thinning grey hair. He was strong and muscular, and kept fit by taking long walks and playing tennis with Cheri. He took breakfast and dinner with the family, and the cook fixed him a cold lunch, which he ate in his cottage so that he need not interrupt his writing midday. Dorothy supposed, as he had no family, he found being with the Armstrongs a pleasant substitute. In the evenings he sat with them for a game of cards or a fireside chat. He seemed to enjoy the way of life so much that if his pension money held out, he might never leave. There was only one thing they did not like about the Inspector: he was too curious about Big Al's death.

One evening the Inspector asked, "Now, at this reunion of yours, I understand that a Mr. Ren Silvestri will be attending. He was the nephew of the man who died here in 1970, isn't that correct?"

Cheri attempted to reply in the positive, but Doctor Armstrong cut her short. He told the Inspector, "Sir, you have referred many times to the night in question, and I have made it plain to you that it was a most unpleasant occurrence for us, and that we therefore do not wish to engage that night as a topic of conversation."

"Yes, of course, do forgive me," the Inspector said, as he lit his pipe. However, one could see that he was still anxious to know more.

In order to divert the Inspector, Dorothy began to tell stories about growing up in Alberta, speaking of what a treat it had been to go into either Edmonton or Calgary, the nearest major cities, which were over two hundred miles across the plains. "I was raised in the middle of the prairies of Western Canada, near the border between Alberta and Saskatchewan, in a microscopic speck on the map called Consort," she recounted. "We had four streets, and they were gravel."

"It must have been a small population," the Inspector ventured.

"Oh, yes," Dorothy replied, warming even further to her subject. "We had a population of less than four hundred for most of the time I was growing up. Consort had a radio station, and one bar, but no movie theater and no police."

"No police," the Inspector parroted. "Imagine that. I suppose everyone was on his good behavior."

The doctor had heard these stories countless times, and was tired of them. He squirmed in his chair.

Dorothy knew her husband was getting bored, but she adored thinking about home and did not want to break the flow of her thoughts. "We had a square little one-story house and a deck over-looking fields of wheat," she continued. "Supper was at six, and as I was the only daughter and there were three boys, on Saturdays it fell to me to vacuum the carpets and dust."

"But the boys had chores, too," Cheri offered. Cheri had been an only child, and had been raised in New York City. She never tired of hearing about Dorothy's brothers and life on the farm. "The boys fed the animals and cleaned the barn."

Squirming even more, the Doctor said grumpily, "Surely the Inspector does not wish to ear about feeding animals and cleaning barns. Perhaps we could speak of things more cosmopolitan?"

But the Inspector ignored the Doctor's comment, asking Dorothy, "And I imagine you were a close-knit family?"

It was Cheri who answered his inquiry. "Oh, they were, they were, until Dorothy was fourteen and her father walked out on them."

"I loved both parents very much, and I was shocked when my father just up and vanished," Dorothy said.

Doctor Armstrong groaned.

But Dorothy was not to be deterred. "Mother would teach in the day and then go down and try to run the grocery store. I also had to take on the responsibilities of working in the store, because the boys ran the farm. I went from being a kid to being an adult very fast."

"And here you are a successful businesswoman with a beautiful island," the Inspector said.

"Despite our financial struggles, my mother managed to send me to Red Deer College in Alberta. I had a good education in business management. Two of my brothers also attended college," Dorothy said.

"Your mother must have been a remarkable woman," the Inspector commented. "She must have been resourceful."

"Oh, she was an angel," Dorothy muttered with tears in her eyes.

The Doctor groaned even louder. "Enough," he said. "We have had the stories of evil dad, wonderful farm life, and even horse manure. Please let us not indulge in any more morbid sentimentality." Turning to the Inspector, he said, "Would you care for an after-dinner drink?"

"I wouldn't mind a spot of brandy," the Inspector replied.

"Oh, Daddy," Cheri said. "Could you make me a Shirley Temple?"

A Shirley Temple is any soft drink with a cherry. It was named after the famous child star, who was often obliged to be at cocktail parties with grownups. Although Cheri was about to turn forty-five, she liked to be treated like a child and to dress like one. At the moment she was wearing a pink and white checked full-skirted dress, and had pink ribbons tied at the end of each pigtail.

Doctor Armstrong smiled and patted her blonde hair. At seventy-three, when he was almost old enough to be her great-grandfather, he actually enjoyed playing "daddy." Just as Dorothy, at seventy-six, enjoyed playing "mommy."

The Inspector had thought this most bizarre when he'd first arrived, but by now he had accepted it as their little game. They were nice people and he enjoyed their company. If he could only get them to discuss that fateful night in 1970. But others were coming who might be more willing to satisfy his curiosity.

CHAPTER NINE

The reunion weekend was supposed to begin on Friday the 16th and last Saturday the 17th and Sunday the 18th of April. Jerome Harrison arrived on Thursday evening, April 15th, because he found that more convenient, and because he didn't want to lose a moment of the special weekend. His job demanded that he be at a board meeting first thing Monday morning, so he would have to say his goodbyes late Sunday afternoon. His position at the Telephone Company did not permit him to miss a board meeting—the meeting could not take place without the Senior Vice President for all of Western Canada.

The ferryboat trip to the island was a rough one. All day there had been a steady wind and rain, and by the late afternoon when Jerome took the boat to the island, it had turned bitterly cold and the wind had reached almost gale force. April was a bad-weather month for that part of Canada, and he hoped the others wouldn't have trouble in getting to the island the following day.

From inside the salon on the ferryboat, Jerome looked out and remembered the very first time he had made the journey to the island. It had been on a police boat. He'd been a lowly telephone repairman at that time, and had been posing as the local Constable. It had seemed a harmless enough impersonation until he had entered Baron Tarrall's mansion to find a dead man on the dining room floor. As a member of an amateur acting group, he'd been studying the plays of Agatha Christie. Her master detective had captured his fancy, had become his hero. Confronted by a body, murder had sprung to mind, and he had metamorphosed, unable to stop himself from acting the part of Hercule Poirot.

Barron Tarrall's yacht had been replaced a number of times over the past twenty-three years. The present replacement was a ferryboat, slow but stable, that took turbulence well but was still being tossed in the high seas. Jerome tied a scarf around his neck, fastened his overcoat, and went out on deck. Better to suffer the cold and wind than to feel queasy. One of the sailors helped him to a bench and motioned for him to strap himself in place. The sailor also tossed him a lifejacket.

He was alone on the rows of benches. They had been especially designed for the large number of tourists the island attracted in the summertime. To avoid lawsuits, seatbelts had been installed and life vests were mandatory for passengers wishing to be on deck.

The addition of tourists had been Dorothy's idea. They paid a set fee for the boat ride, a brief tour of the island, and a picnic lunch. The regular guests did not seem to mind, and the scheme brought in a good revenue. Oddly enough, the biggest selling point seemed to be that persistent rumor that there had been a murder on the island.

The company would not permit Jerome to work past the age of sixty-five—that was four more years—and he had it in mind to possibly spend his retirement on Escape Island. He had sold his shares and the cottage that had been included in the package Cheri had presented to him and to the others who'd been present on that terrible night in 1970. Perhaps that had been foolish; a cottage would go for much more these days. However, he hadn't been back since the Baron's funeral twenty years ago, so he wouldn't have gotten any use from it in all that time. He'd invested the money from his shares wisely and had no regret on that account. Anyway, the newer cottages might be nicer.

He would take a good look at the situation, the investment brochure, and the condition of the structures. He could afford to live well, if not extravagantly, in his later years. His relationship with Cheri would also have a bearing on his decision. He had to curb his imagination. He often saw himself and Cheri married and happy in their island paradise. The Armstrongs were getting on in age, and Cheri would need someone to look after her. But could their romance be rekindled? Had she gotten over her attraction for rough men like sailors...would she find him dull? He forced these disturbing thoughts out of his mind and concentrated on enjoying the idea of the reunion.

As the boat neared shore, he could see that the family were all there on the pier, waiting for him. Despite himself, tears came to his eyes. He was extremely touched to know that they were so anxious to have him back that they'd all braved the bad weather to wait for him.

Jerome unfastened his seatbelt, stood, and waved with large circular motions, much to the chagrin of the sailors who motioned for him to sit down. On the pier, Cheri, Dorothy, and the Doctor pointed at him, waved, and seemed to be talking excitedly. Jerome's heart was beating with joy.

As the yacht pulled closer, he was shocked to see how the Doctor and Dorothy had aged. But what had he expected after twenty years? The Doctor was all grey, but straight and tall, a fine figure of a man. The rotund figure of Dorothy was even fuller than before, and she now waddled when she walked. Cheri seemed to look the same. He could tell that she was still very beautiful. Even from a distance she could still take his breath away.

As Jerome emerged from the bottom of the ramp, Cheri flung

herself into his arms and he swung her in a circle. Dorothy was close behind Cheri, and stepped in to take her place, enveloping him in a bear hug. Then the Doctor shook his hand, while both hugging him and slapping him on the back. All talking at once, they piled into the jeep for the ride up to the mansion-turned-hotel. The Doctor drove, with Cheri beside him, and Jerome and Dorothy sat in the back.

Cheri turned in her seat to study him with her big baby blues. Dorothy asked the questions about his health, his job, his length of stay. She talked a steady stream, hardly giving him time for his replies. Cheri smiled and hung on his every word.

When they reached the hotel, it was Dorothy who showed him to his suite and told him where everything was located and how to use the in-house phone. Jerome was disappointed that Cheri had not taken him to his rooms; he wanted very much to be alone with her.

Dorothy seemed to read his thoughts and said, "You've arrived at sunset, Jerome. Had it been earlier, Cheri would have shown you to your room. But this is the time when we all change for dinner. We eat earlier in the cold weather months. Cheri likes to have a luxurious bubble bath at this hour, and it takes her longer to get ready than it does us old folks. However, the results are well worth the effort. She always looks so pretty at dinnertime. And you two will have lots of time together." She patted his arm, looked lovingly into his eyes, and smiled sweetly, saying, "Whenever you're ready, come down to the sitting room for cocktails. We will be informal tonight, and Sunday night of course, but tomorrow is Cheri's birthday party and we will be formal for the occasion."

The mansion was a solid structure and wanted no improvement in its appearance, so only repairs to the existing building had been done as needed. The bedroom suites looked much as they had, years before. The furniture, draperies, and carpeting, although newer, had been replaced with much the same antique look. Only the bathrooms had been altered beyond recognition and made thoroughly modern.

Jerome showered and changed into grey trousers, a white silk turtleneck sweater, and a maroon velvet smoking jacket. He then slipped on patent leather Gucci loafers over his grey silk socks. He had purchased the outfit especially for this first evening on the island. He hoped Cheri would appreciate his effort, although he intended to behave as if he always dressed with care and great taste.

Jerome heard no voices as he descended the staircase, and thought perhaps he was the first to arrive for cocktails. However, upon entering the sitting room, he saw a burly man smoking a pipe and looking through a magazine.

"Hello, you must be Jerome Harrison. Your arrival has been greatly anticipated. I am Percival Forsythe," the Inspector said. "I'm staying in the first cottage. The nearest one. I understand that it was originally owned by the famous actress, Babs Cunningham."

"Yes," Jerome replied. "We seem to be the first for cocktails. May I help you to something, Percival…a scotch and soda?" The drinks cart had been set up to one side of the fireplace, and Jerome felt enough at home to help himself and Percival.

"A scotch and soda would be lovely, thank you," the Inspector said. "I'm a Brit, so I don't take ice."

As he walked toward the cart, Jerome said, "Dorothy told me there was one guest. How is it you braved the weather this time of year?"

"I'm an Inspector from New Scotland Yard, recently retired. I'm writing a book and was looking for seclusion. I work during the day, and my evenings are never boring or lonely, because the Armstrongs are such charming, enjoyable people to be with. Cheri and I play tennis several times a week, and I take two of my meals with the family. I hope my being here will not be awkward on account of the reunion."

"I'm sure it will not be in the least awkward," Jerome said, but he was not at all certain that was true. It was a pity to have one outsider when the former owners had so much to discuss. They would be talking about things that the Inspector had no knowledge of…they might wish to bare their souls about *that* night long ago when all of their lives had changed forever.

Jerome had poured the whiskey into the glasses and began absentmindedly putting ice cubes into both drinks. The Inspector played tennis with Cheri several times a week…what else did they do together? Was the Inspector a rival for Cheri's affections?

The Inspector arrived at the drinks trolley. "No ice for me, thank you," he said.

"Yes, of course, I forgot," Jerome said, snapping out of his reverie. "So you are in the number one cottage, which was built by Babs Cunningham. And do you find the accommodations comfortable?"

"Quite," he replied. "Doctor Armstrong originally had cottage number two, right next door to Miss Cunningham's, I believe. That was before he obtained a number of shares and became the proprietor."

Jerome looked at him, but his thoughts were again far away. He muttered, "Yes," remembering where all the original owners had wanted their cottages. His had been on high ground overlooking the sea.

The Inspector continued his train of thought. "Dorothy, too, had become proprietor. Then they married and the entire complex became a family affair. Shortly afterwards they adopted Cheri. It was those three who never deserted the island. Have you missed it over the years, Jerome? I know you have an important position in the telephone company, which keeps you on the mainland, but there must have been a few times when you longed for the island life."

"Indeed," Jerome said, "it was never very far from my thoughts." It occurred to him that the Inspector knew a great deal about the setup. Perhaps he was just making small talk, but perhaps he was curious about the origins of the island and about the reunion guests.

"I understand that you were the only person not present in the room when Big Al died," the Inspector said, without expression.

Speechless, Jerome studied him but could not read his thoughts.

"You entered the mansion for the very first time when Big Al was already on the floor and presumed dead. The body had been stored in the basement freezer. When you returned inside after having repaired the phone, you again saw Big Al's body on the dining room floor. What were you able to see from atop the telephone pole that night? I have climbed up there myself and have found there is a clear view through the dining room windows into the room."

Jerome stared blankly at the Inspector. He seemed to know a great deal. But what was his interest? Why all these leading questions?

CHAPTER TEN

O n that same Thursday night in April, Ren had arranged a dinner party at the Rainbow Room to introduce his mistress to his friends and so-called "business partners." This was not a night for wives; each of his friends was bringing his mistress, and this was the test for Tammy Sue. Ren had seen her every night this week, every night since Madam Betty had declared her the ideal one for him. He had been filling his mistress in on their bogus past, training her to behave and speak just as he wished. He didn't have to teach her anything about the bedroom. Tammy Sue was an expert. She knew how to please in a dozen different ways, and best of all, mostly without any exertion on his part.

Tonight she would have to pass with flying colors in front of his friends. He would only take her to Escape Island if she appeared perfect in every way. He was a big man, the biggest man in New York, the boss, and he had to have the best mistress available. But he felt sure that Tammy Sue would pass. She was smart and educated. She was beautiful and stacked. She knew how to dress and behave. And best of all, she was great at pretending that she loved Ren, admired him above all others, and would die to please him.

Tammy had masses of light red hair, startling green eyes, and a peaches and cream complexion. She was soft, voluptuous, and sexy as hell. For the special night at the Rainbow Room, Ren had purchased for her a lavender chiffon evening gown and a short purple cape. That was on top of the seven G's she got for the week, plus the ten G's she would get to accompany him to Escape Island. When he picked her up with his limo outside her building, she looked gorgeous, worth every cent.

The driver opened the door for Tammy Sue and she slid into the back seat beside Ren. "Ren, darling," she said, "I adore my new outfit. Isn't it beautiful? Purple and lavender are so good with red hair. You are clever to choose such a perfect combination of colors." She kissed him softly on the cheek, her hair tickling his ear.

"You look great," Ren replied. "Beautiful, but not cheap. Remember, when you're with my friends, never take your eyes off of me. You can't tear your gaze away from my face. You can look at the women once in a while, but never at the men."

"Maybe I should only look at the men the one time…when you introduce me…otherwise it might seem rude," she suggested.

Ren laughed and agreed. "You are some smart cookie. I probably don't have to coach you at all. I think you know exactly how to be a lady and a loving mistress." Then he roughly grabbed her left breast and squeezed it. With his other hand he undid his fly. "There is going to be a lot of traffic at this hour. It'll take us fifteen, twenty minutes to get to Rockefeller Plaza, so you might as well service me," he grunted, pushing her head into his crotch.

When Ren's limo pulled up outside the NBC entrance of Rockefeller Plaza, Tammy Sue had to repair her hair and lips before she could get out of the car. Ren wiped himself off with a handful of Kleenex and then zipped his fly. He looked over at Tammy Sue, who had her compact open, and she smiled at him. "Was that good, baby?" she asked. "Did Tammy Sue please the big bad man?"

"You bet," he said, and he thought, *"What a great dame. Why can't all women be like her?"*

Tammy Sue was still adjusting her dress as they got into the elevator that would take them to the top. He could see that the new dress was wrinkled and that her makeup was still smeared. She faced the rear of the elevator and appraised herself in the mirror. They both agreed that she would go immediately to the powder room upon reaching the top, and then join him at the table.

Ren's table was one of the best in the Rainbow Room, a circular one for twelve—half booth, half chairs—and was at the windows, with a spectacular view of Manhattan. It was also within easy access to the dance floor. There was a live orchestra, and the place had an elegance not often found these days. The five other couples were already seated when Ren arrived. That was the proper form. His associates arrived early so that nobody kept the boss waiting.

On other occasions, when wives weren't welcome, Ren had come alone or with a call girl. This was the first time that Ren ever felt the need for a mistress—a mistress who would impress Jackie Le Roir and the others on the island.

Ren looked around at the other guys' mistresses and decided that his was the best looking and that Tammy Sue would outshine them all. She was prettier, and definitely classier. Besides, she was new to the group; the other mistresses had been around long enough to be almost as boring as wives. They more or less blended into one: they were all dyed blondes, voluptuous, and four of the five were wearing black and diamonds. The fifth had on a flashy red gown that was out of place in the elegant room.

Like estranged couples, all the women sat together in the booth section and the men sat side by side on the chairs. For dinner, they would pair off into couples, sitting side by side. But for the cocktail hour, which was the longest part of the evening, as they all liked to have a few drinks, the women felt more comfortable talking to one another and the men had business to discuss.

In the powder room, Tammy Sue took two tranquilizers and washed them down with a swig from the small silver flask of whiskey she kept in her purse. The powder room attendant helped her off with her dress and then pressed it with a handheld steamer to get out the wrinkles. The attendant also arranged for her to be brought a triple scotch on the rocks. Her face was a mess, she thought, and she spent a long time redoing the lower half of her makeup—the nose, cheeks, chin, and lips. It took time, but she emerged looking fresh again.

She walked up to the headwaiter and asked for Mr. Silvestri's table. It was all the way across the dance floor by the main windows, which overlooked lower Manhattan. The headwaiter asked another waiter to accompany Tammy Sue to the table, and on the way, she instructed that waiter to bring her a triple whiskey on the rocks.

As Tammy Sue approached, Ren's table grew silent and his friends looked her over thoroughly. Everyone then turned to smile at Ren and nod their approval. Tammy Sue was tall and elegant and a real eyeful. It was hardly noticeable that she walked rather too slowly and rather too carefully in order not to sway.

The men stood while the introductions took place, and the two women at the end of the booth section got up and made room for Tammy Sue in the center of the ladies' group. She smiled beautifully and graciously at everyone, and then never looked again at the men.

All his buddies complimented him on his choice of mistress, with much backslapping, so Ren felt satisfied and proud of himself.

The drinks flowed, the waiters served the group again and again without interrupting any conversations, and Ren failed to notice how much his mistress was consuming.

The ladies were leaning on the table and stretching to be close to Tammy Sue. A great deal of whispering was going on. The women seemed to be taken with Tammy Sue's charm and wit. Especially her wit. Ren noticed that they giggled a lot. They often giggled and looked at him, but he assumed the looks were to reassure him of how terrific she was, and what a lucky guy he was to have found such a perfect woman.

Before ordering dinner the group rearranged themselves into couples at the table. Ren scooted across the booth to sit next to Tammy Sue. "What have you and the girls been giggling about?" Ren asked his mistress good-naturedly.

"We've been giggling about you," Tammy Sue replied in a loud voice. "I told them all about what a prick you are."

The table became silent, and the waiter who had been standing by to take their orders suddenly pretended he had something urgent to do and fled the scene.

But Tammy Sue had a drunken surge of energy and had no intention of stopping. She said, "I told them how you ruined my dress and makeup by making me go down on you on the way here. How you want me to pretend I'm a great lady in order to impress the French woman who threw you over on Escape Island, when you are nothing but a pig."

Ren was devastated, but he, too, was high and unable to react.

Tammy Sue took the opportunity to continue, "I told them, 'He likes to pretend that he's a big man...well, not in the genital department...most times I can't even find his thing...and not in the act—that lasts about two seconds.'"

Ren grew more and more red in the face until he looked a dark plum color. Never had anyone spoken to him this way, at least not in public—not in front of his associates and their mistresses. He had paid Madam Betty in advance for this past week, but she would get a tongue-lashing tomorrow. He would never dream of taking this terrible woman to Escape Island. Tomorrow at the airport, he would cancel her ticket and travel alone. He thanked all his lucky stars that he had found out about her before he'd made the mistake of taking her to the island. But he had an immediate problem—he could not think of what to do, for now, with this vindictive woman. How to shut her up, how to get rid of her. He just wanted her to vanish.

He was saved by his first lieutenant, who stood and took Tammy Sue by the arm. "I think this one wants to excuse herself," he said in a quiet but threatening voice.

Tammy Sue took one look at the big hulk of a gangster and said no more. She got to her feet and let him lead her away from the table and out of the room. If she kept her mouth shut and was lucky, maybe he would just put her in a taxi and let her be swallowed up by the city.

CHAPTER ELEVEN

O n that same Thursday evening in April, Jane Tiddles was preparing to pack Babs Cunningham's suitcases for her trip to Escape Island the next morning. She had a variety of appropriate outfits laid out on the bed awaiting Miss Cunningham's approval. But Babs was getting ready for a dinner party at home that evening and had no time to make the selections until after everyone had gone home.

This sort of last-minute decision-making drove Jane Tiddles mad. She could not understand why her employer let everything go until the last minute. True, Miss Cunningham had gotten up at the crack of dawn and had done a long day's worth of filming. But knowing this might happen, why had she arranged a sit-down dinner the night before they were to travel? Now there were all the dinner arrangements to worry about as well as getting ready for a morning flight.

The sit-down dinner was to be relatively small, for Hollywood. There were to be two couples, a gay dress designer coming alone, and a recently divorced actress also coming alone, Miss Cunningham, and herself. That was dinner for eight, and cook always found eight a manageable number. Any more, and cook always insisted on bringing in another server besides the regular housekeeper, who worked overtime to help on such occasions.

Normally, Jane enjoyed these dinner parties at home. Her opinion was always sought for the flower arrangements and such. She loved to design the table decorations. For tonight she had a Spring theme. The cloth was yellow and the napkins were yellow and white. Daisies would be arranged as a centerpiece between yellow candles.

Jane Tiddles was nervous and uneasy and she couldn't quite put her finger on why she felt that way. The dinner table looked beautiful, all the dinner arrangements were proceeding smoothly. None of the guests had cancelled. The wine had arrived on time and was being chilled. Cook had the meal under control and the housekeeper was not fighting with anyone, for a change. So why was Jane so upset? Surely the fact that she couldn't finish the packing until later was not so upsetting. She had a list for reference, and later Miss Cunningham would look over the outfits on the bed and make quick decisions. The prospect of a late night was not disturbing. So what was the matter?

Babs looked over from her vanity table and wished Jane would stop fussing and leave to get herself ready for the dinner party. "Jane, dear," Babs said, "we are not going to decide which outfits to pack until after the guests leave. You're making me nervous with your fussing. Why not go to your room and get ready for this evening?"

"Well, very well, Miss Cunningham," Jane whined. "If you don't mind leaving *everything* until the very last minute. I thought you might be tired after the guests leave tonight, and that it would be nice to look at the outfits on the bed and simply point to the ones you want to take. Then I would have them off the bed and hung in a special place for the packing. Then I would do the flowers for the center of the table. I want to keep the flowers in the fridge until the very last minute, so they stay fresh."

"I do appreciate that, Jane, so please go and do the flowers and get ready. I would like to relax for a few minutes before the guests arrive. I can't, with you fussing, or with the thought of packing. You are giving me travel fever and I simply do not want to discuss or think about the trip until later tonight."

Jane Tiddles snorted and left the room in somewhat of a huff.

Babs had not yet made up her mind whether or not to take Jane with her tomorrow. Jane was expecting to go, because they went everywhere together. Babs had been far too democratic in the beginning of her employment. She had not wanted to treat Jane Tiddles like some ordinary hired help, because Jane was really a trained nurse. Often Jane had to help Babs with intimate physical chores. Babs did a great deal for herself, but she was wheelchair-bound and at times needed to depend on a nurse. This was especially true when she got overtired and the exertion of some routine tasks just loomed as too great.

They both had started out pretending to the outside world that Jane was a secretary and companion. Jane Tiddles soon became obsessed with show business and took her own participation far too seriously. Babs knew she hardly ever rested, and she did things like fan mail that should have been passed on to a service. Jane now almost believed that she was the secretary and companion rather than the nurse. "Nurse" was obviously the least attractive of her duties, and Babs had allowed the relationship to become too friendly, not professional enough. Now it was difficult to switch into reverse.

Babs was seriously thinking of going to Escape Island by herself, but she hadn't mentioned a word to Jane, and Jane was fully expecting to tag along. But the more Babs thought about it, the more convinced she became that she should not bring a stranger into the group. Jane would be nosy and often in the way. But how to tell her?

Babs was certain that she could manage without special help for the one weekend. For years she had been without a nurse and had managed very well. It was only when she had gone back to work again that she felt a need for a nurse to be standing by. Her work was demanding and required long hours of physical exertion and concentration. At times she just got exhausted and then could not find the extra strength that being an invalid took. She had to do everything with her arms, and that required special maneuvers that ordinary people did not have to go through, except perhaps in a gym.

On the island, someone would help her if she needed to be helped. Both Cheri and Jackie had been wonderful about assisting her, and so had Lorraine Hurley when she wasn't too busy managing the hotel. Then, of course, when she and Harlan had been lovers, the Doctor would come to her rescue. A pity it hadn't worked between Harlan and her.

As she put the finishing touches to her makeup, Babs thought again about her hesitation in telling Jane something as simple as the fact that she wished to go to Escape Island on her own. Why should it be difficult to tell someone who is employed by you to take a nice weekend off for themselves? But Babs was dreading the moment. Jane would take it personally. She would be crushed. Maybe she would cry and make a pathetic scene. Babs didn't think she could stand an emotional outburst, so she was delaying the discussion till the very last second…late tonight.

Of course, Jane would already be packed, but Babs would offer extra money for a special weekend and even help to arrange it… perhaps a three-day cruise, or longer. She might offer her longer. Yes, a week's cruise might be just the thing. Jane had often hinted that they should take an exciting cruise and get some sea air.

The dinner party had gone off beautifully. Everyone had had a good time, nobody had drunk too much, and everybody seemed satisfied to go home at a reasonable hour.

Over dinner Babs had again weighed the possibilities and had firmly decided that she wished to travel to the island alone. When she and Jane were once again in Babs' bedroom, she knew she had to tell Jane. "Jane, dear," she began, "Escape Island has special memories for me. I am going to again be with some people who are very dear. We will have much to talk about. We are close enough that I can ask for help if I find anything that is physically too difficult—"

But Jane did not allow her to finish. "You are not taking me, are you? I knew it. I knew something was wrong…. I have been feeling nervous and upset all evening long."

"Jane, dear, please don't be upset. I am going to arrange and pay for a special cruise for you…for more than a weekend…for a week or ten days. You can go wherever you want. Won't that be lovely?"

Jane suddenly turned into a person Babs did not recognize. Her eyes flashed with hatred, and she threw Babs' clothes off the bed. She shouted, "Stick your cruise! And stick your job! I'm sick of doing everything and not being appreciated. You don't want me to go to that island because you are guilty of killing that man, Big Al! I know it!"

CHAPTER TWELVE

On Escape Island that Thursday in April at cocktail hour, Jerome had the distinct impression that the ex-Inspector from New Scotland Yard planned to question him in detail about the death of Big Al. But just then a maid entered with a tray of hors d'oeuvres. Jerome handed the Inspector the drink he had made for him, and then helped himself to a stuffed egg. He was glad for the interruption. The questioning had begun to make him uneasy. He wondered if it was a professional habit, this questioning, or was the Inspector after real information about that night long ago, and if so, what was his motive?

Dorothy and the Doctor then entered the room arm in arm. It was charming to see such a close couple. Dorothy said, "Oh, good, you have helped yourselves to a drink. I hoped you might, and Sarah has arrived with the hors d'oeuvres...lovely." Turning to the maid, she said, "You have outdone yourself, Sarah, the tray of goodies looks tempting." Dorothy helped herself to a napkin and a dainty smoked salmon roll.

The Doctor waved the maid away when she offered the tray to him. "I meant to tell you, Jerome, that the Inspector has an unhealthy curiosity. He can't seem to stop himself from asking questions, and in detail. I would advise you to do as I do and tell him you refuse to be subjected to any form of interrogation. Otherwise he will make your stay here an exceedingly unpleasant one."

The Inspector grinned and held his pipe in the air as a gesture of approval. Jerome could not understand why the Inspector had not been offended. Doctor Armstrong's condemnation had been quite strong and he had made it without a smile or a trace of humor.

Cheri descended the staircase just then, and to Jerome's utter dismay, the Inspector walked briskly to the stairs, took her arm, and escorted her into the dining room. Jerome might have done the same thing if the Inspector hadn't pre-empted him. He'd hesitated a second too long because the first sight of her beauty had rendered him motionless.

Cheri had done her hair in a mass of broomstick curls cascading around her face. She wore a shocking pink satin cocktail dress with a tight bodice and a full skirt. Her cheeks and lips were painted the same color of pink as the dress, and she had replaced the ribbons in her hair with two real gardenias.

"Hello, Mommy, hello, Daddy," she said. Then to Jerome's great delight, she moved away from the Inspector and over to him. "Good evening, Jerome," she lisped shyly, staring at him with her big blue eyes. Then she stood on her tiptoes and planted a kiss on his cheek.

Jerome thought he would die of happiness. He thought about kissing her hand, but he seemed unable to move a muscle. He wanted to say just the right thing to her, but he was tongue-tied.

He felt himself become apoplectic when the Inspector stepped over to them, took Cheri's hand and kissed it, saying, "My dear, have I told you how utterly beautiful you look tonight?"

Such hate welled up inside Jerome that he began to imagine the Inspector dead. Some death involving excruciating pain.

Then Jerome heard Cheri say, "Jerome, did you smell the gardenias in my hair? Aren't they heavenly? They were a present from Percival."

Jerome managed to nod but felt like crying. Why hadn't he thought to bring her flowers or candy as an arrival present? Of course, he had brought a birthday gift, a stunning and very expensive present. But why hadn't he thought to also bring something as an arrival gift? Also, he should have brought candy or flowers for Dorothy. What was wrong with him? He supposed he was just too much out of the habit of being with women. His secretary should have reminded him to bring some small gifts for the ladies. But that was one of the drawbacks of hiring an old maid. She had probably never received flowers or candy in her entire life, and so the thought would never occur to her. He would be sure to make her aware of her shortcoming.

He felt someone take his arm. He woke from his thoughts to see Dorothy at his side. "Jerome," she whispered, "is anything wrong? You have been standing in a daze and haven't said a word for the past five minutes." She looked at Cheri, the Doctor, and the Inspector, deep in conversation at the fireplace, then back to Jerome. She turned him slightly away so that his back was toward the others, and again whispered, "Don't worry, I have seated you next to Cheri at dinner. The Inspector will be across from you, sitting on his own without a partner."

At that moment, Dorothy and Jerome turned as Doctor Armstrong approached them. "Can the three of us step into the hallway for a moment?" the Doctor asked under his breath.

The three of them went out into the hall, without the Inspector and Cheri giving more than a cursory glance and without halting their conversation. Jerome wondered what Cheri and the Inspector were so involved talking about.

Once in the hallway and out of earshot, the Doctor said to Jerome, "Isn't he the most annoying fellow?" And to Dorothy,

"Can't we stop him from spoiling the weekend? Must he take meals with us?"

Dorothy looked stricken. She supposed it was her fault for not finding a way of encouraging the Inspector to leave the island. "Oh, dear, I would also prefer that he remain in his cottage, but I don't see how I could arrange that. What could I possibly tell him?"

"Just tell him that the weekend is a gathering of intimate friends and we would prefer not to have an outsider present. Would he mind if we sent his meals to his cottage?"

"If we use the word *outsider,* he may feel we have something to hide. We do have to consider his position as an Inspector, even if he is retired," Dorothy said, frowning deeply.

Jerome felt tremendously close to the Doctor and Dorothy at that moment, privileged, like family. They had taken him into their confidence, asked his opinion. He wished he could think of something positive to say other than simply agreeing with the Doctor, but agree he did. "He is the world's most annoying chap, that Inspector. I would like to hit him over the head, knock him out for the entire weekend," Jerome said, without really meaning the part about the hitting.

"Jerome, you are a clever fellow," the Doctor said, putting his arm around him. "You are, indeed, very clever."

Jerome felt so proud he could have burst, but he had no idea why the Doctor considered him clever. What had he said?

"That, of course, is the solution," the Doctor said. "I shall slip a potion into his food, some mild poison, nothing with a long-term effect. Just something to keep him in his bed for the weekend."

"Oh, dear," Dorothy said. "I don't think you should do that. What if something goes wrong? What if he gets truly ill?"

Ignoring Dorothy's protest, Jerome asked the Doctor, "Where would you find the right potion?"

"I have my medical bag," the Doctor said, "and a well-supplied medicine cabinet. Don't forget that we are often isolated here on the island for days on end when a storm is in full force. I am compelled to keep a rather complete pharmaceutical supply on hand. Also we grow herbs and bulbs in the conservatory. I believe I could process them."

Jerome hadn't thought about the conservatory since his arrival. He remembered it well from that night long ago when he, pretending to be the Constable, had made accusations about the herbs to be found there. "So you have kept up the Baron's conservatory?"

"Indeed," Dorothy replied. "It is as marvelous, if not more marvelous, than ever. We grow a large variety of plants. I'm surprised that you didn't notice the leaves through the stained-glass wall. It looks exactly the same as it always did from inside the sitting room."

Jerome, too, was surprised that he had been so unobservant. The Inspector had upset him so much, first with his questioning and then with his overt behavior toward Cheri, that he really hadn't noticed anything else. This could not be allowed to continue. He would offer to assist in rendering the Inspector incapacitated with a malady during the weekend. He said to Doctor Armstrong, "When do you think we should slip the Inspector this potion? Please allow me to help you in whatever way I possibly can."

"I will work on the problem first thing tomorrow morning. It must be carefully thought out. No mistake must be made."

Dorothy said nothing, but her face took on a worried expression.

CHAPTER THIRTEEN

Babs ordered a dry martini the moment she was seated in first class on the flight from LAX to Vancouver. She was exhausted and her nerves were completely frayed. Last night had been the worst night of her life since she had been attacked and crippled by Big Al's hoods. Jane Tiddles had turned out to be a maniac. How could she have so misjudged someone's character? Jane had seemed mild and retiring. Babs had thought Jane might possibly cry at the news that she wouldn't be going to the island, but she never expected to be attacked verbally, have her clothing flung around the room, and for the nurse who earned an exorbitant salary to walk out on her in the middle of the night.

Stranded, Babs had phoned down to the housekeeper, but she had gone to bed. It was cook who came to the rescue, picked up Babs' clothes, packed them, and then helped a distraught Babs to get ready for bed.

She had slept badly. Her body had ached and so had her head. She had been afraid to take anything other than aspirin because of the trip the next day. She'd had to get up even earlier than planned and do the last-minute packing. Cook had also gotten up very early, made her tea, helped her down in the elevator and taken her out to the waiting limo.

Babs gratefully accepted the martini from the stewardess. She sipped it slowly and let her head sink back against the headrest. She looked out the window at the passengers coming up the ramp to board. Because of the wheelchair assistance she needed, Babs had been the first on board. She took the aisle seat, hoping she would be sitting alone.

The most disturbing thing about Jane's temper tantrum had been that terrible thing she had said about how Big Al died. Jane had said, "You don't want me to go to that island because you are guilty of killing that man, Big Al. I know it." How could she possibly know such a thing? The woman was absurd.

A tall heavyset man excused himself and squeezed into the seat next to Babs. He smiled broadly at her, but Babs had nothing but a scowl for him. How annoying to have the seat next to hers occupied. She looked for one of the hostesses but they were obscured by the line of passengers still filing into the plane. When she was able to speak to one of them, she would ask for the man's seat to be changed.

Babs suddenly felt his hot breath on her neck and she jumped. "Sorry, I didn't mean to frighten you. You were really deep in thought," he said. "My name is John Glover."

Babs gave a strained smile, but did not reply. She took the sunglasses from her handbag and put them on…picked up a magazine, buried her head in it, and swallowed the rest of her martini.

The hostess took the glass from her hand and asked if she wanted a refill. Babs said she did. The man beside her said he would like a glass of orange juice. The hostess then hurried away without giving Babs a chance to talk about the seating arrangement.

The man started to talk a blue streak: he never drank…he used to drink…nowadays he stuck to fruit juice…he supposed in her business people drank all the time…and on and on.

Babs did not answer the man. She didn't want to encourage him to keep talking. She buried her head in the magazine and turned him off. Her thoughts returned to Jane Tiddles and her dreadful accusation. Babs was aware that periodically over the years the supermarket tabloids brought up the subject of the unsolved mystery on Escape Island. Murder was always hinted at in those rags. Jane read all the gossip magazines…Babs knew she did, because although she never read them openly, they were always to be found in the trash, and once Babs had seen them under Jane's bed.

The hostess brought Babs her second martini and that terrible bore next to her, his orange juice. He was still spewing his inanities, and Babs continued to ignore him. Passengers were still filing in, and Babs still did not find the moment to ask about the seating. However, the first-class section was filling up to an alarming degree and Babs feared that there might not be an extra seat…that she might get stuck with the bore for the entire trip. She could hear sounds coming from his direction. He seemed unaware that she was not listening.

She thought with alarm that Jane Tiddles might go to the rags and sell her story. She might tell of the intimate details of Babs' incapacity. She could be sued out of existence if she dared to state that she knew Babs had killed Big Al. Yes, sued out of existence, but the harm would already be done.

She again jumped as she again felt the bore's breath on her neck. "I recognize you," he said. "You are Babs Cunningham. Look, I have a beautiful niece. She looks like Jane Russell." Holding the photograph under her nose, he said, "Doesn't she look like Jane Russell?" Then he added, "She wants to get into show business."

Babs took off her glasses, looked icily at him, and snapped, "Jane Russell would also like to be back in show business."

Ren, too, had spent a bad night. First he had drunk far too much to try and erase from his mind what that bitch Tammy Sue had said, and then he had not been able to sleep during the night. He'd even thought of postponing his trip until the following day. But the whole gang would be arriving on Friday, and why should he miss out on one of the evenings of the reunion? He knew he would feel better as the day wore on, it was only this morning that he had to get through. Maybe the plane ride would be uncomfortable, but the boat trip to the island, the sea breeze, and the island air would surely clear his head.

He hadn't had a chance to telephone Madam Betty. He would give her a piece of his mind for sending that terrible bitch Tammy Sue. Maybe he'd put Madam Betty out of business. Maybe he'd get one of his guys to mess up Tammy Sue's face. But he couldn't think about that right now, because his head hurt too much.

In his limo on the way to the airport, he fixed himself a Bloody Mary, thinking if he had the hair of the dog it might help, but he had to put his head out the window and throw up. After that he stuck to cold mineral water.

Jackie Le Roir had started out from Paris on Thursday. She changed planes early Friday morning at Kennedy and ended up on the same flight to Vancouver as Ren Silvestri.

Ren's face dropped when he saw her. He knew he looked green in color and he had wanted to look well again before he saw Jackie. Ren had not returned Tammy Sue's ticket, but had kept both first-class seats so he could nurse his hangover in peace. Jackie had spotted him, and had come to sit in the aisle seat beside him.

He was surprised by how friendly she was willing to be, and that gave him a good feeling. She was smiling, being warm, and charming. Well, well. Maybe in time she had realized what a "catch" she had jilted? Maybe she was ready to come back to him? But he wouldn't take her back so easily. She would have to pass every test...suffer a little for his affection. She would have to prove herself.

Ren was also taken by how beautiful Jackie still was—no longer a girl, but one knockout of a mature woman. He was fed up with the young ones, they were fickle and unreliable. They were like Tammy Sue and didn't appreciate a real man.

Jackie settled in, fastened her seatbelt. So she had come alone to the reunion? That was interesting. Now maybe she wouldn't think that there was anything strange about him traveling alone.

"I decided to come alone," Ren said quickly. "I didn't want to bring my wife. Thought this weekend should be only for us original owners." He added, "I didn't feel like bringing my mistress, either."

"I, too, wanted to come on my own," Jackie said. She pressed his hand and repeated what she had said earlier, "It is really good to see you again, Ren. I realize that I have missed the island and everyone."

She had said she'd missed everyone...but didn't she really mean that she had missed him? He thought he'd probe. "So you decided not to bring your lover, huh? To leave him in Paris?"

"Her," Jackie said, "to leave her in Paris."

The Hurleys rushed from the dock to the airport. They had no time to spare if they wanted to catch the early morning flight. Actually everyone on the cruise ship had stepped aside and allowed them to go first. Still, it had taken a long time to disembark. Major James Hurley had been the hit of the voyage. The passengers shoved one another to get close to him and say their personal goodbyes.

Lorraine Hurley could still not believe what a sensation her husband had made with his bogus hunting stories. People had hung on his every word. They had never had to buy their own drinks because his admirers would fight over who would be allowed to bring the great white hunter his next round. Women envied Lorraine for having such a dashing, exciting husband. She was constantly asked questions about living with a legend, a daredevil...and didn't she feel herself the luckiest woman in the world to be married to him?

James reveled in the attention. He regretted having to leave the ship and was looking forward to the return voyage. He also never tired of his storytelling. They had gotten their trip free in exchange for two evenings of informal talks in the lounge. But his talks went over so well that he had been asked to speak also in the main ballroom and for that they had received a cash payment of a thousand dollars. The rest of the time, he told his stories gratis... on the deck...in the bar...in the dining room. In fact, he never stopped.

And his stories got taller and taller, but nobody noticed except Lorraine. James was absolutely shameless in his effort to hold his audience. He stole famous stories from Hemingway and no one noticed.

One night he told about a rhino chase: "We had wounded this rhino. A huge bruiser, he was...one of the biggest rhinos I had ever seen...and mean. I could tell instantly that he was positively vicious. It is not an animal you can wound and then leave. You don't dare leave a wounded rhino if you care anything about your own life and the lives of the members of your party.

"You see, a rhino never forgets. Never. He will go into hiding and then chase down the hunters...deliberately stalk them until he finds and kills them. He will never let up...will even follow you great distances or wait until nightfall and attack your camp.

"I tried to tell that to the tourists I was leading. 'You can't go back to camp,' I'd said. 'We have got to stay out here until we find the rhino and finish him off.'

"But the leader of the group refused to listen. He said his group was tired and wanted to return to camp...the next day was time enough to track the rhino.

"So we started back to the camp for the night. The light was fading. We were in two jeeps and traveling slowly over the pock-marked savannah. Suddenly I heard thundering and turned to see the rhino emerge from behind a clump of trees. He was heading straight for the end jeep, fast as a locomotive. I yelled for our driver to stop, but he was too frightened. Both jeeps speeded up, but the rhino was outrunning us. I turned and took aim. The rhino was almost upon the jeep behind. I knew there was time for only one shot. If I didn't fell him, he would overturn that jeep with his body and the tourists inside would be injured or killed."

James paused here, and his audience held their breath. Finally he said, "My shot rang true. The rhino skidded and fell with a thump."

Later that evening when they were alone, Lorraine asked James, "Where did you get that exciting rhino story? It sounded familiar to me but I can't quite place it and I haven't heard you tell it before. In what book did you read it?"

"I never read it," James said sheepishly. "I saw it.... We both saw it...some years back."

Lorraine could not remember. "I give up," she said.

He gave her a clue: "John Wayne?"

"*Hatari!*" she exclaimed. "You were playing the part of John Wayne. Of course, the famous scene when the rhino attacks the jeep."

He laughed and nodded his head.

"Oh, James," she said, "retelling a scene from a John Wayne movie. You really are shameless."

Early on that Friday morning in Vancouver, Trish was in a sour mood. Friday was her biggest day at Tresses By Trish. To close the hair salon on Saturday in order to spend it on the island was bad enough, but to close half a day on Friday was a huge monetary loss. About half the week's revenues were taken in on Friday. Originally she had planned to go after work, but the weather was bad and she did not dare wait. If she did, the boat might not be able to take her until the next day, and Trish did not want to miss the first evening. Also she wanted to travel to the island with all the others. That would be between noon and two, when everyone had gathered. She worked furiously all morning, not understanding her irresistible urge to get to that ferry and be with the others. She was getting soft with age.

CHAPTER FOURTEEN

This time of year on Escape Island, the only live-in help were the maid, Sarah, and the cook, Mrs. Bloodsworth. A handyman came once a week to take care of repairs, or he might be called more often if needed. As in the past, the sailors on the island's ferryboat did the heavy cleaning when the ferry was not running full time. There was no gardening to be done in the cold weather and the pool was empty. Without guests, the hotel did not need a large staff.

Early on that Friday morning, Dorothy was going over the shopping list with Mrs. Bloodsworth and Sarah. They were both ready to go to the mainland for the shopping and a bit of an outing. Mrs. Bloodsworth and Sarah would return on the same ferry as the former owners; it would leave the dock sometime between noon and two o'clock in the afternoon, once everyone had gathered. Dorothy hoped that Trish would close her shop early and also be on that first ferry back. The weather was still stormy and might get worse toward evening. She did not want her daughter-in-law to miss the first evening of the reunion.

"Now, let's see," Dorothy was saying, looking yet again at the list. "We should have an extra smoked salmon…just to be sure… and it keeps. Then did I say that when you pick up the birthday cake and the bread, to also buy two dozen breakfast Danish?"

"Yes, ma'am, you did," Mrs. Bloodsworth replied. "Please try and calm yourself, Mrs. Armstrong. Everything has been thought of. Everything will be taken care of, and it will be a memorable weekend for all concerned. When Sarah and I are in the market we will telephone you, in case you've thought of anything else. But please rest easy."

Jerome walked into the kitchen in his robe, looking for coffee, surprised to see everyone dressed at such an early hour. "I make it five-thirty," he said, looking at his watch. "Is that the right time? I thought I might be the first one up."

The three women laughed. "Good heavens, no," Dorothy said, "Sarah and Mrs. Bloodsworth are ready to go down and wait for the ferry. There is the last-minute shopping to do, and they have to return to the dock on the other side by noon. Coffee is on the stove, Jerome, sit down and I will get you a cup, and make you some toast."

Both Sarah and Mrs. Bloodsworth already had their boots on and now they put on their scarves and rain slickers. Dorothy escorted them to the back door and handed each of them a vinyl shopping bag and some money. "Now don't forget, you must be on that first ferry back. I will need you here this afternoon, and also the weather might make the trip impossible later on in the day."

She returned and poured Jerome a cup of coffee. "The milk and sugar are on the table," she said. "I'll make you some toast. There is cereal in the cupboard. We will have a proper hot breakfast when the others come in. Did you sleep well?"

"Yes, thank you, very well," he said, yawning. "Where are the others? What did you mean when you said about them coming in?"

"The Doctor is driving Mrs. Bloodsworth and Sarah to the pier to wait for the ferry. Cheri and the Inspector are playing tennis."

"Tennis at this hour?" Jerome gasped. He went to the window and pulled the curtain aside. "But it is still pitch black out, and pouring with rain. How can they possibly be playing tennis?"

"We have an indoor court that is well lighted. Both like to get their exercise early. Then after breakfast Cheri goes to her studio to paint, and the Inspector returns to his cottage to write."

Jerome began to tremble. The kitchen was drafty and his robe was lightweight, but mostly he trembled at the thought of Cheri spending her early mornings exercising with the Inspector. The dinner last night had not gone well. Although the Inspector sat across from them, and Jerome was seated just next to Cheri, the Inspector managed to hog the conversation and most of Cheri's attention. Good lord, the man was insufferable, Jerome thought. He hoped Doctor Armstrong would go through with his plan to incapacitate that terrible man until the reunion weekend was over.

Dorothy served him his toast and then excused herself...there were so many preparations to be made for the arriving guests, she'd said. Jerome ate the toast and then poured himself another cup of coffee. He saw an array of rain mackinaws on the coat stand by the back door, and he chose one to throw over his robe to keep in his body heat. Then, with his coffee in hand, he strolled down the hallways, past the sitting room, and into the conservatory.

The conservatory faced the out-of-doors on three sides, and the rain beat down on those glass walls and the glass roof. The only protected wall was the one it shared with the sitting room. It was a spooky place in the dim storm light, a mass of plant life with huge ominous-looking overhangs. Jerome wondered which of the plants might be made into a potion. Probably it would be one of the most harmless looking, something with a lovely flower or aroma.

He heard the front door open and hurried into the hall to say "Good morning" to Cheri. She was alone. She had a beautiful smile for him.

"Good morning, Jerome," she said, taking off her mack and

hanging it up on the clothes tree by the front door. "I'm going to have a shower and change into my work clothes, then we will have breakfast. After we've eaten, I am longing to show you my latest paintings. Will you come to my studio with me? Will you spend some time alone with me? We haven't had a real chance to talk yet."

Jerome was so happy that he was unable to speak. He simply nodded his head at everything she said. At last he had an appointment to be alone with her. If all went well while they were alone, maybe he would drop his grudge against the Inspector...stop fantasizing about murder.

Cheri kissed him on the cheek and hurried down the hallway. He stood looking at her and thinking about what he wanted to say once they were alone. He had to stop being tongue-tied, had to let her know how he felt about her.

The front door again opened and a gust of cold wind made Jerome pull the mack he was wearing closer about him. It was the Doctor this time. He had parked the jeep and was returning for breakfast.

As he removed his wet raincoat and hung it up, he greeted Jerome warmly. "I have been thinking about our conversation of last evening," the Doctor said, as if Jerome were his oldest and dearest friend. "And giving our plan a great deal of consideration," he added, drawing closer and putting his arm around Jerome. "First thing this morning I was in the library," he continued. "I own a selection of very good books on serum therapeutics."

Jerome knew that serum therapeutics also included poisons, and he wanted to withdraw from the plan. He wanted to say that Cheri and he were finally going to be alone and work out their relationship. That he was no longer sure it would be necessary to slip the Inspector a potion to keep him away from the reunion. But words did not form and were not said...they remained only in his thoughts.

The Doctor was still speaking. "I've ruled out arsenic, and

most vegetable toxin that is too virulent. We don't want to cause gastrointestinal inflammation or hemorrhaging."

Jerome was horrified at the very thought of gastrointestinal inflammation and hemorrhaging. Maybe this had gone too far.

"Let me show you something," the Doctor said, his arm still around Jerome's shoulder. "Come into the conservatory."

The Doctor led Jerome into the conservatory and closed the door behind them. He then led the way to a far corner. "You see this plant…rather hidden in the corner. Looks harmless enough, does it not? I am talking about this umbelliferous herb, related to the carrot family. It has an inflorescence that appears to sprout from the same point to form a flat or rounded flower cluster with spotted stems, finely divided leaves, and small white flowers…pretty, too. It is used medically as a sedative."

"How powerful a sedative?" Jerome asked, although that was not what he really wanted to know. He wanted to know how poisonous it was and if the Doctor could be trusted to use the plant with safety.

The Doctor saw the frightened look on Jerome's face and laughed. "It can be a very powerful sedative indeed," he said. "A deadly poisonous drink may be made from the herb. But if we decide upon this plant, we shall make a very mild drink and cause only temporary sleepiness."

But Jerome no longer wanted any part of the plan—a plan that might go wrong. What if they gave the Inspector what they thought was a harmless sedative, but it ended up killing him?

The Doctor was now at the other side of the conservatory and Jerome heard his voice coming from a distance. He was talking about ricin, a vegetable toxalbumin from the castor oil plant, extracted from the seed. He was talking about poison and antidotes…how they save lives and how they kill. How anti-ricin taken in small doses formed antibodies, and produced immunity. How a patient systematically injected with small doses developed that immunity. And he was talking about the morbid result of over-consumption.

Jerome walked over to him, thinking how obsessed the Doctor had become with serum therapeutics. Would there be any turning back? Could he even suggest that they might consider changing their minds? He didn't think he could face Doctor Armstrong's disapproval and certainly not his scorn. Perhaps he would wait for the others to arrive…discuss the plan with them, and if no one wished to proceed, they could face the Doctor as a committee to reject the idea.

When Jerome walked over to stand next to the Doctor, the Doctor stated, "C21 H22 N2 O2."

Jerome realized that he must have missed part of the conversation, because the Doctor was looking at him as if he expected a response to the list of numbers.

"Well," the Doctor repeated, "C21 H22 N2 O2. Can you guess what this combination represents?"

Jerome looked completely lost.

The Doctor gave him another clue. "A kind of nightshade."

Jerome still looked lost. He had missed just enough of what the Doctor had been saying to make the question incomprehensible.

"Strychnine!" the Doctor said triumphantly. "It is a colorless crystalline poison which can be used in small quantities as a tonic to increase the appetite."

"Maybe we shouldn't," Jerome blurted out, but he was incapable of finishing his thought. He had to wait and be part of a committee, he told himself. He couldn't countermand the Doctor on his own.

"I know," the Doctor said, agreeing. "I also have my doubts about strychnine, as an overdose can cause convulsions."

Jerome gulped and touched his throat.

The Doctor said, "You are absolutely right, it is bitter…very bitter. The bitterness is difficult to disguise even diluted to the one-thousandth part. But there are cases of its being hidden in a strongly brewed coffee. The Inspector drinks such a coffee."

A few minutes later at the breakfast table, Jerome watched the Inspector put a cup of rich black coffee to his lips. The kitchen was damp and cooking the hot breakfast had made it steamy but not warm. However, Jerome felt his flesh burning as he watched the Inspector drink the espresso that Dorothy had brewed especially for him. Jerome imagined a time when that espresso might contain a potion that the Doctor had concocted, and his blush grew even deeper.

Dorothy was in charge of the kitchen while the cook and the maid were on the mainland. They had their breakfast at the kitchen table for convenience.

"Isn't this lovely, Jerome?" Dorothy asked him. "I always think eating the first meal of the day in a wonderful old kitchen like this one makes one feel good."

The kitchen was huge, and a combination of the modern and the antique. For example, a modern electric range stood beside the old coal stove, which had been kept for emergencies such as a loss of electricity. There were modern stainless steel sinks, but they had been added next to the large double cement ones that were originally in the house. There was a wall of big refrigerators and freezers, but even the quaint old icebox had been kept and tucked away in the corner.

Cheri was bubbly as she talked about her latest ideas for new paintings, and she was attentive to Jerome, announcing to all that she planned to give him a tour of her studio and her work.

Jerome, however, could not take his eyes off of the Inspector. The man was gorging himself with eggs and bacon and toast, and drinking yet another cup of that strong coffee. He was obviously a bull of a man, with a bullish appetite, but Jerome could almost imagine him writhing in convulsions after the next meal. It made Jerome so uneasy that he could not even begin to eat his own breakfast. So that Dorothy would not notice his lack of appetite, he got up from the table and took his plate to the sink, where he quickly disposed of the food.

The Doctor followed him to the sink with his own empty plate and took the opportunity to whisper into Jerome's ear, "I am considering, and may be leaning toward hemlock."

Jerome began to tremble.

The Doctor laughed. "You are unaccustomed to our island chill. Cheri will take you to her studio, where it is always very warm."

Jerome felt queasy, sick to his stomach. All this talk about poison had gripped his imagination and made him feel as if he had been poisoned. He was afraid that he might throw up, even though he had only eaten some toast earlier on. He excused himself, telling Cheri that he would find her in her studio later, and fled to his quarters.

After Jerome left the kitchen, the telephone rang and Dorothy answered. It was Mrs. Bloodsworth. "I'm sorry, Mrs. Armstrong," Mrs. Bloodsworth told Dorothy, "but two unexpected things have occurred that will delay Sarah and me till later in the day."

"Oh, dear," Dorothy said, "not on this important weekend."

"I'm afraid we are both going to miss the first ferry back."

"Oh, no," Dorothy moaned. "You must not miss the ferry."

"Well, ma'am, you decide. Sarah has a toothache but the dentist is not in his office until after two. I really think she should have it looked after," she said breathlessly. "And Miss Cheri's birthday cake will not be ready for me until about the same time. I should check it myself to make sure it is as lovely as they promised."

"Very well," Dorothy sighed. "We must have a perfect birthday cake. After the guests have arrived on the island, I'll send the ferry straight back for the two of you."

CHAPTER FIFTEEN

Shortly after noon the former owners began to arrive in town. The ferry was tied up to the dock, and rocking quite pronouncedly. The waves were high, the wind fierce and cold as an arctic blast. The captain paced the deck, anxious to shove off before the storm got any worse.

Babs Cunningham had been the first to arrive, and she was joined shortly thereafter by Ren Silvestri and Jackie Le Roir, who had met on the plane trip to Vancouver. The three were sitting at a window table in the port coffee shop, which overlooked the dock where the Escape Island ferry was moored.

Babs, Jackie, and Ren were talking about old times, but all three were careful not to mention that Ren and Jackie had once been romantically involved. However, Ren couldn't keep his eyes from undressing Jackie. She was still such a beauty, and he remembered how good she used to feel. Also there was a daring, an excitement, about Jackie that he had never found in any other woman. He felt sure that she had been pulling his leg by telling him that her latest lover was a woman. She'd just wanted to see his shocked reaction.

Jackie was also thinking at that moment about the shocked

look on Ren's face when she had told him about her latest lover, a woman. Imagine a crime boss from New York being so provincial? She knew about the Mafia. They were thugs and murderers who had mistresses, but pretended to worship their wives and children. She knew from Dorothy's letters that Ren had a devoted wife of many years' standing and no less than six children (to her mind a crime in today's world with its huge overpopulation), but Ren had not even mentioned them to her.

Ren had spoken to Jackie at great length about his fantastic mistress, Tammy Sue, who almost sounded too good to be true. He'd told of how they had spent their last night in New York together at the Rainbow Room atop Rockefeller Center. He had surprised Tammy Sue with a lavender chiffon evening gown and a short purple cape, and described how beautiful she had looked that night. He'd said that Tammy Sue had masses of light red hair, startling green eyes, a peaches and cream complexion, and she was stacked. He'd gone on to say that on top of all that physical beauty, she was smart and well educated. She knew how to dress and behave, had class. Best of all, she loved him, admired him above all others, and would die in order to please him.

Ren had neglected to tell Jackie that Madam Betty had arranged the call girl and that she arranged all his hookers. He'd never ever had a proper mistress. He couldn't keep a woman satisfied because of his problem with premature ejaculation. A woman had to service him, like Tammy Sue had that night, with her tongue. Maybe that's what had pissed her off? He had ruined her hair and makeup, and wrinkled her new dress. She had gotten falling-down drunk and had humiliated him in front of his lieutenants and their mistresses. She had even told them that he had hired her because he wanted to impress Jackie.

He tried to put the memory of that evening out of his mind. But Ren *did* want Jackie to think that he was a big man.... Well, he was, sort of.... He was the boss, although only as a figurehead, because of his name being Silvestri, and his having inherited the position. He had money and he had power, and he could spend his time any way he liked. He thought of how much he liked his office, where the door was always locked and his secretary let no one in without an appointment. Inside his office he had a sliding paneled wall, behind which were the latest arcade machines. He played those machines all day long, and nobody knew how he occupied his time but his secretary, Mary, and she would never give him away.

The coffee shop door opened and Major James Hurley and his wife, Lorraine, entered, interrupting Ren's contemplations. There was great excitement, and hugs all around.

It was coming up to twelve forty-five, and that left only Trish Saks to be accounted for, but the weather was turning even nastier. Snowflakes had begun to fall, the wind had picked up more speed, and the captain had sent one of his crew into the coffee shop to tell the passengers that he would like to leave as soon as possible.

"We should telephone Trish and make sure she is on her way. I have her telephone number here in this letter from Dorothy," Lorraine said, holding the letter up. "Her salon is called Tresses By Trish."

James Hurley said, "Yes, why don't you do that, Lorraine? I shall order you a coffee in the meantime." Looking at the others, he said, "Fancy it snowing this time of year. Fancy it snowing at all. I wonder if it will stay on the ground at Escape Island?"

"Don't you remember once in the early years of the development on the island when it snowed in April?" Babs asked. "I believe almost all of us were still living there then."

"I do," Jackie exclaimed. "The snow only lasted a short time but it was beautiful and great fun to play in.... Remember, Ren? You were complaining about the fact that the fittest of the men were asked to shovel off the front walk."

It was Babs who replied for Ren, "Of course, Ren remembers. He finally swept the front steps because Doctor Armstrong insisted."

Babs felt odd saying the Doctor's name. She could no longer quite remember why their romance had cooled off. Harlan claimed it was because she had received the work offer that was to take her away, but she recalled feeling that his love was not enough to sustain her. However, thinking of him now, she knew she was going to have trouble adjusting to the fact that he was married to Dorothy. Poor, sweet, lovable but fat and ugly Dorothy. Babs would have difficulty reconciling herself to the fact that Dorothy, of all people, had become her replacement. And when her job became too strenuous or too stressful, Babs sometimes fantasized about that island life she had given up, and that wonderful man she had once called her own. She had never found a man to replace Harlan, had never married. Now she seemed doomed to be alone forever.

The thought of being alone reminded her of the nurse/companion problem she would have to face as soon as she returned to Hollywood.

As if reading her thoughts, the Major asked, "Did you come on your own, Babs? One thinks of you these days as a famous woman who always travels with an entourage. Lorraine and I don't see television much…don't even have a set in the bush…but we certainly do read a great deal about you in the newspapers and magazines."

Ren took the opportunity to say, "Babs probably felt just like me about bringing into our group someone who doesn't belong. I have a great mistress who will be crying for me all weekend, but I just didn't want to bring a new face to the reunion."

Unlike Ren, Babs told the truth when she said that she, too, had not wished to bring an outsider to their reunion. Babs then shuddered as she remembered Jane Tiddles' reaction to being told that she would not be coming along to Escape Island. Now she realized that Jane's hysterical reaction was founded in more than just mere disappointment at missing the trip. Jane Tiddles must have a morbid curiosity about Escape Island. She read all the scandal sheets and maybe was obsessed about the gossip that surrounded the island and the mystery of Big Al Silvestri's death. Thank heavens she had decided not to bring the woman. She would no doubt have made a pest of herself, snooping for information, and who knew if she could be trusted to keep her mouth shut once they were back to Hollywood? After the way Jane behaved, Babs wouldn't put it past her to sell gossip.

As Lorraine came back to the table, she heard James talking about how they lived in the African bush. They did not live in the bush. They lived in a perfectly civilized English inn, just a short trip from Nairobi, in a lovely cottage of their own which was part of the complex and had all the modern comforts. She spent her days tending to her cottage garden and doing volunteer work for the local hospital, and James spent his days at his club in Nairobi, telling tall tales. But his ability to tell adventure stories had gotten them a free cruise from Nairobi to New York and back, and without that assistance with the fare, they never could have afforded to attend the reunion. Not to be present at the reunion would have broken both their hearts. The island had meant so much to them. They had been very successful at running the hotel for the first five years. Then the money they had received from selling their shares had enabled them to move to East Africa, a dream come true as a way to spend their retirement years. Perhaps she would not contradict James, not dispel the spell he cast. She only hoped he wouldn't go too far in his tall tales and force her to correct him in front of the others. They were her best friends in the world, and she couldn't have them think of her and James as fools.

"Trish doesn't answer," Lorraine said. "I got only an answering machine. She must be on her way."

At that moment the coffee shop door opened and they all turned, thinking it might be Trish arriving. It was the ferry's captain. He was a short muscular Greek named Demetri, a man of about fifty with a full head of wild black hair and a large mustache. His face was red from the cold and he looked agitated.

"We must leave now," the captain said. "The forecast is for the wind to rise to gale force in about an hour's time."

"Couldn't we wait just a few minutes longer?" Lorraine asked. "We are only expecting one more person and she should be on her way."

"We can just get the boat to the island and back to the mainland by leaving now. We cannot wait a minute longer, and I would like for everyone to get on board," the captain said with authority.

Lorraine again spoke up. "In her letter, Mrs. Armstrong said that the maid and the cook would be traveling with us. What have you heard from them? I don't think we dare leave the help behind."

"We received a message that Sarah and Mrs. Bloodsworth will be unable to make the trip until later," he said. "Now, please, everyone, come with me."

Ren paid the bill and everyone followed the captain out of the coffee shop and across the dock to the ferry.

Outside the wind was very strong and the snow lashed at their faces. Everyone pulled their collars up and the brim of their hats down, and walked briskly after the captain, with the Major and Ren taking care of Babs and her wheelchair.

The moment they were up the gangplank, the captain gave the order to start the engines. The guests piled inside the lounge. It was not a day to be on deck. The boat was rocking badly and they were still in port. No one was looking forward to the rough trip ahead.

Just as the two sailors were about to pull up the gangplank, they heard shouting and saw a woman running at full speed toward the boat. It was Trish, and she had made it just in the nick of time.

CHAPTER SIXTEEN

Jerome knocked on the door of Cheri's studio. There was no answer but it was slightly ajar, so he let himself into the room. Originally this had been part of the mansion's attic. He could see where walls had been taken down to make one large studio from three smaller rooms. It was now a very, very large space with three skylights, which had been placed in the roof at equal distances. The place was a mass of paintings. They hung from every wall and in places were piled perhaps ten deep. Even the side windows were mostly hidden by some framed and some rolled canvases. The walls were also lined with an odd assortment of chests-of-drawers. No doubt any chests no longer needed for the hotel were brought here and used for painting supplies.

In the center of the three-space loft was a massive wooden table with paints, brushes, and palettes, and dotted around the center of the floor space were easels of all sizes. It looked more like an art school, where dozens of students were in the process of creating their works of art, than it did the studio of just one painter.

The walls had been basically white-painted plaster, but they were now splattered with colors and had taken on a weird, uneven design. Here and there one saw evidence of once-lovely polished wooden floors, but now they were scuffed and covered in spilled paint.

There were only two hardback chairs, and they did not look welcoming. Between the chairs was a cabinet of tiny drawers that contained tubes of paint. The top of the cabinet had an ashtray, a glass of water, and a dirty cup. Jerome sat down in the closest of the hard chairs and lit a cigarette.

He looked around at the masses of artwork but decided not to study any of the paintings. Cheri would want to conduct him on a tour of her work, she had said as much, so he tried not to take in any of the details of the artwork.

His nausea had passed and he was feeling much better now. The loft was indeed warm, much warmer than his bedroom suite or the rest of the house. In looking around, he could see the large central heating pipes just above the skirting board and could hear their slight hissing sound; no doubt the hottest air rose into the former attic space. He would have taken off his jacket, but there was nowhere to hang it, so he settled instead for unbuttoning it and leaving it open. The jacket was a Gucci navy blue blazer with real gold buttons. He wore it with yet another pair of grey trousers and his Gucci loafers of the previous night. For daytime he had chosen an open-necked white shirt with a tie. He had also purchased a silk scarf to go with this outfit, but in his hurry to get to Cheri he had forgotten to put it on. He thought now that it was a shame he had not worn the paisley scarf, because it would have added a dapper touch that he had wanted Cheri to notice.

He could not imagine where Cheri was, and then he heard a flushing sound. Obviously the loft had a bathroom.

He puffed on his cigarette and continued to look around the loft. All at once there was white confetti at the windows, and looking up, he saw it also swirling around the skylights. It took him a few seconds to realize that it was snowing. Then he heard the howl of the wind. The attic was also, no doubt, insulated better than most of the rooms.

A door at the end of the loft opened and Cheri emerged. He could smell her perfume before he could see her. She was wearing a white linen jumpsuit and an apron with paint splatters. Her blonde hair was braided and twisted around her head to form a crown. She had put on a great deal of eye makeup and rouge, and her lips were a vivid red. She had on a pair of red clogs that alternately clopped and scraped the floor as she hurried toward him.

"Jerome, you are here at last," she said, grinning from ear to ear. "Are you feeling better? I do hope so. I am longing to show you my paintings and get your opinion. Look, it is snowing. How super!"

"I feel much better, thank you," Jerome said, rising from his hard chair and putting out his cigarette. He noticed that Cheri's speech had improved, or at least that she no longer spoke with the crude New York accent and phrasing that once had been so much of her personality. It would take some getting used to, this proper English coming from her lips. He imagined it had been the influence of living for so many years with the doctor and Dorothy, who both spoke a proper English and with English accents...particularly the Doctor.

She was standing beside him now and taking his hand in hers. "Before I show you my paintings, which will take forever," she said, "I want to show you something down the hall and ask your advice."

With that, she led him out of her studio and down the drafty hall to the next doorway. "Watch your head," she said, as she led him into a section of the original attic. It was loaded with old furniture and boxes and it was filthy. Jerome was concerned about his new clothing, which had cost him a fortune, getting ruined.

"What I want to do is get Daddy and Mommy to renovate this space. It doesn't have to be fancy like my studio. I won't need skylights or anything that grand. But I would like to have a small, comfortable sitting area and use all the side walls for storage. Maybe with some pretty curtains and nice lampshades it could be a storage room but still be a cozy place to rest, think about my work, and entertain. What do you think, Jerome?" she asked, looking at him with her huge innocent blue eyes. "Percival thinks that it could be a super place to relax, away from the crowds when they arrive in the season."

She had spoiled the moment for Jerome by mentioning Percival. Damn the man, he had all but taken over Cheri. Jerome blurted out, "What does this Percival, this ex-inspector from New Scotland Yard, mean to you? Are you and he serious? You seem to spend a great deal of time together, and he seems to figure into all your thoughts."

Cheri looked at him for a long moment without replying. Her big blue eyes seemed transparent as she stared at him. Then she put her hands to her lips and giggled. "Oh, Jerome, you are jealous."

"I need to know where I stand, Cheri. Are you serious about this chap, or is there still a chance for me?" Jerome said fiercely.

Again Cheri stared at him for a long moment without replying. Then to his utter dismay, large tears formed in her beautiful eyes and freely cascaded down her painted cheeks. "Oh, how can you be so cruel?" She sobbed. "How can you be so insensitive and say such terrible things to me? You have neglected me for years and you turn up after all this time and demand to know my feelings for you."

Cheri turned and fled down the hall—not to her studio, where he might have followed, but to her bedroom suite, where he dare not go. He stood watching her retreating form and felt confusion and defeat. What had he done? Had he been insensitive? Had he said things she might not forgive him for? What had he said? It seemed fairly innocent at the time. He had just wanted to know if she were serious in her affections for the Inspector, or if he still had a chance.

Try as he might, he could not remember what exactly he had said, but he did recall her words: "You have neglected me for years" rang in his ears. And that was true. He had not written or telephoned her directly. He always had sent his messages for her in his letters to Dorothy. He had never made his intentions clear, told her outright that he loved her and wanted another chance. His fantasies had never been conveyed directly to Cheri; they remained just that—his fantasies—and he had expected her to know what had been in his head all these years. Realizing that now, he knew that he had been wrong to demand an explanation of her feelings.

What a fool he had been. He only hoped that he could correct the situation and get back into her good graces, but the weekend was short, partly gone. Time was running out and he might have ruined his chances for good. However, if he were to have any hope at all, he would have to lay down a careful plan and follow it to the letter. Surely he could come up with a plan? After all, he had risen to become the Senior Vice President of the telephone company for Western Canada. So he couldn't be stupid…only slow to come to terms with his feelings, and awkward in his treatment of women. He couldn't afford to lose another second and he didn't intend to. From now on, a plan to win Cheri would be uppermost in his thoughts.

CHAPTER SEVENTEEN

On board the ferry, the former owners were experiencing a rough ride. It was so rough, in fact, that they were being tossed from side to side inside the salon. A sailor entered and insisted that everyone put on a life vest. He also passed around airsickness bags, but so far everyone had been able to control their growing nausea. The sailor began to put away small objects and to tie down some of the loose pieces of furniture. Major Hurley was advising that they would feel less sick if they sat outside in the fresh air, but the sailor said that the captain would forbid them to leave the safety of the salon.

From the salon window, a frigate could be seen passing, and some of the guests wondered if they shouldn't hail the large ship and ask to be taken aboard. But the Major gave them a pep talk and asked Lorraine to try to find a bottle of vodka, claiming that it was the best sea sickness medicine one could possibly take.

Lorraine staggered to her feet and headed for the bar. Ren rose and helped to steady her as she went. Lorraine found the bottle, handed it to Ren, and he helped her back to her seat on the couch. Trish grabbed the bottle from Ren's hands and took a large swig;

then she held the bottle out for someone else to take. Lorraine waved the bottle away but Jackie took it, drank some, and then offered it to Babs, who took a dainty sip and passed it back to Jackie. Next Ren gave the bottle to the Major, who took a big swallow. Lastly, Ren helped himself to a generous gulp.

"I know what," Trish said, again taking the vodka and drinking from it, "let's sing. That always seems to help in bad situations."

"Good idea," said Babs. "Anything but 'Row, Row, Row Your Boat.'"

Dorothy paced up and down by the sitting room windows, looking at the swirling snow and fretting about the guests. She only hoped the ferry had taken off in time to beat the storm, and would be bringing them to the island soon. A gale-force wind had been predicted for around two o'clock, a little over an hour from the present.

The Doctor entered the room. He moved to Dorothy and embraced her. "You mustn't worry yourself so, my dear. I'm sure the ferry with our reunion guests is on its way. The winds are high, but they are not at gale force yet," he tried to reassure her. "I think I will go down to the pier early and wait. I'll take the station wagon for the people, and Jerome has agreed to drive the sedan and get the luggage."

"I should come with you," Dorothy said.

"You'll do no such thing. Jerome and I can handle the situation. I want you to stay here where it is warm and comfortable and wait for our guests. You can get some hot drinks ready and see to the stocking of the bar. Perhaps a high tea might be in order after their trip."

Just then Jerome entered the sitting room. He had changed into his warm traveling clothes and was putting over them a rain slicker he had found hanging in the kitchen.

"I'm ready to start out whenever you are, Doctor," he said.

They heard the front door opening, and in another minute Percival had entered the room. "What a storm!" he said. "You didn't tell me it snowed on the island. Surely it is unusual to have snow this time of year. I mean, we are past the middle of April."

"It is a rare occurrence," Dorothy said. "But it does happen every few years here on the island. April is perhaps the worst month."

"Surely not worse than January and February?" Percival said.

"Yes, it can be," the Doctor replied, "because we can get these freak storms that we are not necessarily prepared for."

Percival had on a heavy overcoat and a cap with flaps that covered his ears. He also had on high gumboots, and looked like some disaster relief worker. "I came over because I thought you might need a helping hand with all the guests arriving in this wind and snow. I will be happy to go down to the pier and wait with you for the ferry."

"That won't be necessary," Jerome said. "I am here and have been invited to help. We don't need another person to come along."

"Well," Dorothy said, "it is kind of you to offer. Maybe a third hand with the luggage would be welcome? Don't you think, Jerome?"

"No, it will not be necessary and would not be welcome," the Doctor said with sharp decision.

Percival was taken aback. "Surely, you don't mean to say that in this ferocious weather, you are refusing another strong man to help with the ladies and the luggage?"

Both the Doctor and Jerome spoke at once, saying the same thing: "It will not be necessary."

But Percival was dressed for the occasion and would not be put off. He insisted, saying, "But I am ready to brave the storm and I insist upon helping. You need not treat me like a paying guest when an emergency arises. I want to do my bit."

The Doctor shook his head. His voice was strong and stern. "These are our very special friends. We do not wish your help, nor do we want your presence on the pier when we greet our friends after so long an absence."

Percival looked at the Doctor and was momentarily speechless.

Dorothy tried to ease the atmosphere by saying, "It is just a matter of our friends seeing familiar faces when they arrive at the pier. We will be having high tea and alcoholic drinks as soon as they get here and I shall call you. I hope you will join us then."

Jerome, having gathered even more courage, said, "Or perhaps it would be better if you waited until this evening to join us. I think you can appreciate that we would like to greet our friends in private. We have much to say at the first tea-time we have with them."

"That is a very rude thing to say, Jerome," Cheri said, entering the room. "I'm sure Percival has become like one of our family and will always be welcome at any of our gatherings."

"Thank you, my dear," the Inspector said. "But I quite understand the feelings of the Doctor and Jerome. If I cannot be of practical help, then I would wish to return to my writing. I am not accustomed to being here for tea, and would prefer to keep on writing until the cocktail hour." He looked at each of them in turn, and then addressed himself to the Doctor. "If it is all right with you, Doctor, I shall retire now and join you all about the usual time, six-thirty?"

"Yes, thank you," the Doctor said, taking a more civilized tone.

"We will be very pleased to have you join us at cocktail hour," Dorothy said, smiling her most conciliatory smile.

"Yes, we insist that you join us then," Cheri said.

Once at the pier, Jerome parked the sedan and went around to get into the station wagon with the Doctor. As he climbed in beside the Doctor, the wind caught the door of the station wagon and it took all of Jerome's strength to close it behind him. The Doctor had kept the motor running and the heat on. Jerome took off his gloves and rubbed his hands near one of the hot air vents.

They both searched the sea in front of them, but saw no sign of a boat of any kind on the horizon. Large snowflakes were falling and the wind seemed steadier now. There was a light coating of white that was staying on the boards of the pier.

Jerome said, "I understand that Sarah and Mrs. Bloodsworth were detained on the mainland."

"Yes, worse luck," the Doctor replied. "If this storm keeps up they may not be able to get back today. Of course, there is always a chance that the weather may not permit a crossing tomorrow."

"How concerned is Dorothy about the supplies that the ladies were due to bring with them?" Jerome asked.

"Not having a birthday cake for Cheri's party tomorrow night would be a big disappointment for her, but as far as supplies are concerned, we have enough in the cupboards to see us through an emergency of a month or more. No worry on that score."

"But I'm sure Dorothy ordered some special items and will be sorry not to have them," Jerome commented.

The Doctor grinned. "Dorothy will never be satisfied no matter how many supplies we have…. She will continue to fuss till the end."

Jerome rubbed his coat sleeve on the inside of the windshield and peered out. "Look, Doctor Armstrong, isn't that a vessel? It is still far out on the horizon, but I believe I do see something."

The Doctor also rubbed his coat sleeve on the window to clear the mist, and gazed steadily at the horizon. "Damn difficult to see with this snow and the windshield fogging over, but you could be right."

However, moments later they saw the ship more clearly and it was a frigate. Both were disappointed and just a touch worried, even though they had arrived at the pier early. It would be too terrible if the ferry had not already taken off from the other side.

Doctor Armstrong tuned in the shortwave radio and got some scratchy sounds. He fiddled with the radio for about ten minutes and finally got the weather report. The airwaves were full of static, but the report was understandable. Nothing had changed; the gale-force winds were still due to arrive in about forty-five minutes' time.

Then they saw another ship far out in the water. They both left the comfort of the station wagon to go to the end of the pier and watch. The snow was falling heavily and staying on the ground. In some places it had formed considerable drifts. The Doctor had his binoculars and within a few more minutes was able to determine that it was indeed the Escape Island ferry approaching. At that point they got back into the warmth of the station wagon to wait until the ship got closer to docking.

The swells were very high by the time the ferry docked, and getting the passengers off was a tricky proposition, because the gangplank rode up and down in the waves and gave no steady runway, making it especially difficult for Babs Cunningham's wheelchair.

The captain of the ferry stood at the top of the gangplank and the Doctor stood at the bottom; in between, Jerome and the two sailors made a human chain. Lorraine was the first to work her way down by holding on to them, and she was followed by Jackie and Trish. After much persuasion, the Major was coaxed to exit next. Ren passed Babs' wheelchair down the ramp, and then he and the captain made a seat with their arms and carried her down, helped each step of the way by the human chain.

At the bottom of the ramp, Doctor Armstrong forcibly took Babs into his arms and carried her to the station wagon, with

Jerome following behind and then running ahead to open the passenger side door. The Doctor had been determined to carry her by himself and no one interfered. Babs and the Doctor looked closely at each other's face, and memories of their past romance surfaced powerfully in this most dramatic of all settings: the hero coming to the rescue of the damsel in distress. They were both shaken by the feelings it awakened.

Jerome held the station wagon doors for the other ladies to enter. The Major went around to the other side of the wagon and let himself in, as did Ren. They all watched as the luggage was passed hand over hand down the ramp by the captain and the sailors, and piled at the bottom in the snow. The sailors then carried it to the sedan, where Jerome helped them to load it into the back and the trunk. Then the sailors hurried back on board and the ferry began to pull away.

The Doctor pulled his station wagon out first and started for the mansion. Jerome watched the station wagon full of people ahead and felt left out. He could hardly wait to greet everyone properly.

CHAPTER EIGHTEEN

Dorothy and Cheri were beside themselves with joy as they watched the station wagon pull up to the front porch. Both had bundled up and come outside to wait for the guests. Jerome pulled the sedan up right behind the station wagon, got out, and ran to help the ladies from the wagon. This time it was Jerome and Ren who made a seat with their arms and carried Babs up the steps. The Major carried Babs' wheelchair.

Everyone seemed to arrive on the front porch at the same moment and there was much hugging and kissing, while they all talked at once and no one could really be heard clearly. Finally Lorraine said, "Couldn't we continue this inside, out of the storm?" They all laughed and Cheri held the front door open for them to enter. The Major was the last in the door, and Cheri turned to look at Jerome in the driveway, her expression a mixture of sadness and defiance, before also turning and going indoors. The Doctor had already driven around back to park the wagon in the garage, and Jerome got into the sedan and followed. They would bring the luggage in through the garage.

Dorothy and Cheri escorted everyone upstairs to show them their accommodations: Cheri, Trish, Ren, and the Major took the stairs, while Babs in her wheelchair, Lorraine, and Jackie went up in the elevator with Dorothy. Once they were all gathered in the hallway, Dorothy said, "Please, everyone, take off your wraps and then hurry downstairs to the sitting room. There's a lovely warm fire blazing in the fireplace and I've made us what I hope is a delicious high tea."

"Yes, please do hurry down," Cheri echoed. "I've got a thousand things to tell everyone and a thousand questions to ask."

Cheri then started down the stairs, but Dorothy paused in Trish's doorway to talk to her. When they were alone, Dorothy threw her arms around her former daughter-in-law. "I'm so glad you're here," she said tearfully.

Trish dropped her harsh expression and hugged Dorothy back, a tear also in her eye. "I'm glad to be here. I have missed you, Mom."

Dorothy was so overwhelmed by the fact that Trish had called her "Mom" that she was afraid she would bawl loudly, so she stepped away, saying, "Thank heavens you didn't miss the first ferry, there may not be another one today...or even tomorrow."

"I know," Trish replied. "I broke my neck to make it, but thank heavens I did. It's been a long time...and I didn't want to miss a minute of the reunion."

"You look beautiful," Dorothy said with genuine admiration, "and I can't tell you how happy I am to see you."

"I know, Mom, me too," Trish said. "Now get out of here and let me repair myself and use the bathroom. If we don't stop being mushy, I'll be bawling my eyes out and all my makeup will come off."

"Yes," Dorothy replied, "get yourself ready, darling, and hurry downstairs. We have so much to catch up on."

At that moment, the elevator made its whirring sound and descended. When the doors opened again, they revealed Jerome, the Doctor, and the first of the luggage. Ren opened his door just then, saw them, and offered to give them a hand. It took the three of them another couple of trips to get all the luggage into the house, up in the elevator, and delivered. On the final trip, the Major also lent a hand. Soon afterwards, everyone congregated downstairs. The unpacking could wait.

The sitting room was large, but with everyone seated around the fire it seemed cozy and intimate. Dorothy had made a splendid high tea of shrimp cocktails, cucumber and dill sandwiches, stuffed celery and olives…also warm scones, plain cake, and good strong China tea.

Trish sat close to Dorothy and talked earnestly. Cheri sat close to the Doctor and watched very carefully to determine just how much attention her mother was paying to the prodigal daughter-in-law.

Doctor Armstrong noticed how Cheri was clinging to him, noticed how her gaze constantly went toward the couch where Trish was seated close to Dorothy, both women talking intently.

"Trish is Dorothy's daughter-in-law, don't forget," he said.

"I know…she was married to Dorothy's son, William, who was murdered by Big Al's gang. But Dorothy is my mother," she whined.

"That's right. She learned to love you and chose to adopt you. We both did…you are our little girl. We cherish you," the Doctor said, taking hold of Cheri's hand and kissing it. "Don't forget that your mother has not seen her daughter-in-law for many, many years. They have a great deal to catch up on. Trish will be gone on Monday and you will have your mother all to yourself again. But for this one weekend, let Dorothy and Trish catch up. Be just as generous and sweet as I know you are…try not to pout or make Dorothy feel that you are unhappy because she is spending a little time with Trish. Will you promise me that you will do that?"

"Okay," Cheri said. "I'm sorry, Daddy. I was about to act very selfishly…to deny Trish some time with Mommy. But I will be a big girl about the whole thing. I promise."

Babs was studying Harlan from across the room and noting the Doctor's relationship with his adopted daughter. Cheri had never been bright, but now she seemed almost retarded. Babs would have loved to have been able to talk to Doctor Armstrong without Cheri being in the middle, but Cheri was clinging to him and Babs knew she would have to wait for another opportunity.

My God, Babs thought, *Cheri dresses like a child.* For this special tea-time, arranged to greet the guests, Cheri had actually chosen to wear a fluffy pink sweater, a short white skirt, and, of all things, pink bunny slippers! *And imagine,* she thought, *wearing your hair in pigtails at the age of forty-five?* The image struck Babs as bizarre, but she observed Harlan closely, and he seemed to dote on the child-woman, adore her as if she were a normal daughter.

Babs was also very sensitive, careful of Dorothy's feelings. She didn't want to seem to be vying for Harlan's affection. She just wanted to talk to him. Of course there was still an attraction. She could still feel his strong arms carrying her from the ferry to the car. But she had no intention of trying to revive their long-ago sexual relationship. She would never do that now that he was married to Dorothy. She had too much respect for Dorothy, and, yes, even love, for the heavyset woman who seemed able to mother them all.

Jerome, too, was watching Cheri with her father. He had not yet had time to formulate his plan to win Cheri back, but he must hurry. He only hoped it would be possible to make amends and declare his intentions, now that all the guests had arrived and there would be so many distractions, so many people who demanded her attention and his.

Jackie was watching Jerome. He intrigued her. He was a good-looking man and she liked the stylish way in which he dressed. She knew that he had on Gucci loafers and a Gucci sport jacket with real gold buttons. She'd been thinking a lot about him even before seeing him again, because he was a successful man—a very successful man—with money and position. Jackie found money and success a real turn-on and decided to go over and start a conversation with him.

Jerome was rather startled when Jackie settled into the chair next to his, giving him a beautiful smile. He was not accustomed to women taking an interest in him. She complimented him on his excellent taste in clothes. That delighted him, because he had made a concerted effort to look dashing, and was thrilled to be appreciated. Then she began asking him about his position as Senior Vice President, and when he replied, she seemed fascinated by all that he had to say. Encouraged by her rapt attention, he talked more and more about his work. He thought with surprise, *I'm not boring her. Her eyes are alert. She is truly interested.* And he thought, *What a remarkable woman she is.*

Jackie's physical beauty was not lost on him, either. Her eyes were large, a liquid brown. Her dark hair was short and feathery, framing her perfect oval face with its smooth olive skin. She was taller than he remembered, and thin, but with large breasts that were tantalizingly outlined beneath her sheer white blouse. Each time her suit jacket opened, he had difficulty pulling his eyes away from those luscious breasts. She appeared fit and healthy, and she exuded charm.

Jerome was completely wrapped up in Jackie and their conversation, and would have wished to stay that way for the entire tea-time. However, Ren suddenly pulled up a chair and came between them.

Trish was satisfied that she had received, for now, a full share of motherly affection from Dorothy, so she turned her eyes to Jerome. He was much better looking than he'd been years ago when they had been lovers. Jerome now had a flattering and expensive haircut, his clothes were tailored and even designer-made. When she'd known him, he'd been poor. Trish had never been with a truly successful man, and she wondered what her chances of reviving her love affair with Jerome might be. *Damn Jackie for taking up so much of his time,* she thought.

When Trish saw Ren pull up a chair and put himself between

Jerome and Jackie, she thought it would be a good time for her to also go and insert herself into that group. *Maybe Jackie and Ren will get together again,* she thought, *and that would be one obstacle out of the way in my pursuit of Jerome. I only hope that Cheri has not set her sights on him, also.* She remembered all too well how Cheri had stolen Jerome from her all those years ago. But she also remembered that she and Jerome had made hot and heavy music together. Surely he would be mature enough now to appreciate how great she was in bed. Trish felt that under the sheets she had no real competition from Cheri and perhaps not much from Jackie, either.

Trish walked over to Jerome, picked up a chair, and placed it between him and Jackie so that she commanded an intimate view of his eyes and mouth...and he of hers. She tossed her luxurious red locks close to his chest, so that he could appreciate their luster and smell their perfume. She had worn a tight-fitting emerald green wool dress, and knew her full figure was shown off to the best advantage. Trish crossed her legs and let her skirt ride up to mid-thigh.

"Jerome, I can't tell you how marvelous it is to see you again. I have thought about you so often over the years. Imagine that we both live in Vancouver and have never gotten together. You are naughty for not calling me. Just think, it took this reunion for me to get a chance to visit with you again. Of course, I know what an important job you have and how busy you must be, but I can't help feeling neglected," Trish said, pouting her lips and parting them enticingly.

Jerome was again stunned. No women had shown him any attention in years, had not seemed to even notice him, and now two devastatingly attractive ones were throwing themselves at him. Maybe it was true that clothes made the man. He began to think that his money had been well spent. How else could one explain his changing fate?

Once Trish had gone to speak to Jerome, Dorothy sat alone for a minute. Babs was talking to the Major and Lorraine, and Dorothy studied her. *How elegant and beautiful Babs is,* Dorothy thought. She was painfully aware that Babs and Harlan once had been lovers. But they had broken off their relationship before Dorothy entered the picture as Harlan's amore…long before. Her problem, she knew, was that she could not believe Harlan had chosen her. She was so plain, next to what he had been accustomed to in women…like the famous soap opera star. She couldn't possibly compete and had never tried. She had not gone after Harlan…had not even in her wildest dreams thought of herself and Harlan together.

When he proposed marriage, she thought that it was because he wanted her shares of the business to merge with his own. And that was fine with her. Even a marriage based on a business arrangement would have been fine with her. Just to have a wonderful man like Harlan to call her husband was more than she had ever hoped. Then he amazed her by showing her deeply felt emotion, by desiring her, by consummating the marriage and being devoted to her. She only hoped that it would not now be ending. She hoped that Harlan and Babs would not rekindle their love and that he wouldn't desert her for the younger, more glamorous and beautiful woman. Dorothy sighed, because she had to concede that she had been in heaven all these years and if it was about to end…well, she had already had more love than she had ever dared ask for…and from a divine man whom she once could only have fantasized about. Dorothy sighed again and then got up to offer everyone more tea.

The Major was telling one of his tall tales to Babs. Lorraine had heard this particular story more than once and excused herself to help Dorothy collect the cups and pour more tea. But the Major had captivated Babs' attention with his story:

"Hippos come out of the water and cross the fields at night," he was saying. "They often travel great distances. It is as if they are too heavy and lazy to get out of the water when the sun shines, and the weather is hot, but they get their exercise at night, and perhaps satisfy their wanderlust, who knows. And they are like two-thou-sand-pound freight trains when they rumble by. Anyway, we were sleeping in a tent near the Zambian border and close to a stream that runs off Victoria Falls, when suddenly we were awakened by a thundering noise. A herd of hippos cut a path on either side of us, but by some miracle did not run over the tent."

"My God," Babs exclaimed. "What did you do?"

The Major smiled and said with deep irony, "Naturally, the next morning we moved the tent."

"Next morning?" Babs said, flabbergasted. She had fallen com-pletely for the story. "You waited till the next morning? You didn't, of course, get back to sleep that night?"

"Oh, yes," the Major said. "We got in a few more hours of shuteye. We'd had a long and tiring day tracking leopard, and had to be up with the sun. It had been unsuccessful, but we were on their trail and felt surely we would find them on this day. But that is another story—the incredible camouflage of the leopard and how difficult they are to find. Of course, they sometimes find you, and then you're in trouble."

Lorraine was now standing over them, asking if they wanted a refill on their tea. The Major accepted but Babs refused, saying that she wished to go to her room and unpack, perhaps take a rest before changing for dinner.

Shortly afterwards almost all the guests followed suit and went to their rooms to rest and unpack. Only the Major stayed in the sitting room, where he found an audience for his tales in Dorothy, the Doctor, and Jerome.

Jerome was sorry to see that Cheri had also gone to her room. It might have been a perfect opportunity to get her by herself in a corner and apologize for his crude manners of earlier that day… perhaps tell her of his feelings for her…. Now he would have to wait for another opportunity.

CHAPTER NINETEEN

Jerome was the first to arrive at cocktail time, actually almost half an hour before cocktails were planned. He was hoping to see Cheri alone if the opportunity arose, even though that was unlikely, as Cheri was always one of the last to be ready. She cared deeply about how she looked, and he liked that. He had learned his lesson about the importance of dressing well. Hadn't both Jackie and Trish made a play for him? He could scarcely believe that they had actually found him attractive, and he was secretly hoping to cause more of a stir with the outfit he had purchased for this Friday night. It was not to be formal. Saturday, the night of Cheri's birthday celebration, was the only night that was to be formal. So for this evening he had chosen to wear black wool slacks, a black velvet jacket, and a white silk shirt with a ruffled collar and ruffled cuffs. He had hesitated to buy anything so far-out, but the clerk in the finest men's store in Vancouver had assured him that it was the height of fashion. He had purchased the outfit, along with another, a plain grey that was traditional and conservative, thinking that he might not wear the more daring one. However, encouraged by the reactions of the two beautiful women, Jerome had dressed in the daring one for this evening. If he'd made a mistake he would soon know.

The fire was low, so he stoked it and put on more logs. The wind was howling and rattling the windows. It was not quite dark at six and he could see the snowflakes whirling madly about the pine trees and the house. The phone rang several times but no one answered. Finally on the fifth ring Jerome decided to lift the receiver.

The line was full of static and the woman's voice on the other end was difficult to make out. After she had said "Mrs. Bloodsworth" a few times, he understood that it was the cook. She was reporting that the weather on the mainland was brutal. The captain did not want to run the ferry in the storm and so she and Sarah would not be coming tonight. He was to please tell Mrs. Armstrong how sorry they were, and that they would try to get to the island tomorrow, weather permitting.

Dorothy entered the room just then, but it was too late; the connection had already been broken.

Jerome said to Dorothy, "I'm sorry, but no one seemed to be picking up so I thought I should answer the telephone in case you were in the shower and unavailable."

"Oh, that's all right, Jerome," Dorothy said. "You are one of the family and must feel free to answer the telephone at any time."

"I'm afraid it is bad news about Mrs. Bloodsworth and Sarah. They won't be able to get here this evening. The captain doesn't want to take the ferry out in this weather."

"I was afraid that would happen," Dorothy said, walking to the windows and looking out. "What a storm!"

"How will you manage without a maid and a cook?" Jerome asked.

"Oh, we will manage," Dorothy said good-naturedly. "Everyone will have to make their own beds and that sort of thing."

"I'm sure we will all pitch in and help," Jerome said. "Please feel free to call on me for any help you may need. I've been a bachelor for years now and have learned to do many a domestic chore out of necessity. I wash dishes like a professional," he laughed.

Dorothy then turned away from the windows and went to warm herself by the fire. "I believe we can thank you for not letting the fire die out," she said. Then for the first time frowning, she added, "I am just a touch concerned about the meals if Mrs. Bloodsworth doesn't get here by tomorrow. We have plenty of provisions, but she is such an excellent cook, and I am only a fair one. We will have to have much simpler meals than the ones that were planned."

"I'm sure that just being here together is what makes this weekend special. The meals are a secondary consideration. And I dare say that even those, if we put all the talents of the guests together, might be a delightful surprise. I make a mean omelet and salad," he said.

They heard the front door open and a few moments later Percival entered the sitting room, carrying an armload of logs wrapped in an old rain slicker. "I thought you could use some more fuel," the Inspector said. "And since I had to brave the weather to get here from my cottage, I thought I might as well bring in a few logs."

"That was very kind of you, Inspector," Dorothy said. "I'm sure we will be putting them to good use."

"Before I take off my coat and boots, I thought I might bring in a few more loads," he said, heading back toward the door.

"Yes, thank you," Dorothy called after him. Then, turning to Jerome, she said, "He really is a nice chap. I'm sorry Harlan finds him so offensive. We can't just ask him not to come to dinner, can we?"

Jerome didn't answer her. He was thinking about the Inspector and what a nuisance he was going to present. Jerome had forgotten all about the man, but now here he was back again like a bad penny.

"I don't think it is too early to fill the ice bucket and bring it in to the drinks table," Dorothy said, making a move to go.

Jerome put his hand up to stop her and went himself to the hall, saying over his shoulder as he went, "Dorothy, you stay here and greet the guests. I will bring in the ice bucket."

"Thank you, dear. Oh, and also bring the tray of hors d'oeuvres that are on the counter," she called as he left the room.

The Doctor, the Major, and Lorraine arrived next. The Doctor went directly to the drinks table and made two scotch and sodas, and poured a sherry for Lorraine. "Are you going to have a sherry, my love?" the Doctor asked Dorothy.

"No, thank you, my love," she replied. "I'll wait for a bit. Jerome is already down and has gone to get the ice bucket and the hors d'oeuvres. The Inspector has arrived and is bringing in some logs."

"The Inspector?" James and Lorraine both asked at once.

"Yes, his name is Percival Forsythe, and he is a retired Inspector from New Scotland Yard," the Doctor said. "He is a paying guest. He's rented the nearest cottage and doesn't have any plans to leave."

Dorothy added, "He is writing a book. He takes his lunch in his cottage but is in the habit of taking his breakfast and dinner with us. I didn't think I could ask him—"

"Certainly not," Lorraine interjected. "You could not have asked him to eat alone if he is in the habit of taking two of his meals with the family. I'm sure it will work out fine."

Jerome entered with the ice and the hors d'oeuvres. The Doctor returned to the drinks table and poured himself another scotch and soda. Then the Doctor looked up as the Inspector entered with another armload of logs. "Are you having a scotch and soda, Inspector?" he asked. "It seems that I am bartender for tonight."

Dorothy stepped over to the fireplace where the Inspector was just putting the logs down. "These are our friends, Major James and Mrs. Lorraine Hurley. Percival Forsythe, a retired Inspector from New Scotland Yard."

"Pleased to meet you," Percival said. "I won't shake hands until I've taken off these wet clothes, and I thought I'd bring in another load of logs before I do that. Might as well, since I'm dressed for it. Then, yes, Doctor, thank you, I'll be ready for a scotch."

Jerome wondered if he should offer to give the Inspector a hand, but then thought better of it; his new clothes might get ruined.

Lorraine said, "Jerome, you really are a snappy dresser. That is such a fine outfit you are wearing tonight. So becoming."

"Thank you," he replied, grinning from ear to ear.

"It certainly is a fine outfit," Jackie said, coming into the room. "It is what the men in Paris are wearing for evenings such as these. I'm delighted to see that Vancouver is keeping pace with the fashion world." She noticed Harlan at the bar and went over to him. "Good evening, Doctor, I see that you are pouring. I'm very thirsty and would love to have a tall drink of some sort. A soft drink or even water would be fine. Perrier if you have it, or a diet Coke?"

She was wearing a chic cocktail suit. A black velvet dress with a large grosgrain bow at the side, and a bolero jacket trimmed in grosgrain. The dress was strapless and showed off her figure. Her breasts rose and fell over the top of the dress as she breathed.

Jerome walked over to the bar to be near her, unable to keep his eyes off her décolletage. "You look amazing," Jerome said, and then worried about his choice of words. He wanted to compliment her, but was "amazing" the right word to have used?

Apparently it was the right word, because Jackie turned her face to his and said, "What a lovely thing to say, Jerome. Thank you."

"What lovely things are you saying?" Trish asked, as she entered and went straight to the drinks table to stand on the other side of Jerome. "I see Jackie has gotten to you before I, this evening. But you must promise to sit beside me at the dinner table. I have so many things I must talk to you about."

"What may I fix you to drink, Trish?" the Doctor asked. "Would you care for a glass of sherry?"

"None of those precious female drinks for me," she laughed. "I like what men drink. If you've got a scotch on the rocks, that would be more my style."

Cheri entered at that moment and witnessed Jackie on one side of Jerome and Trish close to him on the other side. She wasn't exactly jealous...but was surprised to find that she didn't much like the fact that they were showing him all that attention. She started over toward Dorothy, but saw Babs coming off the elevator and went to help her out the doors and wheel her into the sitting room.

Ren came down the stairs at that moment and took over Babs' wheelchair from Cheri. "Ren, how are your wife and children?" Babs asked.

"They're fine, thanks," he replied, and wheeled her to the fire.

The Inspector entered again with yet another armload of logs and Dorothy rushed to him. "Now, really, Inspector, that will be all. We have plenty for tonight and Harlan has the central heating turned on. You must take your outer clothing off now and join the party. Harlan has your drink ready," she said. "This beautiful lady beside you is the famous actress Babs Cunningham...our favorite celebrity."

"I'm honored to meet you, Miss Cunningham," the Inspector said. "Just let me get out of these wet clothes and I will be very pleased to come back and kiss your lovely hand."

"And this is Ren Silvestri, another of our favorite people," Dorothy said, introducing them.

The Inspector stopped dead in his tracks and studied Ren. "Well, well, you are also famous in your own right," he said. "And you come from a famous—and if you'll forgive me for saying so, it might be called an infamous—family. I'll be most interested to talk to you, Mr. Silvestri, most interested."

Ren looked at the man with sheer hatred. He loathed anyone

connected with the law and he took offense at what the man had said. He was an outsider. How dare he presume to talk about the Silvestri family and to use the word *infamous. I will have to avoid him from now on or else be forced to give him a piece of my mind,* he thought.

When Percival returned after having taken off his outer clothing, the room became rather quiet as everyone seemed to watch him enter, get his drink, and walk over to Babs at the fireplace. Ren made a wide and rather obvious circle around the Inspector in an effort to avoid him. Jerome witnessed this, thinking Ren's behavior curious.

Jerome followed Ren as he walked over to stand by the windows. "Anything the matter, Ren?" he asked.

But before Ren could answer, the Doctor had approached with a scotch and soda. "I believe you still drink scotch," the Doctor said, handing Ren the drink. "I couldn't help but notice the wide berth you gave the Inspector. Did he say something out of the way?"

Ren was still flushed with anger. "You better keep him away from me or I'm likely to ruin the party by punching his face in for him," Ren said between gritted teeth. "He's far too curious about my family and has already insulted the name Silvestri."

As Jerome stood by helplessly, the Doctor outlined to Ren the plan to slip the Inspector a potion during the dinner tonight, a sedative that would knock him out for the rest of the weekend. To Jerome's horror, Ren was immediately in agreement with the plan and offered to assist the Doctor in any way he could.

Jerome had also been caught off guard. Somehow he had not expected the potion to be given this soon. Actually, with all the unexpected attention from Jackie and Trish, his own attention to his wardrobe, and his concern over getting back into Cheri's good graces, he had forgotten about the Inspector, and had even forgotten about the dreadful plan which he had hoped to stop by getting support from the others. Now the Doctor had one of them on his side, Ren. But there was still the Major to be consulted, and the women. Dorothy, he knew, was against her husband's plan, and he felt surely the other women would also be against taking such a severe measure. However, Cheri might side with her father, and Trish had always been a tough cookie. Those two might go along with the plan, he thought. But he might still get a majority against by enlisting the Major, Lorraine, Jackie, Babs, Dorothy, and himself. That would make the vote six "against" to only four "in favor." But now he would have to spend the rest of the cocktail hour going from person to person in an effort to enlist their support.

Actually Jerome had put the dreadful man completely out of his thoughts, and had even been surprised to see him when he'd entered the room for cocktails. It was annoying to have to give up his socializing in order to make a concerted effort to save the Inspector from the discomfort that awaited him. But then Jerome remembered all the discussion about various poisons that he had had with the Doctor, and his own gut feeling that something could go wrong. He must try to prevent a potion from being put into the Inspector's food or drink because he wanted no part of an accident...an accident that might even be considered murder.

As Jerome was deep into these thoughts, Babs wheeled herself over to their group—the Doctor, Ren, and himself. She was in a state of agitation. "Who is that annoying bore?" she asked. "And why must he be here? Surely we are not going to have to suffer him for the entire weekend celebration. He actually began to interrogate me about the night Big Al died. I felt as though he was accusing me."

Again Jerome stood helplessly by while the Doctor explained to Babs about knocking the Inspector out for the rest of the weekend, and again he was horrified when she also seemed delighted and went along wholeheartedly with the dangerous plan.

CHAPTER TWENTY

B ut surely you see how dangerous such a plan might be," Jerome was saying to the Major and Lorraine. "It could go wrong and we could inadvertently kill the man."

"Oh, I don't think so," the Major replied with a smile, as if they were talking about some matter of little importance.

"I'm sure the Doctor has thought out the potion very well, and no mistake will be made," Lorraine concurred with her husband. "The chances of something going wrong are about a million to one."

"But surely, even if it is a million-to-one chance, we dare not take that chance," Jerome said, trying to keep the hysteria out of his voice. "Surely having him around is not that objectionable?"

"You know, in Africa we shoot the animals with tranquilizer darts and they survive ninety-nine percent of the time," the Major said, by way of reassuring Jerome.

In the meantime, Cheri had gone along with her father's plan, as Jerome had thought she might. And Trish had given her consent, also as he had thought she might.

So far, those in favor were the Doctor, Ren, Babs, Cheri, Trish, the Major, and Lorraine. That meant that the plan had a vast majority. Jerome's only hope was that he, Dorothy, and Jackie might object so strongly that some of the others might change their vote. However, when Jackie approached him, before he could go to her, and talked to him enthusiastically about the doctor's solution to the annoying outsider, Jerome gave up hope. Dorothy wouldn't go against everyone's wishes, and frankly, neither would he. It seemed the die was cast.

Dorothy had put place cards out for dinner, and Jerome knew that a few of her trips into the dining room had been to change those cards. In considering the final seating arrangement, Jerome decided that Dorothy's plan was a brilliant one and could not have been any other way. No one wanted to sit next to or even near the Inspector, so Dorothy put him between Cheri and herself, and across from Jerome (the people who found him the least objectionable). Jerome could look over at Cheri, but Dorothy had seated him between his two admirers, Trish and Jackie. That meant that Trish was near her mother-in-law, as she wanted to be, and that Ren was next to Jackie. Otherwise he would have objected. The Doctor sat at the head of the table. As they were the uneven number of eleven, no one sat at the foot of the table, which was normally Dorothy's place. Dorothy gave the seats of honor to Babs and Lorraine, with Lorraine on the left of the host and Babs on his right. Jerome found it touching how Dorothy was willing to share the Doctor with his old flame, Babs. *Dorothy is quite a woman,* he thought.

Right		_Left_
	Doctor Armstrong	
Babs		Lorraine
Ren		The Major
Jackie		Cheri
Jerome		Percival
Trish		Dorothy

The meal was leg of lamb, roast potatoes with gravy, and Brussels sprouts. Most of the women had helped to prepare, cook, and serve.

The Doctor carved, while Jerome and Ren took care of the wine. A hot soup had been planned as the first course, but the women agreed that a homemade soup would be too time consuming, so they opened some tins of consommé and heated it, and for dessert they saved preparation time by opening jars of fruit salad. The lamb would be used for another easy meal the following day. Lorraine and the Major had learned from years of living in East Africa to make an excellent lamb curry.

Jackie and Trish were each vying for Jerome's attention. Under normal circumstances he would have enjoyed himself, especially with Cheri looking on, but he couldn't take his eyes off the Inspector. Every mouthful that the Inspector ate, Jerome expected to be the fateful one. He kept waiting for the man to keel over, fall onto the table, and ruin the meal.

"Jerome, you are not listening to me," Trish said, pulling at his coat sleeve. "I was asking if I could get you some more broth, or if you are ready for your main course?"

Just then his soup dish was whipped away and a plate with the entrée placed in front of him. Trish had asked, but Jackie had been the one to serve him. "You have an empty wineglass," Jackie said. "I will get the bottle and pour you some more."

This time Trish jumped to her feet, saying, "Stay where you are, Jackie, I will get the wine for Jerome."

"Why don't we just put some bottles of wine on either end of the table?" the Inspector asked. "It would save everybody from jumping up and down. If you place one here," he said, pointing to a spot in front of him, "I will serve all the ladies near me."

Jerome wondered if that arrangement with the wine bottles would foil the Doctor's plan to put the potion in the bottle of wine that the Inspector was being served from. Or maybe there was no tainted bottle—maybe drops had already been put into the Inspector's glass?

"How clever you are, Percival," Cheri said flirtatiously. As she flirted with the Inspector, she looked over at Jerome to see his reaction.

Under other circumstances her behavior would have wounded him, but he knew for certain that she was pretending. Cheri had been strongly in favor of knocking the man out for the weekend— he had heard her say it in no uncertain terms. *And it only stands to reason that if you were interested in being with a man, you wouldn't want him to sleep for two days of the celebration,* Jerome thought. He watched the Inspector take the bottle of wine from Trish and stand to pour some into everyone's glass at their end of the table.

Jerome was surprised to learn that he had finished his glass of wine without knowing that he had consumed it; and the next time he looked at his glass, he wondered if he had finished a second glass without realizing it. He couldn't take his eyes off Percival's mouth, or any bite or swallow the man took. He supposed his concentration was so intense that he, himself, was eating and drinking without registering the fact.

He was startled when Trish poked him, saying, "My goodness, Jerome, you have belted down another glass of wine and you are tearing through your food. You must have been so hungry and thirsty."

Jackie leaned into his other side and said, "Your concentration must be somewhere else tonight, Jerome. You haven't said a word. And as Trish pointed out, you are racing through your meal and your wine. Is anything worrying you?"

Jerome shook his head, looking at first one of them and then the other. He couldn't believe that they would be asking him if anything was worrying him. Of course, the plan for the Inspector was worrying him. But why wasn't it worrying any of them? How incredible that they had made the dangerous decision...had all been in favor of it…and no one was in the least anxious or concerned. Apparently they weren't even giving it another thought. No one else was watching the Inspector to see if the potion was taking effect. Did they know something he did not know? Did they know at which point it would be administered? Jerome wished that he had asked the Doctor when and how it was to be given; then he wouldn't have to suffer through this terrible suspense.

The next time Jerome looked down, he saw an empty dessert dish in front of him. Had the dessert been served? Had he already eaten it? He wondered. Then he remembered watching every mouthful of fruit salad the Inspector had eaten. He supposed that he, too, had been given fruit salad. So he must be finished. He also noted that his wine glass was empty. How much had he had to drink? He didn't feel drunk…he didn't even feel mellow or relaxed.

"You've been very bad company throughout dinner," Trish pouted. "You are a very naughty boy to neglect me that way. You seemed only to be staring straight in front of you. And I can't be jealous of Jackie because you didn't talk to Jackie either."

"Tomorrow you must make up for your neglect of me," Jackie chimed in, "by going for a very long, early morning walk with me."

"Well, I insist upon your company this evening," Trish said, taking his arm and practically lifting him out of his chair.

Jerome asked, "Where are we going?" Then he looked around the room and realized with a start that they were the last two to leave the table. Everyone else was already heading out the dining room door, including his other dinner partner, Jackie. She had apparently given up on him as a hopeless bore.

"We are going into the sitting room to have coffee, brandy, and smokes," Trish said, pushing him along.

When they entered the sitting room, Dorothy and the Doctor were taking beverage orders. "How many would like decaf and how many real coffee?" Dorothy was saying. "Raise your hands for decaf…now for real." All around him, people were raising their hands for one or the other, but Jerome was unable to move a muscle. Now he knew. That was where the potion would be, of course, in the coffee. Hadn't the Doctor said that the Inspector drank strong black coffee? Wasn't strong coffee the best way to hide the bitter taste of some potions?

"Jerome? Jerome?"

He looked up and Dorothy was standing over him...her lips were moving. It took him a second to decipher what she was saying.

"Jerome, what kind of coffee will you have? You didn't put your hand up for either decaf or real. Neither did Percival, because he takes a special strong coffee. I make for him a small pot of espresso. Perhaps that is what you want as well. Do you want espresso?"

"Noooo!" Jerome exploded with the answer, and everyone turned to look at him. He was embarrassed with all eyes on him, and he blushed. Then he repeated calmly, "No, thank you. I'll take decaf."

Dorothy was heading toward the kitchen to prepare the dreadful beverage in which to hide the potion, and the Doctor was heading there with her. Jerome knew it was to measure the potion into the cup.

"Major?" the Doctor said as he left the room, "Would you be kind enough to pour the brandies? I am going to the kitchen to help Dorothy with the coffee."

Percival seemed not to notice anything strange, but Jerome did—none of the women offered to help. They let the Doctor go to the kitchen. That was most odd. The Doctor would never, under ordinary circumstances, help his wife in the kitchen with so many ladies present. And it was odd that none of the ladies offered to help Dorothy, when they had all helped with the rest of the meal. Jerome began to think that the Inspector was a rather dim fellow.

The wind howled at that moment, and Jerome jumped.

"Fierce wind we are getting," the Major said. "Let us hope that it doesn't do any damage to the roofs, especially of the cottages, which are most vulnerable."

"Being here again has caused me to miss my cottage," Babs said.

That gave Percival an opening. "That is where I am staying," he said, "in the cottage that used to be yours. You must come over and see it.… Visit me any time the mood strikes you, Miss Cunningham."

"Now then," the Major called out, "who is ready for a brandy?"

Shortly after the after-dinner drinks had been handed out, the Doctor and Dorothy entered, he wheeling a cart with the various coffees. One cup was much smaller than the others, an espresso. Then a strange ritual took place: each person, before taking their own coffee, picked up and held momentarily the small espresso cup. It was as if prearranged, in order that all present would have, literally, a hand in giving the Inspector his potion. In order to test his theory, Jerome did not touch the espresso cup when the tray was wheeled in front of him. Dorothy then leaned into him and whispered, telling him to hold it for a moment. He did, but his hands were shaking so badly that he was in danger of dropping the specially mixed brew. The Doctor quickly took the espresso cup from him, replacing it safely. Now Jerome was a full participant in what was to come.

He watched the Inspector closely—he was talking and not paying attention to the ritual. Jerome wondered how good a cop he could have been when he was so unobservant. Just as the Inspector was reaching for the small cup, a gasp escaped from Jerome's lips. Everyone, including the Inspector, turned to look at Jerome.

But Cheri stepped in and took hold of Jerome's arm, saying, "You burned yourself on your coffee, Jerome, it is too hot." Then, turning to the room in general, she said, "Be careful, everyone, the decaf is very hot. Perhaps wait a moment before drinking it."

Dorothy also stepped in, taking Jerome's other arm. "Cheri,

why don't you take Jerome up to your studio and show him your paintings?"

"Yes," Cheri said, "I have been meaning to show you my work. Will you come now, Jerome? I'll only take you away for about fifteen or twenty minutes. Everyone, excuse us, please. I would invite the rest of you, but I want you to see my painting one person at a time so that I can answer any question individually."

Jerome felt that they had decided to get rid of him, that he was being too emotional and might give the game away if they allowed him to stay in the sitting room while the Inspector drank his espresso. He fully expected Cheri to turn cold toward him as soon as the elevator doors closed and they were out of sight of the others...but she did not. If anything, she clung more closely to him, smiling brightly.

Once they had entered the door of her studio and turned on the light, without letting go of his arm, she turned and placed herself in front of him and puckered her lips. "You may kiss me," she said. "I know I don't deserve it because of the mean way I treated you and all the terrible things I said to you, but kiss me anyhow."

But Jerome did not kiss her. He stood looking at her and wondering why she was behaving this way. It occurred to him that she was being insincere...just trying to keep his mind off what was happening in the sitting room. Perhaps she'd even been encouraged to keep him calm and out of the way until the dreadful deed was done.

When he didn't respond, she said, "I've been such a silly little girl. I have missed you, too, Jerome. I can't tell you how I've been looking forward to seeing you again. For years now I've known what a mistake I made by losing you. Will you forgive me? Will you give me another chance? I believe we could be happy together."

Jerome was convinced, because Cheri was not bright enough to be that deceptive, he knew. He folded her into his arms and kissed her with all the longing he had known for her. He felt overcome by both passion and deep love. She was a child-woman and he might have had a real woman, but he had always loved Cheri. She was the one he wanted.

Meanwhile, in the sitting room, the Inspector had begun to yawn in an uncontrollable manner. "You must all excuse me," he said. "I'm afraid that I am overcome with fatigue, with sleepiness, despite the strong espresso that I have drunk. I apologize, but I must go to my bed."

"The Major, Ren, and I will walk you to your cottage, Inspector," the Doctor said. "We were going for an after-dinner constitutional, at any rate. So we might as well all go together."

"You're going to take a walk in this weather? In this high wind?" the Inspector asked incredulously, and again he yawned violently.

As the Inspector rose from his chair, he stumbled, but the Doctor was there to catch him under one arm, and Ren quickly took hold of him under his other arm. The coats for all of them had appeared as if by magic, and the women were efficiently helping the men to dress for the out-of-doors. None of them, however, dealt with the awkward business of putting on boots. They would dry their feet later. Right now it was important to get the Inspector to his cottage as fast as possible.

They did not leave the Inspector at his cottage door as they'd said they would. By the time they got there, he needed assistance getting inside, undressing, and getting into bed. While Ren and the Major helped the Inspector onto the bed and off with his clothes, the Doctor took from his overcoat pocket a thermometer and a stethoscope. He then made sure that the victim was not running a fever and that his heart was beating as regularly as could be expected, and forced him to drink some water. Before leaving the now-sleeping man alone, the Doctor checked his pulse. Then they turned off the lights and left.

CHAPTER TWENTY-ONE

The next morning Jerome awakened early, trembling and in a terrible sweat. He'd had disturbing dreams…dreams about death. Why had he had those dreams? Perhaps because today they were all going to the island gravesite to pay their respects at the graves of the Baron and Foster? Or perhaps his bad dreams had been because of last evening after dinner, when he'd known that the potion must be in the espresso that had been prepared for the Inspector. He had not witnessed the drinking of that espresso. Cheri had taken him upstairs to her studio, and when they had returned downstairs twenty minutes later, everyone had been playing a word game… everyone but the Inspector. Dorothy had smiled and said in the sweetest of voices that the Inspector had been feeling sleepy and had excused himself to go to his cottage and retire for the night. She'd also said that the Doctor, Ren, and the Major had gone with him, and seen him safely inside and into his bed. The Doctor had then checked him to make sure he wasn't ill…but he was fine and just needed some rest. She'd added that the Inspector would probably sleep for the rest of the weekend…or until about Monday morning.

Jerome got up quickly from the damp sheets, and, shivering,

ran into the bathroom. Before using the toilet, he turned on the shower and let the water get boiling hot. When he took his shower, it was as hot as he could stand it, without burning himself. He let the water run over him for a long time and then he soaped, shampooed his hair, and rinsed with cooler water. Afterwards he rubbed himself off vigorously, and wrapped himself in the thick terry robe provided for each hotel guest. He was feeling much better.

He rubbed the mirror with the sleeve of his terry robe to clear the steam. Then he shaved, brushed his teeth, and combed his hair. As he groomed, he thought about Cheri...pleasant thoughts, remembering how he had held her...how it had been like old times... as if the years had not passed. They had not made love. That would come later, perhaps tonight after her birthday party. It would be then that he would ask her to marry him, and he had reason to believe that she would consent. Then what bliss to know that his retirement years would not be spent alone.

There were certain details that might be sticky...such as where they would live until he retired. He had to be in Vancouver for his work, but Cheri might not want to leave her parents. He could probably get to the island every weekend, and of course, there were always holidays and vacations when they would be together. He might have to settle for that for the next few years.

He would remodel one of the cottages for them, if she liked the idea. But he knew she would wish to live in the mansion as long as Dorothy and the Doctor were alive. Actually she might never wish to leave the mansion, and he thought that might be even more sensible. They would have to supervise the running of the hotel when the Armstrongs got too old to continue the management. He could remodel an entire wing of the hotel for him and Cheri...why not? He knew in his heart that he would end up doing whatever Cheri wanted. She was so childlike that at times to reason with her on an adult level was difficult. But, like a child, once she agreed to marry him, she would cling to him forever, he knew.

He thought about the sex life they would have, not with excitement or a sense of urgency, but as a constant comfort. Cheri was passive. She was not passionate and did not particularly enjoy sex. She loved to be held, to cuddle. Everything sensual would be up to him. But he also knew that she would never refuse his advances. Theirs would be a mutual understanding of his needs, and he would, in a sense, father her. It occurred to him that he would father her long after his own sexual needs had diminished. She would never make him feel less of a man, never make him feel inadequate after his manly vigor was gone, because that would never have been important to her in the first place. Their mutual affection could only grow stronger.

Jerome selected his heavy woolen trousers and thick turtleneck sweater. The central heating was slowly heating the house, but it wouldn't be warm for a few more hours. Also, the trip to the gravesite was going to be an endurance of the wind and cold. He also got out his heaviest socks and the high boots he had brought for hiking. He could smell the bacon cooking in the kitchen, and it made him feel hungry. He hurriedly dressed, grabbed his leather jacket, and went downstairs.

As he entered the kitchen, he was surprised to see that everyone except Cheri and the Doctor had already arrived for breakfast and were seated at the kitchen table. He was greeted warmly as he sat down. They all seemed in fine spirits and were looking forward to an invigorating hike to the gravesite.

He inquired about Cheri and the Doctor.

"Cheri isn't down yet," Dorothy said, "and Harlan has gone to look in on the Inspector, make sure he is comfortable this morning."

Comfortable, Jerome thought. *In what way was she using the word?* Wasn't comfortable a term they used to reassure you when someone had been in a car crash? "The patient is resting comfortably." How could you define the effects of a drug in the short term and the long? He was sorry he had not been downstairs to witness the effects of the espresso. He wished he'd seen the condition of the Inspector for himself. It might have allayed his fears. Perhaps the man was only sleeping off a sedative, as the Doctor had planned. The Doctor knew what he was doing and had thought of every possibility. He had been in the kitchen himself to measure the amount of the potion to go into the Inspector's coffee.

Perhaps no harm would come to him whatsoever. The Inspector would wake up refreshed and not understand or even truly care that he had missed the weekend. If he did suspect, he could never prove that he had been given a potion. But Jerome knew this was all wishful thinking. He should have gone with the other men to the Inspector's cottage…should have seen for himself what was happening. That might have put his mind at ease. And he should have been a part of what was happening. After all, he was already involved. He had participated in the ritual of lifting the cup, just as all the others had done. He had not wanted the man to be drugged, and had tried to win the support of the others. But when no one but Dorothy had sided with him, he had not objected. He had not stood his ground and said that he would not condone any plan that endangered a man's life. He had not bucked the tide of opinion when it had gone against him, and that made him just as guilty as the rest…maybe even more guilty than the others.

The back door opened and the Doctor came in from outside, taking off his overcoat. "He was sleeping soundly as I left, and everything seems to be fine," the Doctor said, as he hung up his coat.

Dorothy turned from the stove and asked, "Will he be requiring any food, dear? Or any liquids other than water?"

"No, my love," the Doctor replied. "I have given him water and the bedpan. He was conscious for a while. Everything is functioning. He is just very tired. He will not need solid food or any special liquids. I shall make several trips a day to give him water and make sure he does not become dehydrated. He'll be awake and right as rain on Monday."

"That's lovely, dear," Dorothy said. "Now sit down and have your coffee. Breakfast will be ready in a minute."

Jerome broke out in a cold sweat and began to tremble. He rose and went over to look out the window. He thought it best that none of the others notice the reaction he was having to the conversation that had just taken place between Dorothy and the Doctor. He was afraid that they would turn on him. But why was he the only one who had found that conversation chilling? True, the Doctor appeared confident that all would be well, but was he? The Doctor was treating this as if the man had always been a patient, and not someone who had been violated. Dorothy was behaving as if it were natural for a man to have to be given a bedpan, and forced to drink water and to sleep for hours at a time. How odd that none of the others even inquired about the Inspector. They behaved as if he were no concern of theirs, as if he were a nonperson, as if he'd already ceased to exist. Why did he, and he alone, have this feeling of dread?

"Everything is ready," Dorothy called. So Lorraine, Jackie, and Trish got up from the table and collected the plates. They went over to the stove, holding the plates out for Dorothy to fill, then brought them back to the table, serving the men and then themselves.

As Dorothy was piling her own plate with food, Cheri entered. "Mommy, don't give me quite so much," she said, before turning and saying "Good morning" to everyone.

Once Cheri had her food, she sat down, motioning for Jerome to sit next to her. When he did, she kissed him. Meaningful looks went all around. Jackie shrugged and smiled. Only Trish appeared to be jealous.

Babs had decided not to visit the gravesite this morning. Harlan had offered to drive her there later in the afternoon. She could not have negotiated the wheelchair over the rough terrain, and the others wanted a brisk walk. Also, she was feeling exceptionally tired. She had come without Jane Tiddles, the nurse, and had been forced to do everything for herself. Washing and dressing could be exhausting without a helping hand. She might have asked Lorraine for some assistance, but she hadn't wanted to...she hadn't wanted to take away moments of the reunion from Lorraine. She hadn't wanted to be a burden.

There was a large flower box on a chair by the door. Jackie got up, collected it, and placed it on Babs' lap for her and everyone to see. As Babs opened the box, there were "Ooh's" and "Aah's."

"Aren't they beautiful flowers?" Jackie asked. "They are Chinese silk, the finest in the world, and ruinously expensive. I was able to get them wholesale through the art gallery where I work."

The box of artificial flowers was then passed around the table. Everyone had a closer look at their splendor. Jackie wanted Dorothy to choose a bouquet for the house from among the flowers. The others, she wanted to divide among the women so that each of them had some to place on the graves of the Baron and Foster.

After breakfast, they bundled up and started out. The weather had warmed up by several degrees and the snow had melted. The only signs of snow were in the drifts that still remained. The wind was strong, but not as strong as it had been. Nevertheless, everyone had to clutch at their scarves and some had to hold their hats on.

The gravesite was on the more barren end of the island. There were no cottages on that side, and the view was of open ocean that seemed to stretch forever. The beach was strewn with heavy boulders that had not been removed, and they made regal monuments for the dead, although both graves were marked with a proper chiseled stone stating the name and the dates of birth and death.

Jackie was the first to kneel down in a central spot at the foot of the graves, place flowers on each, and secure them with rocks. Then, bowing her head, she said prayers for both her departed friends. Soon everyone was praying. Only Dorothy found kneeling too difficult. She remained standing, and bowed her head to pray.

After they had each paid their respects individually, it was

Cheri who suggested that they all stand, hold hands in a semicircle, and pray together. Jerome thought it was a wonderful idea. It brought them all so close together, standing at the graves, holding hands, and looking out to sea. They were friends with many shared experiences. Even when parted by long distances, they had remained somehow united. They were tied together by this island and a myriad of memories.

Trish began to sing a hymn. Her voice was low, rich, and very beautiful. Jerome wasn't sure how many of the others knew that Trish had such a splendid voice, but he remembered how lovely it was from the times when they had gone dancing together and she had sung in his ear. He hoped Trish would one day forgive him for again choosing Cheri over her. She was a great gal and he hoped he would get an opportunity to tell her so and extend his friendship. The fact that he loved Cheri was something beyond his control.

When they returned from the gravesite, they came into the house through the back door, leaving their muddy boots on the back porch. Babs was in the kitchen at the stove. She had made a large pot of coffee. Everyone took off their outer garments, hung them up on the pegs and clothes rack, and again sat at the kitchen table. The house was much warmer now and the kitchen was absolutely toasty.

"How was it?" Babs asked. "Was it lovely? Jackie, did you say a prayer for me...for the Baron and for Foster?"

"Of course, I said a prayer from you to both of them," Jackie replied. "And we stood in a semicircle and all prayed together."

"It was so beautiful," Dorothy said. "And Trish sang a hymn that made us all cry...it was so lovely."

The Doctor walked in the back door and said, "Dead."

"Yes, dear," Dorothy said. "A lovely hymn for the dead."

"No, dead," he repeated. "I'm afraid the Inspector is dead."

CHAPTER TWENTY-TWO

Dead!" Jerome cried out. "Oh, my Lord. Oh, my Lord." he screamed, and continued to scream for what seemed like minutes.

No one else reacted to the news of the Inspector's death. They all turned to observe Jerome with cold stares. They observed him as if he were having some physical difficulty, perhaps an epileptic fit… nothing to do with emotion…nothing to do with the tragedy of a death…a death caused by them…in other words, a murder. They were in total denial. Only he was admitting that they, and he, had actually killed a man. It was a barbaric act and they were all guilty.

Still no one reacted. They continued to look at him as if he were the crazy one. Maybe it was a bad dream from which he would wake? All was silence now that he had stopped screaming, he noted. Everyone was silent and still observing him. Then he watched as the Doctor went to the kitchen telephone and dialed a number.

"Police?" the Doctor said. "I would like to report a death on Escape Island. One Percival Forsythe, a British national, an ex-Inspector from New Scotland Yard. This is Doctor Harlan Armstrong. Yes, I'll hold," he said.

After a moment he continued, apparently talking to someone else. "Yes, Doctor Harlan Armstrong, owner of Escape Island. Yes, I am a medical doctor. Yes, as his attending physician I will have the authority to sign the death certificate. Cause of death?" He paused. When he continued, his voice did not falter as he said, "Perfectly straightforward. He died of natural causes. It was a cardiac arrest."

No sooner had the Doctor hung up than the phone rang. It was the captain of the ferry, saying that the weather was due to improve and that he felt he could make the trip to the island by the afternoon. He had been in touch with Mrs. Bloodsworth and Sarah and they would be returning with him. Were there any instructions?

The Doctor told the captain that a police boat would also be coming as soon as the wind died down, as it was expected to, during the afternoon. He was to alert the cook, the maid, and the crew not to be alarmed. The man had died of natural causes... peacefully in his sleep.

Peacefully in his sleep, Jerome thought—*a sleep induced by a drug that the doctor had stirred into the man's espresso. The man had been a victim. A murder victim.*

When the Doctor told them that Sarah and Mrs. Bloodsworth would be arriving this afternoon, Dorothy was thrilled. "Isn't it wonderful," she said. "We will have a marvelous meal tonight. And Cheri's birthday cake will be here." Then she and Cheri hugged and did a little dance. The others, too, were in a joyous mood. Everyone began to talk at once and make plans for the evening ahead.

Jerome could not believe what was going on—they had not only not been moved by the Inspector's death, they had actually forgotten all about him. Their thoughts and plans were focused on a celebration. It was cruel and inhumane. Jerome found it unbearable.

He began to recall that night in 1970 when he had entered the house to find Big Al motionless. Pretending to be the Constable, he had declared murder. Now he had reason to review all that he had been told and all that he had witnessed on that night long ago.

The seating arrangement of that night might have some possible significance. He recalled very clearly that the Baron was at the head of the table, and Dorothy at the other end. Cheri was to the Baron's right and Babs to his left. Also at the left-hand side, the Doctor's place (although he wasn't in it, as he had been in the sitting room at the time). Next on the left was Lorraine, and then the Major. On the right, Big Al was next to Cheri, then came Jackie and Ren. In his mind's eye, he visualized the seating:

Right		_Left_
	Baron	
Cheri		Babs
Big Al		Doctor
Jackie		Lorraine
Ren		Major
	Dorothy	

He'd been told that the Major had offered a toast to the Baron, and to the charming and helpful Ms. Dorothy Saks, and to all of them for a weekend to remember.

Big Al's fish had arrived just then, and without waiting for his hostess to begin, he'd taken a huge mouthful. Everyone had raised their glasses in the toast except for Big Al; he'd started eating rapidly, big mouthfuls, and had just about finished his fish when there had been a blackout. Some flashes of lightning had lit up the windows for a moment and there had been a thunderclap. The thunder had been loud, but not loud enough to cover the distinctive sound of a body falling.

The thump of a body had been unmistakable, and several of the women had screamed. The Baron had been heard to ask, "What happened?"

"It's only a power failure, we must all try to remain calm," the Major had said. But everyone had known that a body had fallen.

"But I heard a thump," Babs had cried out.

Dorothy had pleaded, "Please, everyone, as the Major said, we must remain calm. I'm sure Foster is seeing to some candlelight."

The lights had come back on. Everyone had been in the exact same position, except for Big Al. He had been slumped over the chair onto the floor. There had followed a stunned silence as they observed Big Al's motionless form. Everyone had taken a moment to catch their breath and then had moved to him to see if he was breathing.

Suddenly Big Al had come back to life, violently choking, sitting up.

Cheri had stood and lifted Big Al's arms in the air. It had been a useless gesture. Big Al had continued to choke.

Ren had hit Big Al several times on the back. Big Al had seemed to recover, but an instant later he'd stopped breathing, grown red in the face, and grabbed his throat.

The Major had pushed Big Al's upper torso onto the table and had given him artificial respiration, as you would a drowning man. Big Al had again been silent and had appeared dead.

Jackie had pushed Big Al's torso back into a sitting position, leaned over him, and pounded his heart. Big Al had come to life.

Babs had stuck her fingers down his throat, probing for a foreign object. It had been difficult to do because of the large cocktail ring on her right hand. Big Al had stopped choking and breathing.

Lorraine, courageously, had begun giving Big Al mouth-to-mouth resuscitation. The women had watched with distaste, as apparently they wouldn't have touched his lips even to save his life. Big Al had taken a breath and again started choking.

Foster had gripped Big Al from behind, administering the Heimlich maneuver. Big Al had seemed momentarily to recover.

At this time there had been another blackout and that produced a chorus of screams, and a confusion of voices.

The lights had then come back on.

Doctor Armstrong had entered the room. The Doctor had been in the sitting room trying to make a phone call, and had responded to Jerome's tapping on the inside door.

Moving to Big Al, the Doctor had felt his pulse, and then, looking steadily around at the faces, had declared, "This man is dead!"

There had followed screaming and outcries of disbelief, and again everyone had begun to gather round the corpse.

Jerome had been in the entrance to the dining room, and had shouted, "Stay where you are! No one move!"

The guests had frozen in place and had turned to look at him in the entranceway. Posing as the Constable, he had entered the room, saying, "If this man is dead, it could be murder. And each and every one of you is a suspect."

Later he had interrogated them all and found to his amazement that he had been correct. They all had had motive. Big Al had been known to them all, and all had suffered at his hands. They all had been present at the time of death, and each had access to a death weapon.

In reviewing it in his mind, Jerome could see that his theories could have been correct. The Baron grew the foxglove, Dorothy gathered the leaves, and Trish placed them along with the sage in the fish stuffing. Cheri gave Big Al an overdose of his digitalis medication, and after he had already had his prescribed amount for that day, Babs released more digitalis from a secret compartment in her ring. Ren broke his ribs and forced them toward his heart, and Foster gave him a karate chop, also to the heart. The Doctor, while pretending to feel his pulse, gave him an injection of yet more digitalis.

It was more difficult to pinpoint what Lorraine, the Major, and Jackie had done to kill Big Al, but it was probably symbolic…a ritual such as the lifting of the espresso cup with the potion for the Inspector had been…a gesture to make them all equally responsible.

Now he recalled looking in from atop the telephone pole into the window of the dining room and watching the entire thing in replay. Big Al had somehow survived the first attempt…had survived the freezer. He had re-entered the room and they had replayed the entire murder a second time. That is what he had seen from his position high up on the telephone pole. That is why he had entered to again find Big Al's body in the same position. They had killed him. They had all killed him, and not just once, but twice. No wonder they had no feeling for the death of the Inspector. Jerome believed that the Inspector's death had been an accident, but they had killed him nonetheless. And no wonder none of them were shocked or had grieved. They were cold-blooded killers.

He must get away from this island forever. He was exhausted. He would have a short nap, and then pack, and leave…never to return.

Cheri was tugging at his arm, waking him from his reverie. "We are all going to my studio to look at my paintings," she said.

Dorothy took his other arm. "Yes, everyone is anxious to see Cheri's artwork, and we are all anxious to hear what Jackie has to say. She runs the most important gallery in Paris," Dorothy said.

They seemed to form an invincible circle around him. All of them were somehow holding him without touching him. They seemed to be willing him to stay with them…as if they had read his thoughts. Oddly, he did not feel threatened. He felt a warmth and caring generating from all of them. They were radiating love, or so it seemed.

Jerome felt as though he were in a daze, unable to do anything that was outside of being part of the group. He went with them… went with the entire group to see Cheri's paintings. Well, why not, he had the time. The ferry would not be there until the afternoon. There was plenty of time to take a nap, pack, and leave.

Cheri had displayed her paintings in a circle around the walls of her studio. Not all of them, as there were too many, but the latest ones and the ones in which she took the most pride. Even so, there must have been a circle of a hundred or more. They walked that circle, one person in front of the other. There were many compliments and much studying up close of the canvases.

Jackie thought Cheri's paintings were indescribably bad. They looked worse to her in actuality than they did in the photographs that Dorothy had sent. She was at a loss for words. She didn't want to hurt Cheri's feelings, but what could she say? "Interesting," she finally said. "I find them most interesting."

Both Cheri and Dorothy took that as a wonderful compliment. "You see, darling," Dorothy said to Cheri, "the art expert thinks your paintings are interesting." Turning to Jackie, she asked, "Jackie, will you now be able to recommend Cheri's work for your gallery?"

"I'll be happy to," Jackie said, lying. "But please remember that I have no power to buy them. I'm just an employee," she lied again.

Cheri held Jerome back until the others had gone, then she locked the studio door and fell into his arms. "Oh, darling," she said, "I couldn't wait to be alone with you. Last night was not the time, with everyone waiting downstairs for us to return."

Jerome wanted to say that now was also not the time, but he felt her warm body up against his, and the words would not come.

"Jerome, I thought about you all night long. I couldn't sleep for thinking about you," she purred, and pressed her lips to his.

He kissed her softly, but she moaned as if he had done the most thrilling of all things to her. "Jerome, I love you. I know now that

I have always loved you," she whispered. Then she led him to the couch so that they could lie down together.

He had no more will. He made love to her, and also said again and again that he loved her, too. They fell asleep.

When Jerome awakened, he felt refreshed and happier than he had been in years. They had made beautiful love and fallen asleep together. He looked at the child-woman in his arms and wondered if he could possibly leave her. She was the love of his life. He wouldn't walk out before her birthday party. He couldn't. Tomorrow would be plenty of time to pack and catch the ferry as originally planned.

CHAPTER TWENTY-THREE

Jerome was surprised to learn that while he had been asleep with Cheri the ferry had come and gone, and so had the police boat, taking away the body of the dead man.

He'd been about to go into the kitchen for a glass of juice when he had heard the voices of Mrs. Bloodsworth, Sarah, and a butler hired for the day, John Rice. Mrs. Bloodsworth had been outlining the instructions for John and Sarah concerning tonight's formal dinner party. Then they had begun to discuss the removal of the dead man's body. So he had stopped to listen at the door.

"That poor man," Sarah said.

"We all have to go one day," Mrs. Bloodsworth told her. "He wasn't a young man. He'd probably led a full life, and he went peacefully in his sleep. That's the way we all hope to go."

John said, "The police were on and off the island quickly."

"That's because of Doctor Armstrong being a medical practitioner and all," Mrs. Bloodsworth told him. "I didn't know he was the Inspector's doctor, it was all news to me. But apparently he had been treating the Inspector for a bad heart without anybody knowing. Since he was what they call the 'attending physician,' he was able to sign the death certificate, and that's why they were able to get it over with so quickly. And thank heavens for that, now we can get on with the preparations for tonight's celebration."

Dorothy had arrived just then and had seen Jerome standing outside the kitchen door. He'd blushed at seeing her, because he'd felt she must have known that he'd been eavesdropping.

"Jerome, dear," Dorothy said, "why are you standing outside the door? Come into the kitchen and meet the help. We were so lucky to get a butler for the day, John Rice. He wasn't available on Friday, but since the ferry was delayed until today, he was able to join us for the rest of today and part of Sunday. Thank goodness for another helping hand."

After Dorothy had introduced Jerome to the help, he had gotten his juice and left. The weather had improved markedly and he'd decided to take a walk. He had walked quickly by the cottage that had been the Inspector's, but he need not have felt anxious. There had been nothing to see. All had looked normal, as if nothing had happened.

He'd then walked up the hill to the cottage that had once been his. He'd tried to go inside, but it had been locked. He'd sat for a time on the porch and looked out to sea. There he'd remembered the pleasant years he'd spent in this spot, in this cottage, and on the island. Then he'd wandered back to the mansion.

On his way up the stairs, he had stopped at Cheri's studio. She'd still been on the couch, but awake now. He'd laid down again beside her, and again they had made love.

Jerome and Cheri slept after making love, and missed tea-time. At five, she ordered him playfully to go to his own room. She needed time to get ready for tonight's party, she said. He left purposely without asking her to marry him. Now he would be breaking different news to her, unhappy news about his decision to leave the island and her forever. But he needed time to think everything out carefully before he declared his intentions. He wasn't ready yet to face what was to come, all the unhappiness he would be causing her, the others, and himself.

At cocktail time, Jerome was, as usual, the first to arrive. John, the butler hired for the weekend, was just setting up the drinks table. Jerome remembered Friday evening, when he thought he was the first to arrive, but had encountered the Inspector for the first time. The man had been onto something about Big Al's murder. He had been asking too many informed questions. Jerome wondered about the book the man had been writing, had it been about the murder on Escape Island?

The Doctor entered the room. He looked marvelous in his tuxedo, tall and handsome, greying but somehow ageless. The new butler asked if the Doctor wished for drinks to be served now. Both Jerome and Doctor Armstrong ordered their usual scotch and sodas.

"Doctor," Jerome said, once the butler had left the room, "I've just been wondering what the Inspector's book was about."

"He had few possessions with him," the Doctor said. "The police packed up his belongings and will try to contact any next of kin."

"Yes, but what about the pages of the book he was writing?" Jerome asked. "He'd been here months, working every day. There must have been a rather thick manuscript in the cottage."

"Surprisingly, not," the Doctor said, sipping his scotch. "There appeared to be only a few pages of scribbles."

"So you saw his manuscript?" Jerome asked.

"Yes, I was in his cottage before the police got here, looking for important documents. Thought it would save time," he answered.

"But what about the book manuscript?" Jerome insisted.

"There was no manuscript," the Doctor said sternly. Then

his attitude softened. He put his arm around Jerome and walked him to the windows. "There is something I want you to know, Jerome," he said with a tone of confidentiality. "Percival had a bad heart. He didn't want anyone else to know, but he took me into his confidence when he first got here. He'd had surgery and hadn't much time left."

Jerome looked at the Doctor in amazement. "You knew he had a bad heart and you still gave him the potion?"

"The potion enabled him to rest...was good for him," he answered.

Jerome confronted the Doctor head on. "But you told the police that you were the attendant physician."

"And that was the truth," the Doctor said. "He hired me as his physician while he was on the island. The police were given the notes about his checkups and the cancelled prescriptions I had written."

"But I still don't understand about the manuscript," Jerome said. "There must have been the pages of the book he was working on."

"He wasn't working on any book," the Doctor said flatly. "The Inspector didn't want anyone else to know that he had a short time to live. He needed long naps during the day and so he told Dorothy and Cheri that he used those hours in order to write. There was no book."

"You say he was a dying man...the potion only caused him to rest. Then why did we go through the ritual of each lifting the espresso cup before it was given to him to drink?"

"We are a closely knit group of friends, you know that. When we all decide on an action, we all do it together," the Doctor said.

"But why the ritual of the cup if it was harmless?"

The Doctor looked at him for a long moment before replying. "That is a good question. I suppose it is because we were turning away a guest so that we could have two days without an outsider.

But we are people with a conscience, and we were tricking a man. We had all agreed that was what we wanted, and so we all shared symbolically in the deed."

Jerome almost thought he understood.

The Doctor continued, "He would have died with or without the potion. He would have died at any rate. It was just a matter of a short time. The potion did not kill him or speed up his death."

The others began arriving then. Ren and the Major were in tuxedos and the ladies in gowns. The room began to look like the pages of a glossy magazine come to life. Even Cheri arrived precisely on time, looking like a strawberry sherbet. Her gown was pink tulle with dots of strawberry red. It had a tight bodice and a huge ballroom skirt that swept the floor as she walked. By comparison, the other ladies were modern and chic. Even Dorothy was dressed in a chic black gown that she had purchased for the occasion, but Cheri didn't seem to notice, or if she did, she didn't mind.

Dinner was a banquet of caviar and chilled vodka, followed by goose with apple and prune stuffing and all the trimmings, including gooseberries. The wine for the main course was the finest claret that Baron Tarrall's wine cellar had to offer. The cake was three tiers, chocolate with white icing, Cheri's favorite. The top was decorated with forty-five candles and a tiny blonde doll holding a paintbrush and palette.

Jerome might be wrong about what had happened to the Inspector, but it was difficult to believe that the Inspector had not been writing a book. The Doctor admitted to being in the cottage before the police arrived. He could have found the manuscript. It might have been an account of the death of Big Al. The man knew the facts and always asked leading questions. He seemed to be obsessed with the possibility of murder. Was that the real reason they all wanted him out of the way? Didn't the Doctor then look for and find the manuscript, bring it back to the main house and put it in the furnace?

However, Jerome recalled what the Doctor had told him earlier. He was the man's physician. There were the checkup records and cancelled prescriptions to prove it. Therefore it was also true that the man had a very bad heart. Perhaps he'd had that operation...had very little time left. He wanted to spend that time on this peaceful island. But he did not want the women to know how ill he was or to pity him. For his remaining days he wanted to appear normal, even to play tennis, and enjoy the company of a beautiful girl like Cheri. But he required a great deal of rest, so he made up the story about writing a book. He could spend most of the day in bed without anyone's knowing, or disturbing him and discovering his secret. If Jerome thought about it...it all made perfect sense... as much sense as his assumptions.

Then he thought about his own character: wasn't he a pessimist? Wasn't he a fellow who was by nature full of gloom and doom? Wasn't he a loner who had difficulty communicating? Weren't the people at this table his dearest friends? The only true friends he had, or had ever had? Wasn't he a cad to doubt them?

Cheri had blown out the candles on the cake, and each person at the table had stood up and offered her a toast on her birthday milestone. They had raised their glasses and offered her their love and good wishes. He had only half-heard the accolades, because he had been so deeply absorbed in his own thoughts.

Dorothy said, "Everyone has proposed a toast to Cheri except the Major and Jerome. Major, you go next. We must leave Jerome for last," she said, with some deep meaning behind her words.

Jerome was startled back to the present. His was to be the last toast. What could he possibly say? Last meant that it was expected to be the best of all. But he was very bad with words. He began to sweat.

The Major rose and held high his glass of claret. "My dearest Cheri, who made everything Lorraine and I now enjoy, possible. Who changed our lives and the lives of everyone here for the best.

May your days be as content as a giraffe's who has no enemies. May your strength be as great as an elephant's...and your memory. May your courage match that of the rhino, but may your weight never reach that of the hippo. And, on a serious note, we love you now and always."

The Major's toast had received much laughter and then applause. Now they all looked to Jerome. He still had no idea what he would say. He was sweating profusely and his hand shook as he stood and raised the glass, pointing it in Cheri's direction. Then there was silence.

Everyone looked at him...waiting...waiting even longer.

Cheri said, "Just tell me what's in your heart, Jerome."

"I love you," he said. "I want you to be my wife."

"I accept," she said, and all his doubts were put aside.

THE END

ABOUT THE AUTHOR

Carroll Baker starred in more than forty Hollywood and European films, including Tennessee Williams's *Baby Doll*, which brought her an Academy Award nomination and skyrocketed her to international fame; *Giant; Harlow; The Carpetbaggers;* the classic Westerns *How the West Was Won, The Big Country,* and *Cheyenne Autumn;* and the newly released version of the 1961 dramatic film *Something Wild.*

In the 1980s, while living in London and appearing in the theater, she began to pursue another passion, that of writing. She is the author of three other published books—*Baby Doll*, her autobiography; *To Africa with Love,* an autobiographical travel romance; and *A Roman Tale*, a bawdy novel. *Baby Doll* was extensively reviewed and lauded by many publications, including *The New York Times Book Review.*

Carroll Baker currently lives in New York City.